ROD FL

The Y ... 1092
~Cumbria
Invaded~

The Harrying of the North
Book Four

*To Anne,
With all my thanks for
your assistance.
Love, Rod Jan '21.*

Hindrelag Books
www.hindrelag.uk

The Year 1092
~Cumbria Invaded~

Cover photo by Rod Flint
Art work by Woofdog: www.woofdog.co.uk

Other books by Rod Flint

What others say

"Rod Flint has pulled off the difficult task of blending historical accuracy with a pacy, action-packed plot. The background detail is convincing, the dialogue consistent and linguistically plausible and the characterisation empathetic. I am looking forward to the sequels."

"Well researched and evocative of the period and place. Well recommended. I am looking forward to the next one."

"It provides a story of humanity in the midst of violent upheaval and a glimpse of how average people, who are so often my own heroes, might have coped and sought to claim back their own future."

For my forebears: the many generations of Flint and Pattinson families who lived in Glenridding and Patterdale.

Contents

Author's Note

My motivation for writing the tale of Hravn and Ealdgith and their experience of the Harrying of the North, was a desire to leave something for my family's future generations that brings to life an early and easily forgotten period in our past. My parents' families, the Flints, Martins, Wilsons, Mattinsons, Pattinsons, Curwens et al can trace their lineage through 1000 years of life in Cumbria and the Borders, as far back as the nobility of the pre-Norman north, and through Gospatric to Earl Uhtred of Northumberland, King Ethelred II of England and King Malcolm II of Scotland.

Modern Western societies are increasingly equal and diverse in their social attitudes. The Anglo-Saxon and Norse societies of pre-Norman England had evolved from pre-Roman Germanic cultures and followed an Orthodox English Christianity. They were more equal in their attitude to women and their legal status than the strongly Catholic, constraining and more misogynistic society that developed under the Normans. I wanted my two heroes to reflect all that is good about today's society whilst remaining true to their own time.

Whilst writing, I have tried to use words that are authentic and made a deliberate effort to avoid those that have a French or post-invasion origin. That is why 'stake-wall' is used instead of the French word palisade.

I now live in Richmondshire, but spent many childhood holidays in the Eden Valley and on the fells of the Lake District, where I chose to use the traumatic time of the Harrying of the North as a vehicle for this tale. The geography speaks for itself. These are places I have known and loved all my life.

I would like to thank all those who have supported and encouraged me, not least in the laborious task of proof reading and for helping to ensure that the story is understandable to all. In particular, my wife Judith for her support and encouragement; my mother Clarissa, herself a true Cumbrian and incredible font of family history; my daughter Lara, always full of enthusiasm for the tale and in some little way a role-model for Ealdgith; my son Ian, for his calm interest; my granddaughter Serena Orme for her thoughts about Gytha as a girl of her age; my brother Paul for suggesting ideas and proof-reading, and my good friend Anne Wicks for her attention to my grammar.

My thanks are also due to Glenn Bailey from Woofdog for his graphic design and art work, and to Kathleen Herbert whose book 'Spellcraft – Old English Heroic Legends,' recounts the tale of Hildegyd and Waldere, from which I drew in Book 1, and helped inspire the characters of Ealdgith and Hravn.

Cumbraland and Westmoringaland

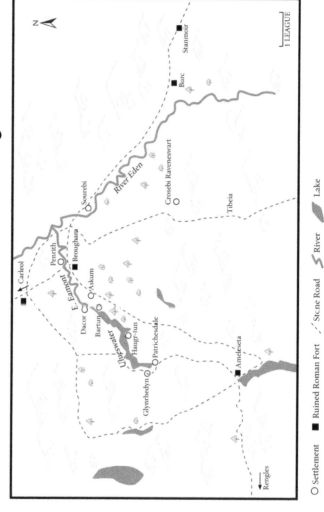

Stanmoir

Burc

Crosebi Raveneswart

River Eden

Tibeia

Sourebi

Carleol

Penrith

Brougham

E. Eamont

Askum

Dacor

Bartun

Haugr-tun

Ulfeswater

Patrichesdale

Glynrhedyn

Ameleseta

Rengles

N

1 LEAGUE

○ Settlement   ■ Ruined Roman Fort   ⁄ Stone Road   ✦ River   ◗ Lake

Place Names

Place names are those shown in the Oxford Dictionary of English Place-Names. I have used the name for the date nearest to 1092. Where a similar name has several spellings, I have chosen a common one in order to avoid confusion. Places that existed in 1092, but aren't listed, retain their present names.

Alnewich. Alnwick. Dwelling on the River Aln.
Ameleseta. Ambleside. Shieling or summer pasture by the river sandbank.
Aplebi. Appleby in Westmoreland. Village where apple trees grow.
Askum. Askham. Place at the Ash trees.
Bartun. Bartun. Barley farm.
Bebbanburge. Bamburgh. Stronghold of a Queen called Bebbe.
Bogas. Bowes. The river bends.
Borgarárdalr. Borrowdale. Valley of the stream by a fort.
Brethstrett. High Street. The ancient British and Roman way over the fells linking the Eden Valley to the Windermere Valley at Ambleside.
Burc. Brough. Stronghold or fortification. OE. Burh.
Carleol. Carlisle. Celtic; fortified town at a place belonging to Luguvalos.
Crosebi Raveneswart. Crosby Ravensworth. Manor with a cross owned by a man called Rafnsvatr.
Cumbraland. Cumberland. Region of the Cumbrian Britons.
Dacor. Dacre. Named for Dacre Beck, a Celtic river name meaning 'the trickling one'.
Dalman. The area now occupied by the Dalemain estate, meaning 'manor in the valley'.
Doolish. Douglas, on the Isle of Man.
Dunholm. Durham. Island with a hill. Also the county of Durham.

Dyflin. Dublin. Norse, derived from Gaelic 'Dubh Linn', meaning 'black pool'.

Eithr's Lake. Hayeswater. The lake by the enclosure.

Ériúland. Eire / Ireland.

Gatesheued. Gateshead. Goats headland or hill.

Ghellinges. Gilling West. Capital of the Wapentake of Ghelliges-scir.

Ghellinges-scir. Approximates to Richmondshire. North Yorkshire local government district embracing Swaledale, Arkengarthdale and Wensleydale.

Glynrhedyn. Glenridding. The valley overgrown with bracken. Cumbric / Welsh. Glyn meaning valley. Rhedyn meaning ferns.

Hagustaldes-ham. Hexham. The warrior's homestead.

Haugr-Gils. Howgills. Hills and narrow valleys.

Hep. Shap. Heap of stones.

Haugr-tun. Howtown.

Hindrelag. Richmond. English name before 1070. Origin not known.

Kircabi Kendala. Kendal. Village with a church in the valley of the River Kent (1095).

Kircabi Lauenesdale. Kirkby Lonsdale. Village with a church in the valley of the Lune.

Kircabi Stephan. Kirkby Stephen. Village with the church of St. Stephen.

Kircabi Thore. Kirkby Thore. Village with a church in the manor of Thore.

Lincolia-scir. Lincolnshire.

Loncastre. Lancaster. Fort on the River Lune.

Lune. The River Lune derives its name from the Old English word Lon which has its origins in an Irish Celtic word meaning health giving.

Melcanetorp. Melkinthorpe. Outlying hamlet of a men called Maelchon.

Morlund. Morland. Grove in the moor.

Mortun. Moreton on Swale. Farmstead on marshy ground.

Novem Castellum. Newcastle

Ofertun. Orton. Higher farmstead.

Penrith. Penrith. Chief ford.

Persebricg. Piercebridge. Bridge where the osiers grow.

Pulhoue. Pooley Bridge. Hill or mound by a pool. The 'Bridge' was added in 1800.

Ravenstandale. Ravenstonedale. Valley of the raven stone.

Rengles. Ravenglass. Either derived from words equivalent to Welsh *yr afon glas*, meaning "the greenish or blueish river", or the name may be of Norse-Irish origin containing the Irish personal name *Glas* and meaning "Glas's part or share".

Richemund. Richmond. Norman name after 1070; meaning strong hill.

Routhebiria. Rothbury. Stronhold of a man called Hrotha.

Sourebi. Temple Sowerby. Farmstead on sour ground. Temple affixed in 1292 due to its early possession by the Knights Templars.

Stanhopa. Stanhope. Stony valley.

Stanmoir. Stainmore. Rocky or stony moor.

Swale. River Swale. Old English 'Sualuae', meaning rapid and liable to deluge.

Tibeia. Tebay. Island of a man named Tiba.

Tinan. River Tyne. Celtic or pre-Celtic, meaning river.

Ulueswater. Ullswater. Lake of a man called Ulfr.

Westmoringaland. Westmorland. District of the people living west of the moors (Pennines).

Wlsingham. Wolsingham. Homestead of a man called Wulfsige.

Principal Characters

*Historical character

Lady Ealdgith. Gifted the lands of Shap and Ullswater by her 'uncle', Earl Gospatrick of Cumberland and Northumberland.

Sir Hravn of Ravenstonedale. Lady Ealdgith's husband. Their children:

> **Æsc**. Known as Bear.
>
> **Aebbe**. Married to William, Lord Ketel's son.
>
> **Gytha**.
>
> **Freja**.

Ulf. Master-at-arms.

Cyneburg. Ulf's wife. Their children:

> **Adelind**. Cynburg's daughter, adopted by Ulf.
>
> **Agnaar**. Adopted.
>
> **Aelfswip**. Known as Eir.
>
> **Leofric**.
>
> **Wassa**.

Godric. Ealdgith's housecarl. Married to Ada.

Ada. Ealdgith's friend and female housecarl.

Osberht. Child. Adopted by Godric and Ada.

Wealmaer. Housecarl.

Brandr. Housecarl.

Dai. Housecarl.

Mungo. Reeve.

Wassa. Housekeeper.

Cedd. Priest.

Neven. Cumbrian village girl befriended by Gytha.

Others:

*King Malcolm III of Scotland.

*Count Alan of Richmond.

*Dolfin. Anglo-Cumbrian ruler of Cumberland. Son of *Earl Gospatrick.

Felix de Kiberen. Norman / Bretton knight.

Aedan. Manx merchant.

*Jarl Buthar. Cumbrian / Norse leader.

The Harrying of the North

The Year 1092 – Cumbria Invaded

Sumor 1091

Chapter 1

Gytha braced her feet on the bough and eased her back against the broad trunk of the old oak. On top of a hill and twenty feet above the ground, she caught the low breeze that was the only relief from the humid heat.

The man that she was watching felt no such relief as he eased his horse to a halt on the hill opposite, unbuckled his steel helm and wiped the back of his hand across his brow trying to stop stinging salty sweat trickling into his eyes. All he achieved was to smear the red-brown dust across his forehead.

With a loud double click of her tongue against her teeth, Gytha cautioned Loki, her Wolfhound, to stay lying at the base of the oak. Loki, not long out of puppyhood, was responding well to Gytha's training, but still possessed the playful spirit of his namesake, the Norse god of mischief.

Gytha unslung the bow from her shoulder. It was long for her height, but the physique of her arms showed that she had the strength to use it. She drew an arrow from the quiver at her waist, notched it into the bow string and waited. Gytha liked to watch, and the high oak was a favourite lookout. The dust from the horse's hooves had attracted her attention. The man was obviously uncertain of his whereabouts, not that he was the first to go astray at the bend in the old stone road that led south from Penrith through the vale of the Eden. She had watched him crest a series of low ridges, pause to scan the land ahead, and then ride out of sight in the little valleys between. Strangers fascinated Gytha; they were rare. Her father's men patrolled the mountainous borders to their south and east, to secure their lands against Norman incursion and to control trade across them. This stranger worried her because he wore armour. Gytha could see the glint of mail under his scarlet cloak, and his black stallion was built for speed and strength. This man had a purpose.

The man tweaked his reins and urged the stallion forward, down towards a dusty track that wound between the two hills.

With a speed born of skill and training, Gytha stood upright on the bough, raised and braced her bow, slowed her breathing and tracked a point twenty paces in front of the horse. Her first arrow hit the centre of the track with a thwack that resounded in the still, early afternoon air. The second arrived unheard as it quivered in the turf two paces in front of the horse. Gytha smiled to herself as the stallion reared in surprise and the man yelled out, struggling to calm it.

The man struggled to calm himself too, recognising the arrows for the warning that they were; he would have been dead already if that was the archer's intent. He sat back in his saddle and scanned the ground to his front, then froze as he caught sight of a person high in the tree above him lit by a shaft of sunlight. A green tunic, leather breeches and cloth bound legs above mid-calf boots. It was a strange dress for a man, but stranger still for a girl just into womanhood. The beauty of her long, wildly unbound fair hair and the glint of green in her eyes attracted him. The arrow that pointed directly at his face chilled him.

Gytha had the stranger exactly where she wanted him. She knew she was safe and her voice expressed her confidence. "You have one chance to tell me who you are and what you seek. Now, speak." She spoke in English, unsure as to whether Norse, Cumbric or even Norman French might serve her better.

The man's accent surprised her. His English was hard to understand, but his condescending tone, that of a man used to giving orders, was obvious. "I am the King's messenger. I seek Sir Hravn. Who might you be? Now, lower that bow else you do more damage than you intend."

Gytha's scornful laugh shook the man's self-confidence. "And which king might that be? There are none that hold sway hereabouts, though two might like to. Of those, one is a bastard whose servants my father is sworn to kill. The other has, I grant you, some claim to my fathers' support." Gytha used the term 'bastard' with relish. It was a favourite of Ulf, her father's closest friend and battle companion, but one that her mother would admonish her for using. "If you are Norman, say a prayer instead of an answer," Gytha added, raising an eyebrow to encourage an answer.

"I am Urgust, young mistress. I serve King Malcolm of the Scots. If you are Sir Hravn's daughter you must be Lady Ealdgith's daughter too. My King has spoken highly of her, though she would have been little more than your age when they met."

As Gytha lowered her bow she said, "I am Gytha. If you seek my father I will take you to him. Now wait a moment."

Urgust took a deep breath, then blew it out with relief watching, surprised, as Gytha grabbed a rope and, leaning backwards, slid quickly down the tree. He swung down from the stallion to greet her, then paused as he saw the wolfhound rise up alongside her, its head touching her hip.

Gytha laughed, "This is Loki, his mischief can be a menace, but you are safe with him."

"Not as safe as you are, Gytha. It's a foolish man that would come between a hound like that and his mistress. I'll lead my horse and walk alongside you. Is it far? Now tell me, are all the women hereabout so fearsome?"

3

Gytha gave Urgust a quizzical look, then smiled. "As to distance, it is but half a league, and as to our women..." She laughed and shrugged, "Some, mayhap. Did you know that my mother once wore armour and led our people into battle? Not that she has to now, but she has taught my sisters and me to hunt with the bow and defend ourselves with sword and seax, as well as to fight and topple a man whilst unarmed. We've also learned to use the sling for hunting. Moder's taught my cousins too."

Gytha giggled when Urgust's jaw dropped in genuine surprise. It wasn't just the girl's obvious martial ability that surprised him, it was the matter of fact way in which she accepted it as normal.

"So, do you have brothers as well as sisters?" Urgust was intrigued.

"A brother, Æsc. We call him Bear, after my ealdfather. He's the eldest and rides alongside my fader. Then there's Aebbe. She married William, Lord Ketel's son, last year and is with child already." Gytha paused, then gave a little laugh. "It's such a Norman name, William, is it not? Moder hates it, but she says it's to be expected seeing as he has a Norman moder."

Urgust shrugged, letting Gytha chatter.

"Anyway, Moder says that Aebbe is like her ealdmoder and namesake, all books and needlework. She's not like moder; though I am, as is Freja. She's only nine but she'd kick your ankle rather than hug you."

"What!" Urgust chortled, grinning at Gytha, "And how old are you?"

Gytha smiled rather coyly, "Fourteen last Aefter Yule, not that I ever want to marry. I want to be like my moder when she was young. I have already tried her mail armour on. It belonged to Queen Aethelflaed, you know. As did her sword, or so she claims."

Urgust shook his head in disbelief. If Lady Ealdgith was like her daughter she must be someone to behold.

As they walked, Gytha studied the King's messenger through narrowed eyes. Though she was still suspicious, his casual charm reassured her. He had

4

removed his helm and slung it from the pommel of his saddle, revealing that his sweat-flattened red hair was shorter than the fashion of her father's men and that he had a close-trimmed beard. She thought he would be approaching twenty and of an age with Bear. She quipped cheekily, "Your English is funny. I can understand what you say, but it sounds odd. Is that the Scots' way?" Before Urgust could answer she added on impulse, "Ydych chi'n siarad Cumbric?"

Urgust stopped, turned and stared at Gytha before bending forward laughing, his eyes creased in merriment. "Wrth gwrs dwi'n siarad Cumbric – *of course I speak Cumbric.*" He continued to speak Cumbric. "Though my people call it Pictish. It is a beautiful tongue, is it not? Unlike that hard Irish Gaillic spoken by others in our kingdom. My king sent me knowing that I speak English and that your father speaks Cumbric. Did you know that Pictish, Cumbric and what the English so rudely call Welsh was the language of the old people and was once common across all our lands?"

Gytha smiled back at Urgust. "Yes I did, and it is a similar tongue to the Normans' Bretton soldiers." She paused, then added, "My fader, like many of our people, is part Norse and I speak that tongue too."

"What?" Gytha giggled as Urgust's jaw eyes widened. "Don't tell me you speak three tongues?"

Gytha shook her head sombrely. "No," then added with a smile, "Four. Moder insisted that Brother Cedd, our priest, taught us all Norman French. They are our enemy and she says if you can understand your enemy's tongue you can understand how he thinks."

Urgust nodded. "That makes a lot of sense. There aren't many who think as deeply as your mother, but she is right. What does your father think?"

"Oh, they are as one. They always are." Then, rounding a corner on the track, Gytha stopped and pointed. "There is our hall."

Urgust shielded his eyes from the glare of the high sun and studied a building that dominated a low rise two furlongs away. He gave a low whistle of surprise. The hall was unusual. Built on a low stone plinth, it formed an H-shape. Two long wings with steep thatched roofs that almost touched the ground, were joined by a large cross-piece with higher, whitewashed, wattle and daub sides and a large wooden door.

"Fader says that it is a mixture between the longhouse of his Norse forefathers and the English manor house of Moder's family. That building in the middle is the old manor house that was here when he and moder claimed the land. He built the far longhouse onto it for all our men-at-arms to live in, and then the nearest longhouse when I was little. If you look carefully you can see the porch on the side with Norse dragons above it."

Urgust nodded slowly, impressed.

Gytha took the opportunity to probe Urgust. Much as she liked him, a king's messenger could not herald good news. "What do you want with my fader? Is it war with the Normans?"

Urgust rounded on Gytha, his eyes pinched together under a low frown, his confidence shaken by the prescience of Gytha's question. "Little mistress. That is between your fader and me. Yes, there is war, but not one that will threaten the peace that you have here. Now, let us hurry."

*****

Gytha ran ahead as they neared the family longhouse and, as she burst through the gap between the high oak double doors, shouted, "Fader, Fader, there's a messenger here from the Scots' King. He says there's war." Then she stopped, suddenly hesitant. Her father was seated at the large trestle table playing neffa-tafl with Bear. Godric and Agnaar were playing too and she realised with trepidation that she had interrupted their championship.

Urgust stood back and admired the carved entwined dragon heads above the door, then walked in with a slow confident step.

Hravn pushed his stool back and stood up. He was taller than most men. Black hair shot through with thin strands of grey hung just clear of his shoulders, and a neatly clipped beard framed his chin.

It was Hravn's eyes that impressed Urgust. Black and piercing like those of the bird after whom he was named, they gripped Urgust's gaze. Bowing with a slight nod of his head, Urgust held out his hand and spoke formally.

"Sir Hravn, I am Urgust mab Oengus. My King sends greetings. I am sorry to interrupt your game."

"Hah! Why is it that I get an uneasy feeling whenever Canmore comes calling? Did your King tell you about the last time he ventured south of the border?" Hravn spoke brusquely.

"No, Lord." Urgust replied honestly, but with sudden reservations about Hravn and a slight feeling of insult that the King's nickname had been used so casually. Although 'Canmore' could mean an imposing head of a kingdom, it also referred to the King's over-large head.

"Gytha, go and fetch your moder, she will need to hear what the Scots' King has to say, then find Wassa and have her bring a horn of small beer and some food for our guest. I can almost see his thirst. Send for a bowl of water and a cloth too."

Hravn gestured for Urgust to sit by the table. "Come, whilst we wait for Edie, I will introduce you to my son, Æsc, though we all know him as Bear because he takes after his ealdfather and is taller and broader even than me...and better at tafl games too. Then there is Agnaar, my adopted nephew. I must add that Canmore bears great responsibility for the loss of Agnaar's family; of this we will no doubt speak more." Agnaar gave a brief nod in greeting. He was the exact opposite of Æsc: squat and sturdy, and with jet-black hair and sharp blue eyes, his face was the image of his dead mother's. "Finally, Godric, Lady Ealdgith's huscarle and my friend in many battles." Godric held out his hand to Urgust. He was of an age with Hravn and as tall, with a clean shaven angular face under thinning brown hair.

"Oh! I was forgetting." Hravn turned and pointed to a man and youth who were just entering the hall from the old adjoining manor. Both had yellow hair and blue eyes, and looked so alike that many mistook them for father and son. "My huscarle, Wealmaer, and Ulf's son, Leofric. They've already been knocked out of the game."

"Aye Lord. My direct approach was mayhap too direct to beat Bear." Of average height, Wealmaer's strength reflected his stocky frame. He blushed as he spoke about his defeat. "Though young Leofric here will no doubt shame us all one day." He laughed as he ruffled the lad's tousled hair.

Hravn turned to the boy. "Go and give Wassa and Gytha a hand to prepare food for our guest, then come and listen to what he has to tell me." Leofric ran off, grateful for an excuse to be with Gytha. They were the same age and spent much of their time together when Leofric wasn't at his father's hall in Patrichesdale, at the far end of Ulueswater.

As Hravn sat down, one of two wolfhounds lounging by the hearth got up and rubbed its muzzle against his upper arm. Hravn wrapped his arm around the hound's neck in a playful embrace then, casually scratching its muzzle, said, "This is Sköll, Hati is by the hearth. Edie and I have bred from their forbears since we were Gytha's age and have trained them to fight and hunt alongside us. A good wolfhound is worth a dozen men, I can tell you."

Urgust glanced around the hall. He had become used to his King's stone built palace but still appreciated the size of Hravn's home. He watched smoke from a low fire in the hearth waft up and out through narrow openings in the sloped thatched roof. As it did so it drew air in from outside, the slight draught giving the illusion of cooling them in the humid summer weather. Colourful woven blankets hung from beams around the edge of the hall, screened compartments behind and brought some brightness to the otherwise dingy space.

Hravn caught Urgust's expression and turned to Agnaar, "Fetch some lamps, Urgust will need to see to eat." Then added with a hint of a smile, "Mayhap that explains why you beat me so handsomely. A sleight of hand in the gloom could explain it." His face was serious when he returned his attention to Urgust. He was about to restart the conversation when a tall woman entered.

Urgust stood immediately on recognising Lady Ealdgith. She wore the same green tunic and mid-calf boots as Gytha. He bowed his head out of courtesy and, without waiting for Hravn's introduction, said, "Lady Ealdgith, you have your daughter's beauty. My King sends you his greetings. I am Urgust, his messenger."

Ealdgith gave a slight smile, appreciating the flattery, but wary of the message to come. "You're very kind, though my face carries lines of age that hers does not."

Godric rose and pulled a chair back for Ealdgith to join them at the table. As he did so, Hravn prompted Urgust to start.

"You can talk whilst you eat once the food comes but please, what is the message that has driven you with such haste?"

Urgust cleared his throat nervously. "Are you aware that in late Thrimilce, King Malcolm led his men into Northumberland and that he has now come south?"

Hravn nodded slowly, stroking his chin whilst he regarded the messenger coldly.

"The King commands...err...requests that you assist him at the siege of Dunholm. He would value your ability to translate the Norman tongue for him and understands that you have done this before." Urgust realised too late that he was misreading Hravn.

"What? In Thor's name! Does Canmore never learn? Whenever the north rises the Normans smash it back down and grind its people even further into the dirt." Hravn's reaction was explosive, and surprised them as he smote the table with the flat of his hand.

Urgust's stool toppled backwards as he jumped up, red faced.

Reaching up, Bear placed his hand calmly but firmly on Urgust's shoulder. "Relax, friend. Whilst your king has little sway here, we all have a common loathing of the Normans. I'm sure my fader will see the benefit of being present at Dunholm..."

"Ahem..." Ealdgith cleared her throat to warn Bear not to get ahead of his father, and Hravn to give Urgust a fair hearing.

Hravn sat back, raised his hands and gestured for Urgust to sit down. "Why has Canmore moved against the Normans?"

"Lord, he fears the rise of strong Norman baronies on the Lothian border and senses that the new king, William Rufus, no longer abides by the agreement that the old King William made at Abernethy. He is minded that he must move to take control of the lands north of the Tinan if he is stop the Normans pushing north of the Tweed."

Hravn shook his head with a look of disbelief. "Canmore is the one to blame for those strong Norman baronies on his Lothian border. It was his raids across it that irked the Normans. You also need to understand that my oath was to Earl Gospatrick of Northumberland and Cumbraland, not King Malcolm. He held Northumberland from King William and Cumbraland from Canmore. Westmoringaland was his in his own right. The Earl was Edie's kin and he conferred these lands on us. Canmore might claim that he rules Cumberland but he hasn't set foot there since well before you were born, and as for Westmoringaland? Well, it is most probably still under the House of Wessex; King Athelstan was the last to claim it. The Normans haven't come here, yet."

Hravn stabbed the table with his forefinger and continued. "Canmore treats our people like pieces on a tafl board. When Edie and I were sent to his court as the Earl's envoys, he promised to resist the Normans whenever they crossed his border. Instead, when the Normans did cross the border in the sumor of seventy-two, he withheld from battle, gave homage to William the Bastard and connived in expelling the Earl to Flanders."

Ealdgith interrupted. "Yes, but to be fair, Canmore did accept my uncle back two years later and conferred the lands of Lothian and title of Earl of Dunbar upon him."

"I know, but by then his health was broken and he was a changed man." Hravn added, sadness in his eyes. "Anyway, it was in the years just after the Earl's death that Canmore sent his army out of Lothian to ravage Northumberland and..."

Ealdgith stopped Hravn with a wave of her hand. "Yes, Gytha, bring the water and cloth for Urgust to wash his hands and face." Ealdgith realised that Gytha and Leofric had been standing in the shadows, afraid to interrupt and agog at the revelation about their family's past.

Hravn watched whilst Urgust washed and drank, then continued whilst he began to eat. "Urgust, it is best you understand the grief your king's actions have caused our people before I give you my decision. As I was saying, in the sumor of ten-eighty the Scots raided Northumberland, taking slaves and pillaging churches. But neither the Norman lords, nor their Bishop who holds the lands of Dunholm, did anything to stop the Scots. Factions in the church fought each other, the people rose against their Norman masters, killed Bishop Walcher and laid siege to Dunholm castle. It wasn't my battle, but we couldn't risk the uprising threatening the peace of our border, so I led most of my men, many more than I have now, to war in Dunholm and then stayed with them as they were forced back into Northumberland. The Normans reacted, as they always do. Bishop Odo, the Bastard King's half-brother, came north and harried the land again. Then the Bastard himself came north and once again accepted Canmore's submission."

Hravn kept jabbing the table with his finger to emphasise his points. "So, what did Canmore's little adventure achieve? He gained booty and slaves, yet lost nothing but his pride. The Bastard King, though, was given an excuse to gain a stranglehold on what was left of the half-free North. But the people of the North lost everything, as did we. Half our men were killed or grievously scarred by wounds. Our families were shattered." He gestured towards Agnaar. "His father and uncle, my closest companions, were killed at my side. Frida, his mother, was so grief stricken that she died broken hearted leaving Agnaar and her infant son, Osberht, to be adopted," Hravn's eyes flicked briefly to Godric. "It was the second time in ten years that the Normans destroyed all that we held dear. So, don't tell me, or anyone here, that your king holds our respect."

The room fell silent, save for the spit of logs in the hearth. Urgust watched eyes flit from him to Hravn, then he stood. "Lord, I have your answer and understand why. I thank you for your food and will convey your answer to my King."

Hravn remained seated as he glared at Urgust. "No, you do not have my answer. I have simply told you the facts from the past. Just as before, I cannot stand by whilst others set light to my borders. If your king is talking to the Normans about matters that affect me...," he gestured to those around the table, "...us, I must be there. Bear and I will come, with a dozen of my men. Stay with us the night and ride with us tomorrow. Gytha, show our friend where he may rest. In the meantime, Wealmaer, stand three sections to, whilst the rest of us plan what we must do."

*****

"Come, let's talk outside. I need to clear my head." The others followed as Hravn walked from the back of the hall into a courtyard formed by the three buildings. They sat around a table made from wide oak planks.

Godric spoke first. "It's happening again, isn't it? A war on our borders that sucks us in whether we want it or not."

"I think there is more to this. We have an old king and a young one, both striving to make their mark and both driven by the same red-haired wilfulness. The politics of kings is driven by big egos and are prone to rash decisions." Ealdgith was more perceptive about the threat facing them.

"Aye, as is Count Alan Rufus," Hravn added, "Although he'll be getting old, I haven't heard that he has died. He will doubtless be at Dunholm to take the battle to Canmore."

"Take care if he is. I'm sure he will hold a grudge. I can't see him forgiving you for spying for the Earl and betraying his king's business." Ealdgith referred to the time, twenty years earlier, when Hravn had insinuated himself into the Count's headquarters as an interpreter and then used the Earl's network of spies within the Church to forewarn him about the King's plan to come north and confront Canmore. At the same time Hravn and Ealdgith had led a resistance that successfully harassed the lands that Count Alan had taken from Ealdgith's father. They had burned granaries and mills and hampered his ability to sustain the garrison that was at the heart of the Norman's military might in the North. Count Alan had a lot to avenge.

"I will, Edie, I will. But what we need to do now is get one step ahead of whatever calamity is likely to befall us. William Rufus won't take the Scots' challenge lightly. We might not consider that Cumbraland is under the Scots' yoke, but he does. If he is provoked into action these lands could be forfeit. After all, Carleol is right on the border and an easy way into Strathclyde, and if he is of a mind to punish the Scots, it could be an easier route to take than fighting his way up through Lothian."

"You're right, Hravn." Ealdgith glanced at Godric as he nodded in agreement. They both appreciated Hravn's instinctive grasp of tactics and geography.

Hravn placed his palms on the table and looked around. "We've talked about this before, though Bear and Agnaar were too young then to be involved. If the Normans raid north from the Lauen valley, or down from Stanmoir, we could probably hold them. But if they are set on taking the vale of Eden there is little we, or anyone else, can do. We need to prepare to fight. Edie, whilst Bear and I are away, get Cenhelm and Gamel to work making more

13

throwing spears, lances, bows, arrows and lead slingshot, and refurbish all the cross bows that we have." He referred to the armourer and blacksmith who had accompanied them from Earl Gospatrick's service. Though both were now well into middle age, their skills were indispensable.

Ealdgith caught her husband's eye. "Let's not forget that if we lose control of the lead mines at Patrichesdale, and our ability to sell lead through the port at Rengles, we lose everything. The rents from the little land we might have left won't be enough to sustain the men-at-arms we will need to hold the lake and protect the mines."

Hravn gave a slight nod. "I know, Edie, I know. Agnaar, take Leofric and return to Ulf. Take the assistant armourer with you too. I want Ulf to build up our armoury in Patrichesdale. If we can't hold these lands we can certainly hold those around Ulueswater...we must."

"Aye, Lord, though I would rather come with you."

Hravn chuckled. "I'm sure you would, Agnaar, but I can't risk taking both you and Bear with me. Where would that leave Edie?" He winked at Godric as he spoke, knowing that the housecarl and Brandr and Dai, his two subordinates, were all the support that his wife would need.

Ealdgith interrupted before her husband could continue. "And Agnaar, please ask Ulf to make our hall ready. We haven't stayed there this year, but I rather think we soon might." She referred to the hall that she had had built nearly twenty years ago, as soon as they started to make a profit from their lead mines. It was situated on a small raised plateau above where the Glynrhedyn beck flowed into the lake.

Hravn nodded agreement, then continued, "Godric, get word to Ketel. He needs to know of the unrest and potential for war. Though mayhap he has already heard through his father in law." Ketel was their daughter Aebbe's, father in law. The son of Elftred, Ketel and his brothers had inherited swathes of land around the

Cumbric uplands from their late father. Elftred had been a powerful English lord who had held Cumbraland for Earl Gospatric and then advised his son, Dolfin. Dolfin now ruled Cumbraland and Westmoringaland from Carleol. Ketel's Norman wife, Christiana de Taillebois, was the daughter of Ivo de Taillebois, a Norman with a brutal reputation. He had been favoured by the late King William and held large estates to the south of Westmoringaland and across England. It was a complicated situation, but the intermarriage of Cumbric and Norman families had probably contributed to the stability of the region.

"Aye, Lord, though I will speak to Ada first. It is best she hears of this from me."

Ealdgith rested her hand on Godric's arm. "Of course. I'll talk to her too whilst you are away." Ada was Godric's wife and Ealdgith's companion. Orphaned when Norman men-at-arms had hanged her father for his inability to pay tax, Ada had then been so badly abused by a Norman knight that she always blamed this for her inability to have children. Hravn and Ealdgith had rescued Ada when she was barely out of girlhood; she had become Ealdgith's maid and been trained to ride and fight alongside her. Life's experience had made Ada hateful of Normans and suspicious of men outside her adopted family. Her childhood friend and subsequent husband, Ole, had been killed alongside Agnaar's father and the trauma of his loss had almost broken Ada. It was only Godric's and Ealdgith's careful nurturing that had released her from the black depths of despair, though her recovery had come at a cost. She had sworn herself to protect Ealdgith and Godric and to revenge Ole's death. When Godric had adopted Orme and Frida's baby son, Osberht, he had hoped that it would help warm Ada's heart. It had, but her hatred of the Normans was undiminished.

Hravn sat back and stretched his shoulders. The tension within him ebbed now that they had come to a decision. "Edie, I'll take three sections, leaving you with seven and the huscarles. I'll be happy with a dozen men plus Bear and Wealmaer. Godric, once you are back from Ketel, set to and train the men hard. Oh! Whilst I think about it, Agnaar, have Ulf recruit more men around the lake and have them trained in using the sling and the bow. Mayhap he should start with those who use both for hunting."

Gytha and Leofric had re-joined them during the discussion and were sitting quietly at the end of the table, rather awed by the talk of war.

Hravn glanced across to them. "Leofric. Ask Urgust to join us again. Tell him we need to discuss the route we will take tomorrow."

As Hravn turned to Godric, Gytha moved next to her mother. "Moder, can I train with Ada? There is a lot she can teach me."

Ealdgith nodded, with a sad smile. She saw much of her younger self in her daughter and knew that Gytha would inevitably be involved in any conflict to come. "Yes Gytha. I will speak to Ada first. I am sure also that it will help her control the demons within her." She paused, coming to a difficult decision. "Go and see Cenhelm and Gamel. I fear that your life will be as mine was at your age; it is time you had a sword. Have them make one as long and light as mine. It will be a challenge for them, but they will have time and it won't need fine decoration, just strength and balance. You will need leather armour too. Sadly, we lack the time and money, and even Cenhelm lacks the skill to make a suit of fine mail. Mine was made for a queen many generations ago."

Chapter 2

As the line of horsemen wound their way steadily up the hillside track, their mottled green cloaks blended with the moorland. Urgust glanced over his shoulder at those riding behind and appreciated that their epithet of 'green men' was well justified.

"Edie and Godric raided that manor back in lencten of seventy-two." Hravn rode next to Urgust and pointed with his spear down the valley to his right as they crossed the headwaters of the river Uuire, whilst making for the high ground above the Bishop of Dunholm's manor of Wlsingham.

Urgust followed Hravn's direction and gave a low whistle. "How old was she then?"

Hravn chuckled. "It was the night we raided right across Dunholm, burning mills and granaries to help confound the Bastard King's plan to march his army north. They came by sea in the end. We must have been sixteen or seventeen."

"Edie must have been as feisty as Gytha."

Hravn pursed his lips, thinking. "Yes and no. Gytha is pretty hot-headed. Edie and I grew up overnight when the Normans killed, raped and burned their way across Ghellinges-scir two years earlier. We were Gytha's age then. Edie thinks everything through before she acts, and she had been forced to fight and kill several times by the time we raided here. Even then, she was driven by the desire to look after those who were left of 'her people', as she calls them. Edie's father was thegn of the manor of Hindrelag and Edie was the only one in her family to survive. She's a natural leader; I'm not yet sure about Gytha."

Urgust cocked his head on one side, thinking. "Lord, you work your men in groups of four and give control to some who seem quite young. Why is that?"

Hravn nodded and chuckled. "Ah! A good question. It's how I've worked from the earliest days. I call them sections. Edie and I were part of the first group of four. My men are trained to scout, patrol and ambush. We move quickly and attack our enemies when they least expect it. It's the only way a small band can survive against a mass of men-at-arms. Two men can support one another, and two pairs work well as a team, supporting each other. My men need to understand what I want them to achieve and then work as independent groups. That way we can cover more land. That's why I choose the brightest and best to lead my sections. Yes, they need experience, but they also need good sense, a sharp mind and the respect of the men around them. Age isn't everything."

They were distracted by a curse from behind as one of the men's horses stumbled on the edge of a peat bog, nearly throwing the rider. Hravn cursed himself, "Hell's teeth! I'd wondered about bringing ponies instead, they're surer footed up on rough ground."

"Really?" Urgust was surprised. "I'd have though you would surely want horses in the event of meeting Normans."

Hravn juggled his hands, as if balancing the pros and cons of the idea. "Mayhap, but on ground like this, ponies will out-run horses and give us mobility, though they would be a liability on the flat fields and tracks around Dunholm. Come on." He urged his horse onward as Sköll ran to catch up with the head of the column. "We'd best catch up with Bear and then find somewhere to spend the night."

*****

Late on their second day Bear held up his hand to halt the column behind. From their position on the edge of a broad spur they could look across to the west bank of the River Uuire. Dunholm town and the castle were less than a league away.

Hravn studied the disposition of men-at-arms, both Scots and Norman. Dunholm was a fortress on a broad craggy plateau surrounded on three sides by a loop of the River Uuire. It was enclosed by high stakes and, in places, recently built walls. In the centre, a stone castle had been built on top of an artificial earthen mound. The north end of the plateau was protected by a high stone wall and gatehouse that overlooked a small town bounded by another stake wall. The defences had been improved a lot since Hravn's last visit over ten years ago. He shook his head slowly, unimpressed by the Scots' King's battle plan.

Urgust spoke before Hravn could comment. "My King split his army and crossed the river much further north. See how he holds the outer bank of the river, preventing the Normans inside from crossing over it and escaping. Yet, he also holds the town and can take the gate."

"Aye," Hravn said thoughtfully as he watched the dust from two score cavalry riding north, a league south of the castle, "but see also how the Normans are reinforcing with several conrois of men, and they have started to screen the far side of the northern gate. Those are Count Alan's colours. They could encircle the Scots on the far side of the river." Hravn watched as a raft was hauled slowly across the river. It was just beyond the range of an archer on the fortress wall. "I can't see how your king could evacuate his forces if the Normans did encircle them. It would take for ever using that raft."

"Yes, but..." Urgust faltered, seeing the logic of Hravn's argument. "Lord, mayhap you should hold your men on this side of the river. I'll take you across to the King on the ferry. You can see his standard flying in the town. He'll have taken a hall there for his use."

"I agree, Urgust. Lead us down there and introduce me to the commander on this side of the river. I'd like him to find us somewhere secure, from where we can come and go as I see fit."

They found the local captain down by the ferry site. He was a dark stocky man whose English was spoken in the lilting accent of the 'Old North'. "Ye ur welcome, laird. place yer men in th' copse oan th' ridge behin' us."

Hravn nodded his thanks and turned to Tófi, the senior of the three section commanders, whilst Urgust arranged a crossing on the ferry. Tofi, a giant of a Dane

19

from Bernicia, was one of the few who remained from Hravn's original war band. "Have the men make camp in the copse, set a watch, and get a meal going. Keep some food back for us. Bear, Wealmaer and I will see the King first."

The raft, three boats lashed together with rough-hewn planks providing a flat surface on top, proved surprisingly stable as the crew pulled it along a stout fixed rope. They shared the raft with a party of men-at-arms and two horses, the latter with their eyes covered to keep them calm. Hravn waited until the men had coaxed them off the raft before he followed Urgust up a slope to the walled town of Dunholm.

Bear looked at his father and grimaced as he wrinkled his nose at the fetid smell that hung in the warm air between the narrow row of shuttered houses. Hravn laughed, "It's not the fresh air of the country, is it? Wait 'til you go to Carleol, that really stinks." As they turned a corner a woman shrieked and pulled two children quickly indoors. A bolt rasped as it was drawn across the back of the door.

Wealmaer chuckled and glanced sideways at Urgust. "Trusting, aren't they? Must have thought we were Scots."

"What's that!" Sköll growled and Bear turned in surprise as he heard a sudden whir and the smack of wood against wood, followed seconds later by a loud splintering crash.

Hravn stopped and, placing his hand on his son's shoulder, pointed to a cleared space beside the Scots' headquarters where a group of men-at-arms clustered around a high wooden frame. "That's a mangonel, and the key to success at a siege. Urgust, we'll take a quick look before greeting Canmore."

Hravn and Bear stood to one side, watching as a long vertical pole within a sturdy wooden frame was winched backwards, down to horizontal. The base of the pole was fixed to an axle held in place by the bottom of the frame. Stout twisted ropes that bound the axle and frame together creaked loudly with the strain of rotation and stretching. Two men heaved a head-sized boulder onto a bowl-shaped bucket at the free end of the pole and, as they stepped backwards quickly, the pole swung upright to smack against a padded cross-brace. The boulder hurtled through the air and struck the centre of the gatehouse door a furlong away on the other side of a shallow moat.

Cheering as the door splintered and slowly fell backwards, the serjeant in charge of the men-at-arms glanced at his appreciative audience, "Watch this, we'll have the skitas now. Doogie, load stanes instead. Tam, raise the aim. I want to drop these just behind the gate."

As the pole was winched back down, a dozen fist-sized rocks were piled onto the bowl, whilst four additional pads of thick felted wool were placed on the cross beam.

The serjeant stood back, briefly checked the alignment of the mangonel, then yelled, "Now!"

Bear watched, mouth agape, as the rocks followed a much higher trajectory, seeming almost to hang in the air before dropping behind the gatehouse.

The men-at-arms laughed as the crack and clatter of rocks and screams of pain and anger showed that they had found their mark. "Same again, lads. That'll stop them reinforcing the gate. You carry on and I'll go and see if the master wants to attack it, or nay."

Hravn laughed at Bear's look of wonder. "We saw one of these in action last time we were here, at the siege in eighty. You were too young to remember then, but Ulf made one to see what we could do. It'll be up at Patrichesdale. Mayhap we should dig it out when we get back."

Urgust was less impressed. "Lord, my King awaits."

*****

Hravn bowed, then stepped forward to greet King Malcolm. Canmore had aged in the twenty years since their last meeting. Now rather stooped, his frame seemed even thicker set, whilst the bushy red hair and beard had given way to a bronze-grey. His balding, over-sized head appeared even larger. "My Lord King, how may I assist?"

The King's eyes held Hravn's for a few seconds, then he spoke in the Brythonic tongue common to Picts and Cumbrians. "Thank you for answering my summons, Sir Hravn."

Hravn didn't hesitate, "I must always react when the peace of my borders and my people are threatened."

King Malcolm's lips twitched in a thin smile, though there was no humour in his eyes. "My people, my borders, by whom are they threatened?" He continued as Hravn remained silent. "I came south when I learned that the young Norman king means to ignore the understanding that we have. You were to speak for me should that be needed, but..." he waved a hand dismissively, "...that is of no concern now."

Hravn frowned, puzzled. "Why so, Lord King?"

"The Bretton count speaks my tongue well enough. I should have remembered given that you were once a spy in his court. We have spoken and have an understanding that he will relay to his master."

"I..." Hravn was about to speak.

"You may take your leave. My stay here is at an end." He turned his head at the sound of the mangonel's thump, "That's just to keep the Count's men occupied until I'm ready to take my leave without their interference. Oh, and Count Alan sends you his regards. He regrets that he won't be able to meet you in person." Hravn felt a nauseous chill. The cold humour in Canmore's expression warned of the intent behind Count Alan's message.

With a curt, "Good day, Sir Hravn. Your service to me is at an end," the King turned and stomped out of the room. Hravn watched, speechless, then left without a word to the guards.

"The conniving bastard!" Hravn cursed as he re-joined Bear and Wealmaer outside. "He's playing me for a fool, and God knows what sort of deal he's struck with the Normans...he's drawn us right into the wolf's jaws. The Count knows I am here. Come, I want to be clear of

22

here tonight, even if we ride after dark." Hravn led the way back through the side streets of Dunholm town and down the hill to the ferry.

The low sun just touched the top of the hill behind the ferry as they waited for it to be hauled across. "We'll eat whilst Tófi strikes camp. I want us across the ford, over the Browney and into the woods beyond before the light fails." Hravn turned as his name was shouted from behind.

"Sir Hravn! My Lord would see you again." A young esquire was running down the hill towards them.

"The King?" Hravn called back, questioning.

"Yes Lord," the messenger shouted.

"You two go on, I'll take Sköll. Get the men ready to move upon my return. I'll see what Canmore wants, but we won't be staying." Hravn clasped Bear's shoulder quickly, then walked up to meet the messenger.

"Follow me, Lord. We haven't much time."

Hravn was surprised at the man's curtness and struggled to catch up with him as he led the way back into the dark maze of narrow streets and alleys.

"Wait! What...?" Hravn shouted ahead as the esquire stepped aside briskly. Too late, he caught a flicker of movement in the black shadow of a doorway ahead.

With a sudden yowl Sköll was flung backwards and collapsed, twitching, two paces behind. Hravn swung around and gasped at the sight of a crossbow bolt embedded in his hound's head. Then he pitched forward, unconscious, as the pommel of a sword struck the back of his helm.

*****

"Bear! Stop! Where's Sir Hravn?"

Bear and Wealmaer stepped back off the ferry and looked up as Urgust ran down the hill.

Wealmaer called back. "Hravn? The King's messenger came for him just minutes ago. He returned with him. What...?"

"No!" Urgust almost cried with anguish. "That was the Count's man. It's a trap."

Wealmaer grasped the gravity of the situation immediately. "I watched them go," he shouted, as he sprinted up the hill past Urgust, his sword already drawn. "Follow me."

"My king has betrayed you. I'll explain once we find Hravn." Urgust shouted through panted breath, slipping on smoothed cobbles as he followed Wealmaer along the twisting street.

"You skita!" Wealmaer screamed in anger as he turned a corner and saw Hravn stumble under a sword blow. He was barely twenty paces ahead. The assailant reversed his sword and was about to strike a death blow when, realising that Wealmaer was almost upon him, he turned and fled. As he did so, a crossbow bolt sliced through the gap between Wealmaer and Bear to embed itself in a door post. Leaving Bear to attend to his father, Wealmaer closed to within two paces of the fleeing man and flung his sword into his back. As the body pitched forward Wealmaer heard the sound of running boots receding ahead of him. He retrieved his sword and rolled the body with his foot. Blood bubbled from the young man's mouth as he lay, glassy eyed.

"Fader's alive, though concussed. We need to get him back to Moder's care." Bear's call drew Wealmaer's attention away from the dead youth.

"I'm afraid his hound's dead. I'll take his collar for you." Urgust carefully unclipped the thick leather collar then gently lifted Sköll's heavy body to the side of the alley.

"Thank you. We can't take him with us." As Bear knelt, cradling Hravn's head, he asked Urgust, "You spoke of betrayal?"

Urgust nodded. "It grieves me to say, but I heard the King talking after his meeting with Hravn. He has agreed with the English king to fall back to Lothian and then wait to meet him on the border. Red William has also promised to reclaim Cumbraland for my King in return

for controlling his barons in Northumbria. This is all to be agreed at their meeting.
Your fader's death was a separate deal with Count Alan. I'm sorry, I came to warn you as soon as I heard."

Bear removed his hand from under his father's head and grasped the Scot's forearm as they knelt beside Hravn. "Thank you. You placed yourself at risk and do so now by staying here."

"I will stay and see you safe across the ferry. The King has no cause to question my loyalty to him, but I have a duty to see you safely away." He hesitated, "I know there are wicker stretchers on the baggage train, across yon side of the river. I'll speak to the master once we cross the ferry. He should have a harness to suspend it between two horses."

Wealmaer touched Bear's shoulder. "We need to get Hravn away from here lest they return, or the King sends men. We'll take an arm each, around our shoulders. Urgust, can you go ahead, call the ferry and get more men to help?"

*****

Bear watched anxiously as his father lay on a stretcher, his head cushioned by a folded cloak. The glow from the embers of their fire threw a red glow, and a little warmth, over Hravn's body. He turned at the sound of muffled talking and caught sight of the silhouettes of two guards as they met and turned, retracing their steps around the camp's perimeter. It had been too dark to move Hravn safely by the time Urgust had obtained the stretcher and he was grateful that the Scot had offered to stay with them until his father was safely away from the King's encampment.

Wealmaer crouched down next to Bear. "You need to get some sleep, Lord. We've a hard, slow few days' ride ahead. Rest now awhile and I'll watch your fader. His breathing is regular so there's nothing more that we can do 'til he awakes, or we get him into my Lady's care."

"Aye, mayhap you're right." Bear nodded. "Shake me at the first light of dawn. I want us to slip away from here as soon as we can see to ride. The men can eat later, once we're over the ford and onto the ridge."

Wealmaer entrusted Hravn's care to Tófi's section, freeing Bear to choose their route, whilst he oversaw the protection of the troop. They bade farewell to Urgust at the ford over the River Browney and thanked him again for the two horses from the King's remounts.

Bear made the most of the late summer daylight, but it was a slow tedious journey with frequent checks that Hravn was breathing. Late on the third day, just after they had forded the Tees at Middeltun, Tófi shouted urgently. "Our Lord is awake!"

Bear wheeled his horse around then dismounted next to those carrying the stretcher. The horses stood still as he moved between them and carefully bent down to his father. Hravn looked up at him, blinking; dazed but conscious. Bear looked back over his shoulder to Tófi, "Lower the stretcher, slowly, and bring some water."

Bear knelt next to Hravn and dribbled water onto his dry lips. "Don't talk, Fader, we'll explain."

Hravn listened, but as his brow became increasingly furrowed Bear realised that he was confused. He leant close to Hravn and looked into his eyes. "Fader. Do you remember meeting King Canmore?"

Hravn's eyes widened as he mouthed, "No."

With a reassuring smile that hid his inner rising panic, Bear said, "We'll move on now and get closer to home before nightfall. You'll be back with Moder tomorrow. I'll send Wealmaer ahead so that she is prepared. She'll know what to do."

Chapter 3

"Eir, go and cut fresh mint please, and gather as many bilberries as you can. Thank God that they are in season. I want Hravn to drink plenty of mint tea whilst he recovers, it will ease any headache, and bilberries will reduce swelling and help his vision." Ealdgith spoke to Ulf's daughter, Aelswip, calling her by her familiar name; that of the Norse goddess of protection and mercy. "And Adelind, we'll make a start preparing him a room and a bed in the middle hall. He'll need peace and rest away from the household's noise."

Ealdgith busied her mind preparing for Hravn's return, thankful for Wealmaer's warning the night before. The stomach wrenching premonition that she had felt when Hravn rode off had been realised. When Agnaar rode to warn Ulf to prepare for war, Ealdgith had told him to return with Ulf's daughters, both of whom she had trained to assist her as herbalists. Fearing that open conflict with the Normans could not go well, Ealdgith wanted to be ready to care for any casualties that might return. She had learned ancient medicinal laws from Hravn's Cumbric grandmother and had added to her skills over the years in order to care better for her people and to tend to the wounds of those who had fought alongside side her in their early resistance against the Normans. It was a heavy burden and, as her household and wider family had grown, Ealdgith had striven to train others to carry out her work. Thankfully, and unlike her own daughters, those of Ulf and Cyneburg had shown a fascination since girlhood. Both already had a reputation as wise women. It was a role that was increasingly at odds with the teaching of the Church but, in the old communities enfolded within the land of fells, dales and lakes, pragmatic common-sense prevailed.

Ealdgith and Adelind worked quickly to prepare a room, moving a bed closer to the hearth, making a second one in the corner for one of the three of them to use every night, opening the shutters to freshen the air and scattering dried lavender over the floor. "Its scent helps soothe a headache." Ealdgith told Adelind, then hesitated before adding, "I'm worried. Hravn took two bad blows to his head many years ago, just before you were born. He was concussed both times and an infusion of mint seemed to help him then. I fear he may have a weakness in his skull, and from what Wealmaer has said this last blow nearly killed him. There is so little that I can do."

As the sun passed its zenith and began to drop towards the western fells, Ealdgith paced restlessly back and forth along the track to the hall, casting anxious eyes towards the hills to the north east from where the men would return. She turned as Godric called to her. "They are here, my Lady, I can see their dust mayhap a league away. Come. Sit a moment and calm yourself before they arrive." Godric was concerned. In twenty years of service to Ealdgith he had never seen her so unsure of herself.

Ealdgith took a deep breath to compose herself and, smiling at his worried face, gently touched Godric's forearm, "Thank you. Stay with me. Hravn will be as reassured by your face as by mine."

Bear urged his horse forward into a canter, drawing ahead of the troop, then skittered to a halt in a pall of dust in front of his mother. Leaping from his horse he hugged Ealdgith to him. "I'm sorry, Moder. I should have stayed with Fader."

Ealdgith pushed him back and looked into her son's eyes. "No. There is only one who betrayed your fader. Come, let us get him inside."

Bear supervised whilst Tófi's men unbuckled Hravn's stretcher from the paired horses and carried it slowly into the manor house to place it by the bed. They stood back, wondering what to do next.

"Leave us now. Thank you. You have cared for him well, but we will now strip him of his mail and move him onto the bed." As the men hesitated, reluctant to leave their lord, Ealdgith ushered them out. "Go, you need food and rest, and I need you ready should we have another fight brewing with the Normans."

Ealdgith knelt by her husband and gently stroked the soft beard on his cheek. Hravn gazed at her, his brow furrowed.

"I don't know what happened, Edie. Can you tell me?"

Ealdgith bit her lip, striving to control the mind-numbing panic she felt within. She willed herself not to cry and forced a gentle smile. "Of course, but first why not tell me what you remember? I'll start from where you begin to struggle."

"I, I... I remember Gytha bringing a stranger, a Scot I think. Yes, yes, Canmore's man. We talked here, in the hall. He wanted me to go to Canmore. There was something about Dunholm and the Norman King, but...that was in the past, surely?" Hravn's eyes flickered wildly. Ealdgith could see that he was becoming distressed.

She cupped her hands around his face to hold his attention. "That's enough for now. Come, let us get all that heavy mail off you, then we'll bathe you and get you to bed." Catching the two girls' sudden embarrassed glances she gently teased all of them, the humour helping to reassure her. "They are almost your daughters now. You've nothing to hide from them, and they have nothing to fear."

The women worked quickly as they unbuckled the mail and eased it carefully off Hravn's body, before progressively removing his grime-stained clothes and washing him with warm lavender scented water. "Now, my beloved, I want you to stand so that I can pull this shift over your head. Also, you need to keep your legs strong, we can't have you lying down all day. Here, take my hands. Adelind will hold your shoulders whilst Eir dresses you."

Hravn stood unsteadily, grasping Ealdgith's hands as she pulled him up, thankful for Adelind's support.

"Good, now we'll sit you on the bed." Ealdgith helped Hravn to sit then, as he lay back against a folded bolster, pulled a blanket and a fleece over him.

"Here, Edie says that this is your favourite brew. You must be so thirsty by now." Eir gave Hravn her sweetest smile as she handed him a cup of warm mint tea. "Would you like me to hold it for you?"

Hravn shook his head and sipped, moistening his lips with his tongue before drinking deeply. He breathed out with a long sigh. "Do you have more? The warmth does me good."

Ealdgith stood in the doorway watching Eir feed Hravn a bowl of broth, followed by the bilberries that she had harvested that morning. The girl had the blonde hair of her father, Ulf, and the wide-spaced eyes and high cheekbones of Cyneburg, her mother. With her hair tied back from her temples in two long plaits, Eir looked every part the earthly embodiment of the Norse goddess. Ealdgith knew why Bear was so attracted to her. It was time the couple were married; both were older than she and Hravn had been.

Eir took the empty bowl from Hravn and, as she stood up, Ealdgith replaced her on the edge of the bed. "I'll tell you now that which you have forgotten. Wealmaer returned here last night with the news of your injury and has told me all that passed whilst you were away."

Hravn listened intently without interruption. As she finished, Ealdgith took Hravn's hand and said, "I'm sorry about Sköll. I think they killed him first to be sure that he wouldn't fight to save you. He saved your life just as much as Bear, Wealmaer and Urgust."

"Yes." Hravn nodded. "I still can't remember, but I understand it all. We owe Urgust a great debt for his warning. I knew Count Alan would want revenge, but Canmore! I must warn Dolfin."

"No, my dear, you must rest. After a blow like that it will be many a day yet before you ride anywhere. I will warn those whom we must."

Hravn kept a grip on Ealdgith's hand as he said, "Edie, when I came around I thought it was ten years ago. I was looking for Orme and Ole and didn't recognise Bear. That really scared me. Everything is still so blurred. Even now I feel like I'm not here, like I'm floating."

Although they were still bathed by warm summer air, Ealdgith lit a low fire in the hearth to provide a focus for Hravn and to ensure that he stayed warm. As dusk fell, she replaced Eir and settled herself in the spare bed. She lay awake listening to Hravn's slow consistent breathing and was just drifting into sleep when she was jolted by a loud indistinct shout: "Hold the wall! Shields together! Orme, there's a gap. Orme...No!"

Ealdgith leapt from her bed and ran across the room, stubbing her toes on the hearth. Hravn was sitting upright, rigid and staring, but silent. She felt heat emanating from him as she placed her hand briefly on his forehead. "Oh, no," she muttered. Although she had never experienced it, Ealdgith knew that if a fever followed concussion it could be fatal. Without hesitation, she pulled all the bedclothes back then lit a pair of beeswax candles before soaking a cloth in water from a pitcher. Next, she loosened the shift around Hravn's neck and trickled cold water over his brow, face and neck, all the while gently reassuring him that he was safe and at home.

Hravn relaxed slowly and gradually lay back on the bolster. His eyes lost their frantic stare, but they didn't close. He lay still, wide-eyed and oblivious to Ealdgith's attention.

Ealdgith opened the shutters to encourage a flow of air then, taking a candle, went to rouse Eir. It would be a long night and they would need to work quickly to reduce Hravn's temperature.

When dawn's golden fingers crept in through the open shutters Ealdgith left to wake Adelind. Ealdgith spoke quietly as the young woman's eyes opened, "Please, help Eir whilst I get some rest. Hravn is full of fever and tormented by visions of his past. We must keep him cool. As the day warms up, sprinkle water across the floor, it will help cool the room as it dries. When the household awakes tell Bear to join me with Agnaar, Godric and Wealmaer at noon, then send Gytha to relieve Eir. I'll take over again once I've held council."

Ealdgith turned as the heavy curtain across the entrance to Adelind's chamber was drawn aside. Her priest, Father Cedd, spoke softly. "Sorry, My Lady, I heard your voice. Is something amiss?"

"I thought you were with Brother Patrick. Is he..."

"Yes, My Lady. He has passed. The canker took him quickly in the end. I have just returned from Morlund. He is buried and at peace in his church at last." Cedd referred to the large growth that had quickly grown on Brother Patrick's neck.

"I am sorry, Cedd. He was a good man and a loyal servant to my uncle. But, we have a crisis here now. Hravn has returned from Dunholm gravely ill after a blow to his head. Please join Eir in the old hall and sit with him. I know he has never been one to ask for Our Lord's Grace, as he has always felt a calling to the old gods, but your presence and friendship will help him now. Stay with him a while, then rest and join me in council at noon."

Godric rose and pulled back a chair for Ealdgith as she approached the table in the main hall. Wan faced and heavy eyed she looked at the worried faces. They all knew that Hravn was in grave danger. She held their gaze, stern faced, then took a deep breath before speaking.

"I cannot say if Hravn will recover, and if he does, I cannot vouch for his state of mind. At the moment, he seems seized by terrors from his past – all our pasts. It therefore falls to me, to us, to decide upon our future. We know that the Scots' King has betrayed not just Hravn, but all of Cumbraland. We know too that the Normans will take our lands as soon as the winter snows clear enough for an army to march." Ealdgith paused and placed her hands on the table to emphasis her point, "Thank the gods that we have had warning. We cannot waste the time that we have been given. Bear, I want you to take Godric and warn Lord Dolfin in Carleol. He knows me and respects my judgement. He knows too that Godric has always spoken for me. Dolfin will listen to you, of that I am sure. You must be back here three days from now." Ealdgith hesitated, aware suddenly that she had a responsibility to friends outside the immediate family. "On your way back, call on Tyr at Morlund. His late father, Gunnar, was the best of our friends when we first came to these lands.

Warn him and tell him to warn Aebbe, his sister. She is married, but lives nearby."

Ealdgith continued as both men nodded. "I will take Godric, go to Kircabi Kendala, and speak to Lord Ketel personally once you return from Dolfin. Now, before you left for Dunholm we spoke about the need to forsake these lands and hold those around Ulueswater. Agnaar, the harvest is almost in. Work with Mungo, the reeve, and decide how much we need to see the manor here through to lencten. Then move all that is left by cart and boat to Patrichesdale. Send warning to Ulf to prepare to receive it, and start now. Ignore the other manors, I will tell you momentarily what I have in mind for them."

She cleared her throat. "I haven't discussed this with Hravn, but I am sure he will agree. Wealmaer, call all those who hold lands from us to a folkmoot here, two weeks from today." Ealdgith used the English term, rather than the Norse 'Thing' to describe a meeting of freemen. "I will give them warning of what is afoot and offer those who want it the option of moving to new lands around the lake. There is unbroken land in Martindale, Boredale and Bannerdale, and more along the north shore of the lake around Wethermeloc. There is time yet for them to move with grain and livestock before the winter. I will instruct Ulf to arrange work parties to help with constructing simple houses. Those who are undecided are free to stay and take their chance under a new lord."

Bear sat upright and blew a deep breath, "Moder, are you sure?"

Agnaar was quick to support Ealdgith. "No, you're right, my Lady. The Normans have brought nought but pain to my family, this family. I've heard what the harrying was like. At least this way people will have a chance to leave before they are forced to flee."

Ealdgith gave Agnaar a tired smile of thanks. "Thank you. Let us not forget that in the harrying the Normans struck at Yuletide. They may do so again, though I would hope that the high passes will stop them. Sadly, the vale of the Jor was no such barrier."

Ealdgith looked at her two housecarls, "Godric, Wealmaer, what do you say?"

Godric's answer summed up the conversation and was all the support that Ealdgith needed. "My Lady, I've long known that the blood of Queen Aethelflaed flows in your veins. Whatever you decide, we will make it happen."

Ealdgith sat back in her chair, feeling suddenly relieved and less tired now that the decision to move her people had been taken. She turned at last to her priest.

"Cedd, stay close to Hravn and me please. I rather think I will need your counsel, even if he doesn't."

*****

"Ugh!" Bear spat, waving his hand across his face, "Fader said Carleol stank. By the gods, I see what he meant."

"Aye." Godric agreed. "It's always like this when the mess from the tannery hangs in the river as the tide comes in. It'll get worse the further into town we go, with the garden cess pits and street sewers. Look, do you see that red stone wall in the distance? That's the fort." He rode on, leading their way through the maze of narrow streets until they came to the gate house.

"My Lord Dolfin." Bear bowed slightly as he entered the chamber of the great Norse-style hall within the old sandstone fort at Carleol. "My parents, Sir Hravn and Lady Ealdgith, send you their greetings and bid me to relay news from the Scots' King."

Dolfin stepped forward and took Bear's hand. "Welcome. Ale? God knows the water hereabouts isn't fit to drink."

As they took horns of ale from a servant, Godric realised just how closely Dolfin resembled his long-dead father, Ealdgith's uncle, the Earl Gospatric. Tall, well-built with thinning brown hair and a beard that framed a round face with brown eyes, Dolfin was approaching the age the Earl had been when Godric first served him.

Gesturing for the two men to sit, Dolfin took over the conversation. "I sense that you are about to tell me that my cousin, King Malcolm, has come to terms with Red William. Am I correct?"

Bear and Godric exchanged glances. Bear spoke. "Yes, Lord, but I fear that I may have more to add. Please, what have you heard?"

"That Red William intends to take Carleol from me in order to secure his western border and prevent incursions." Dolfin spoke with a blunt frankness. "My cousin has offered me the earldom of Dunbar, once held by my father, as recompense. Red William will grant key lands here to some of his own barons, retain loyal Cumbric, Norse and English ones, then return kingship to my cousin."

Bear flushed bright red as he choked on a mouthful of ale. "What! That's a cynical concoction if ever I heard one. Do you believe it, Lord?"

Dolfin remained stern faced. "I have no reason to doubt my King's word. As for Red William, he is young but honest, as far as I know."

Bear passed his horn back to the servant then spoke, shaking his head. "I have just returned from Dunholm. Your king held the city in siege and summoned my fader there to help him translate whilst he negotiated with the Normans. We arrived too late, for your king had already reached an agreement using Count Alan as an intermediary. My fader was dismissed. As we prepared to leave, he was summoned back to the King, but the bastard had betrayed him to Count Alan and he was attacked. Thank God, we rescued him, but he is gravely ill and may not live. Is that what the two kings mean by 'securing the borders'? I'm sorry, Lord, but King Malcolm has forfeit my family's loyalty."

Dolfin frowned and placed his hands together at the finger tips as he contemplated the situation. "Sir Hravn, and Lady Ealdgith too, have long held those south-eastern borders peacefully and nipped any disturbance in the bud before it could spread. If Red William is set on taking Westmoringaland, he could well want Count Alan to secure the pass over Stanmoir from Richemund, and he might also want Count Ivo de Taillebois to hold the headwaters of the Lauen and the southern approaches into the vale of the Eden..."

"Which means," Godric interrupted, "that my Lord and Lady's lands would be forfeit."

Dolfin nodded, "Unless they can come to agreement with Count Ivo. Ketel is his son in law, is he not?"

"Yes, and my sister is married to Ketel's son, William." Bear understood Dolfin's line of thought. He realised, too, just how prescient his mother had been. He stood. "We'll take our leave, Lord. I fear that once the Normans arrive they will never leave again. I just hope that our family can withstand the shock."

As Dolfin grasped Bear's hand, he said, "Yes, well, if all goes awry there will be a home for you all in Dunbar. My father always held your mother in the highest regard. Do tell my cousin that, and give her my best wishes for her family's future."

*****

Ealdgith heard the horses arrive in the courtyard and went to greet Bear and Godric. "Come inside, both of you. Hravn is awake. His fever broke last night and he is more lucid; some of his memory is coming back. Tell us both what Dolfin said."

Bear caught his mother's arm as she turned to go back into the hall. "Have you told fader about the folkmoot yet?"

"No, of course not. I need to bide my time. He isn't ready yet."

"Mmm...it might be time now." Bear glanced at Godric who nodded agreement. "You were right, Moder, our lands may well be forfeit." He followed his mother into the hall and Hravn's chamber.

Hravn smiled weakly at his son, "I'm beginning to recall our time in Dunholm. I owe you my life."

"Nonsense." Bear laughed, surprised and embarrassed. "It was Urgust that brought us the warning, and Sköll that took the first blow. Wealmaer and me, well, we just did our job."

Ealdgith looked at her son. "Well?"

Bear pulled up a stool and sat by his father. "If you're looking for a hero, it should be Urgust. If he hadn't betrayed Canmore's confidence, we wouldn't be prepared to outwit the Norman's onslaught. I'm sure, for all his talk of family loyalty, Dolfin would not have sent warning. He already knows what's coming and has been promised the earldom of Dunbar, and Lothian too, no doubt. He has nothing to lose, and mayhap more to gain. He did say that Red William will settle his barons here, retain some Cumbric lords, and that he will no doubt want to secure the passes at Stanmoir and Tibeia."

"It's what we feared, is it not, my love?" Ealdgith took charge of the conversation. "It explains why Count Alan wanted you out of his way. It also shows that he respects your ability as a soldier; one who could really harm his ability to do his King's bidding."

Hravn's eyes narrowed as he concentrated on what Ealdgith was saying. "By the gods, my head's so fuzzy. But yes, Edie, I know what you mean. I can do him harm, but he will win. We have to be ready to withdraw into Ulueswater."

Ealdgith took his hand, "We are, my love. Those plans are in hand. Even now Agnaar is overseeing the movement of grain to Patrichesdale and I have called a folkmoot. We're going to offer land around the lake to all those who want to leave...to leave now."

Hravn tried to push himself upright, then fell back. "What? How can I manage all that?" He sighed resignedly, "But yes. You are right. We must move the people to safety before we can think about dealing with Count Alan."

Ealdgith laughed. "Worry not, you're surrounded by good men, they have it all in hand."

Hravn smiled properly for the first time, "Yes, and they are led by a good woman."

*****

Hravn walked Ealdgith to her horse and then kissed her before she swung herself up into the saddle. "Give my regards to William and love to Aebbe."

"I will. We'll be back by tomorrow nightfall." Ealdgith called Hati to heel, turned her horse's head and spurred the bay mare to a brisk trot. Godric followed, along with Ada and Dai.

They soon joined the Roman stone road that led up the limestone escarpment and wound its way into the Lauen valley, then south into the pass from Tibeia, where Ealdgith stopped briefly to talk to the section of their men guarding the pass from the old stone fort by the river.

They were on the border between Norman and Cumbric lands. Skirting those of Roger de Poitou and Ivo de Taillebois, they made for one of the few Anglo-Cumbric enclaves, that of Ealdgith's son in law, William, and his father, Ketel.

As they rode Godric closed up next to Ealdgith and called across to her, "My Lady, given that we know the Normans, probably de Taillebois, will take this border, I suggest we pull the section back from the fort at Tibeia. They would be overwhelmed in an instant in a deliberate attack, and we would simply lose four good men for no effect. Two could ride out daily from our hall and keep watch from the higher ground, then ride back to forewarn us of any movement up the stone road."

"I agree. I will tell Ketel that if he wants to keep his own lands secure, he must look to himself from now on." She frowned as another implication of the impending loss of control over their lands struck Ealdgith. "When we return from Kendala, take some men and ride to Kelda. It's a while since we last called upon the people there, but Hravn long ago promised Alfr that we would protect them should the Normans threaten the vills at the head of Swaledale. That day has now come and there is little we can do to honour his promise. When the Normans seize the vale of Eden, the people at Kelda will be hard pressed to sell their lead through Carleol or Rengles. They need to know that the Normans will soon surround them."

Godric understood Ealdgith's concern, "Did Alfr not die a few years back? I remember he had a very merry wife." He added, a twinkle in his eye.

"He did that. Edda was a good friend. She's gone too now, so I heard. Aage, their son is headman, and Agata is married with her own family." Ealdgith thought back to the time of their flight along the wilds of Swaledale and how Alfr had helped them set up their first lead mine at Patrichesdale. "Theirs is such an isolated community that I doubt any will want to leave, but if they do, they will be welcome to join us."

It was close to noon by the time they had covered the twelve leagues from their manor at Crosebi Raveneswart to Ketel's hall at Kircabi Kendala, and the horses were in need of a rest. Dai went in search of the groom whilst Ealdgith went into the hall to look for Ketel.

"Moder! What a surprise." A shapely and heavily pregnant young woman with the black hair and eyes of her father ran forward to embrace Ealdgith, then faltered, uncertain. "Is anything wrong?' Is Fader here?"

Ealdgith pulled her daughter to her then, as she released her from her embrace, said calmly, "Fader's at home. He's not well, but better than he was, we must talk. Please find Ketel and William, then I can tell you all together."

Aebbe listened open-mouthed whilst Ealdgith reported all that had happened. Ketel's face was fixed in a stern frown. "As you know, I see little of my father in law and Christiana is uncomfortable in her father's court, so we have heard nothing of this. The last I heard of William Rufus he was strengthening his grip on Normandy. If he has secured his base there, then he is bound to grip his northern borders here next. Canmore's getting old, and when he dies, the Scots' lands will be ripe for the taking whilst they sort out their succession."

"You're right," Ealdgith spoke quickly, "and I don't blame Dolfin for forsaking these lands. If his King won't fight for them there is no point in any of us trying."

"Yes, Edie, I can take steps to get closer to Ivo and I doubt he will go against his daughter, but I fear Hravn, and you too, have been a thorn in the Normans' side for too long. We should be secure here, but the passes and the central valley itself will hold a strategic interest for Rufus. If he has control of Carleol, and has secure supply lines to it, he can threaten Dumfries at his leisure."

Ealdgith's sardonic laugh surprised them all. "Red William's plans be damned. We'll never hold our lands along the Eden and are already moving into Ulueswater. When I return, we'll hold a folkmoot and offer those who want to move with us the opportunity of new land in the dales that feed into the lake, freemen and bondsmen alike."

Ealdgith responded to her daughter's look of surprise. "We have no choice, my love. Count Alan has already made an attempt on your fader's life, though I fear Hravn will insist on giving him a bloody nose when he comes."

"I'm sure he will." Ketel agreed. "I wish that I could too, but that would be the end of this family."

Ealdgith lifted her hand to acknowledge and reassure Ketel that she understood his frustration. "My worry is for the people who we leave behind. Aebbe, your dowry included Hep, Bampton, Askum and Bartun. When we move to Ulueswater we will gift you all our lands in the arc from Ravenstandale right around to Hep." As Aebbe gasped, Ealdgith turned to William. "The lands will be given into Aebbe's name, but it will be for you to hold them. Our only condition is that you treat the people just as we have. Their loyalty and hard work cannot be faulted. Ketel, it'll be for you to make your fader-in-law understand that Tibeia is William's, and not his to control."

Whilst Aebbe's look of surprise turned to a wide smile, her husband promised sternly, "Of course, my Lady. We both know what this means to you. Ravenstandale was Hravn's family's land before the Pendragons took it by force, was it not? My father has told me what it cost you both to win it back." William looked at his father before continuing. "If Hravn does decide to give Count Alan, or even my grandfather, a bloody nose then we will cover any tracks he leaves."

Ealdgith's smile of gratitude turned to one of consternation as she saw Aebbe flinch and grimace, rubbing her stomach. "I think I need to take a look at you, my dear, before I do anything else. I sense your time is not far off now."

Aefter Yule 1092

Chapter 4

Wind howled across the roof vents, blowing blue billows of smoke back into the manor house hall. Ealdgith studied the blackened rafters above, thankful that the hearth fire was of well-seasoned oak. At least it gave off less smoke and smelt quite fragrant. The air in the hall could have been a lot worse.

Hravn sat at the head of the hall's long table drumming his fingers in thought whilst his family and their housecarls joined him at the table. As he ran his fingers through his hair, he cursed the dull ache and fuzziness of thought that still plagued him months after the blow to his head.

Those around the table jumped as the hall door burst open, caught by a gust of rain laden wind. "Ulf, you made it." Hravn stood up and went to help his former master-at-arms as he strove to close the door with his one good hand.

"Aye, just. I stayed at Bartun last night. It was a hard ride along the north shore and I couldn't get any further. The lake is high with all this rain."

Ulf dominated the space between the door and the table. Unusually tall and powerfully built, he was thickening around the midriff. He always joked that it was age telling upon him, but they all knew that the wound he had received alongside Hravn in the shield wall at Routhebiria was the reason. His withered left arm, permanently suspended in a sling, hampered the exercise and physical work that had kept him trim.

He teased Gytha as she handed him a horn of mulled ale. "Thanks, lass. You look more like a Valkyrie every time I see you." She blushed as he added with a wink, "Leofric sends his love."

"And you look more ox-like too, Ulf." Ealdgith chided her life-long friend, defending her daughter as the men laughed. "Gytha, take Ulf's cloak and hang it to dry by the hearth."

As Ealdgith sat down, she asked, "And how was your Yuletide, Ulf? Ours was a little more sober than usual. I've not long returned from attending to Aebbe. She has just given birth to a daughter who they have named Gunilda, as is common within Ketel's family."

"Well, that's news we must toast. As to our Yuletide, it was fair to middling." Ulf had a twinkle in his eye. "Some would say it was quiet. Alv, son of Ragnaar the boat builder, was the only one to fall off the table whilst trying to drink a horn of ale standing on his head, then Leofric threw a sack of hens onto the table in the middle of the feast. There was mayhem when they tried to fly free." Ulf continued whilst Gytha giggled, "He made up for it later when I had him stand on the table and play his lyre for us all. He has a talent, I'll give the lad that."

Hravn returned to his seat and called the meeting to order. "Before I start, Ulf, tell us how those who moved from our lands are faring."

Ulf shrugged and smiled. "No problems to speak of. There are always those who cuss and moan, but I gather most of those are the ones who chose not to move. Those who did are, in the main, content. I'm thankful that fewer came than I anticipated, and they seem to be the ones with some imagination and drive. Most went to Martindale and inland from there. I think they found it more secluded and potentially more defensible than the open lake shore at Wethermeloc, and I agree with them. We felled some of the forest higher up the dales to provide timber for cottages, and most have started to break new ground. I've provided boats to row and there are plenty of trout, char and schelly in the lake. We've enough grain to see us through and provide seed corn too. So, it's good. Your plan worked well, Edie."

"Thanks, Ulf. How about preparing for the Norman threat coming our way?"

"Ah, a matter close to my heart." Ulf beamed, a wide smile across his florid face. "All the men of Patrichesdale are committed. The boats are fully crewed and I have three new sections of archers and three of slingers. We've been casting lead slingshot for months now. Crafting more bows and building up a stock of arrows is taking longer."

Hravn shared Ulf's enthusiasm, "Good, that's much better than I had hoped. When you return take Bear and Agnaar with you. They can fetch a couple of casks of slingshot back with them, so don't stop casting. Now, err, we saw a .... man... mangonel in action at Dunholm, and Bear and I have an idea as to how to use the one we made years ago." Ealdgith glanced quickly at Ulf as Hravn fumbled his words.

Ulf slapped the table with his right hand. "Hah! I'm ahead of you there. I've had the skein of ropes and sinews renewed and set it up below the hall at Grassthwaite Howe. It's a mean beast, young Bear, with some vicious quirks. I'll show you and Agnaar how to fight with it, and we'll train a section to crew it."

Bear glanced across to Ulf and mouthed his appreciation.

Ealdgith caught Gytha's eye across the room, read her expression, nodded and leant to whisper in her son's ear. "Take Gytha with you."

Ulf continued. "Lord, have you decided when you will move from here?"

On looking briefly at Ealdgith, Hravn shook his head. "Not yet, Ulf. I'm keeping a close eye on the weather, but I can't see the Normans moving over the Pennines until they can be sure of a safe line of supply. Whichever route they come, they can't risk bad weather cutting them off. Ketel's been cultivating links through his fader-in-law and now has spies in the Norman castles at Richemund and Novem Castellum. He's just sent warning that troops are gathering at both, mainly Breton mercenaries at Richemund, and Flemings at Novem Castellum. If Red William is funding them, it shows that he is serious."

Ulf's expression lost its joviality. "How much warning do you expect? A spy is all well and good, but he has to be able to get a message out."

"I'm not so worried about Novem Castellum. Any advance from there will be against Carleol, and we know that Dolfin will go north when the Normans come. Richemund is the threat, and the high road over Stanmoir summit. It's not a place for marching troops and a baggage train at the moment, but I intend placing two sections up in the old stone towers on the tops and keeping a standing watch on the new Norman castle at Bogas."

"Phew!" Ulf pulled a face and shivered. "That would be too much for my old bones these days." Then he nudged his foster son sitting next to him. "Agnaar's up for it though, I bet."

Agnaar laughed, "I am. What's more, I picked up talk in Kircabi Stephan yesterday that strangers were seen on the road near Burc the other day, and they weren't merchants by the sound of it."

"Once Bear and Agnaar are back from Patrichesdale, I've told them to create a base in the forest on the high ground north of the stone road between Burc and the summit. They are going to stockpile fodder and arrows there. I intend to hit the Count once he steps off Norman land and to draw his attention away from our lands here. If Edie hasn't moved to join you by then, it will give us a chance to break clean away."

Ealdgith interrupted her husband. "I hope we'll be with you by then, Ulf, but Hravn's right. We don't know when Count Alan will strike and we have to draw his attention away from Ulueswater for as long as possible. Hravn's a marked man now, as far as the Count is concerned. He proved that at Dunholm. It'll break my heart to leave these lands after we fought so hard to claim them, but we'll keep them in the family by gifting them to Aebbe. William assures me he will care for those who remain. I just pray that Ivo de Taillebois's patronage is sufficient to keep the King at bay." She added, with a weak smile, "At least I'll be able to see more of Cyneburg. But, to answer your question, plan on the rest of my household joining you in early lencten if we haven't come sooner."

She shrugged, "Anyway, we'll be down to the last of our food by then. I've already sent the rest ahead."

"Good!" Hravn stood and slapped his hand on the table. "I'm sure you need a meal, Ulf. Join us."

"I will that, and I still need to toast the head of that first granddaughter of yours."

As they stood, Ealdgith attracted Ulf's attention and gestured with her head to a far corner. He joined her, worried by the anxiety in her face. "Ulf, do you ever feel that the terror from moments in your past is still with you? I sometimes relive moments, such as when you sliced Math's body in two with your Danish axe, just down the track from here. But I never wake tormented. But Hravn does, ever since that blow at Dunholm."

Ulf frowned, disconcerted by the question and hesitated. "At times, yes. Cyneburg will tell you of my torments. I was bad for a while after the campaign in eighty. The shield wall at Routhebiria kept haunting me, as did the ghosts from the one at Fulford, with your father in sixty-six. It was always the shield wall. Crushed together, hacking, stabbing, covered in gore, trampling friends when they fell at my side, and without pause, just an endless constant bestial fight..." Ulf stopped speaking, expressionless.

Ealdgith had never seen him like this; she took his one hand in hers. "I'm sorry, Ulf. I shouldn't have asked. It's the shield wall that haunts Hravn too, and a fire."

Ulf nodded, "Elreton Mill. Where we lost Alfric in the explosion. Surely you remember what Hravn was like after that, when you led us away from the Norman patrols and over the bridge at Persebricg?"

Memories of finding Hravn deafened and dazed flooded back. "Yes, I do," Ealdgith said softly.

*****

Bear always smiled to himself when he watched Ulf ride a fell pony. The large stocky warrior on the small equally stocky mount looked so incongruous, but he didn't dare comment. Having seen Ulf and his mother in conversation at the hall he knew that something was amiss.

Ulf slowed his pony to a halt by a gap in the trees above the lakeshore and pointed across the lake to a prominent fell, with craggy slopes that fell steeply to the water's edge. "Do you see, either side of Hallin, those are some of the new settlements for your moder's people. Haugr-tun and Sandrwic, both with a beach for boats and several sheltered dales beyond them."

"They'll certainly be safer there." Bear appreciated the protection provided by the steep fell sides. "Are there any routes out at the heads of the dales?"

"Aye, there's a pass from Haugr-tun to Sandrwic at yon side of Hallin, then another from Sandrwic up Boredale around the back of Place Fell, that high lump to the right. Then it makes its way around and down to Patrichesdale. It's mayhap five leagues in all."

Riding on again, Gytha closed up alongside Ulf. She glanced across to him, questioningly, "I've usually gone to Patrichesdale by boat. I know that this old track is worn and muddy, and is almost completely overgrown in places, but surely, it's quite easy to follow. Do you think the Normans will find it?"

"Aye, they may well do, but they will be vulnerable to an ambush if they do. Your fader and I are masters at that, your moder too."

Ulf laughed at Gytha's sudden grin and pleading eyes, "Hah lass! Yes, you've persuaded me. I'll show you how to plan one, young Valkyrie. Something tells me that one day, you and Leofric will be as big a thorn in the Normans' side as your parents were at your age. Now, bide a while and I'll show you all something that I have in mind."

"Is this what you mean, Ulf?" Gytha asked as she halted just beyond the trees, where the rutted muddy track joined a paved road that swept away from the lakeshore up into the hills to her right. "Are these old roads used much? Here's another in much better condition. It seems to come down from a high pass to the north and lead into Patrichesdale. Surely it means that there are two ways in. Is it not...?"

Ulf nodded, interrupting Gytha, and held up his hand to stop her next question. "You're quite right." He turned to the men as they closed up and stopped by the track. "Now lads, all of you, tell me what you see and what we can do about it?"

Agnaar frowned, puzzled at first by Ulf's question, then said, "The Normans would appear to have two lines of approach. We would need to block them in yon wood, but it's very close to home.".

"It's a threat to your front door, Ulf. I fear that by moving here, we might just be jumping straight from the hearth's fire into the cook's pot." Dai pulled a sour face.

Bear laughed. "I like your analogy, Dai. But Ulf spoke of an ambush just now. I think I can read his mind. What do you think, Gytha?"

Gytha's jaw dropped, then she smiled at her brother, her eyes alight with excitement and the sudden realisation that he had faith in her. She paused for a moment, then her heart leapt as she grasped the simplicity of what Bear had seen. "I don't know what lies over that high ridge to the north, but I'd wager Bear's boots that the Normans wouldn't venture over it in this direction in a hurry. How would they know that the lake lies this side of it? If they come, they'll follow the same track as us from the foot of the lake. From where we stand, we can't see the stone road again after it enters the trees fifty paces ahead. We only assume that it leads to Patrichesdale. Is that right, Ulf?"

He smiled at Gytha encouragingly. "Aye, it does, it follows around the lakeshore for half a league, we just can't see it through the trees. Then the way is blocked by a rocky bluff; you can see it jutting out at the base of The Dodd." He nodded to a broad tree-clad fell with a craggy top. "It turns when it crosses the beck and cuts up around the bluff."

"So why don't we dig up the track between here and the trees and plant scrub and grass to hide where it runs? That would channel any Normans up the track to our right, away from Patrichesdale, and into an ambush."

"Well said, young Valkyrie," Ulf's large hand rubbed Gytha's shoulder affectionately, "you're your moder's daughter, for certain."

She grinned at Bear's wink and then gave an embarrassed laugh at Agnaar and Dai's looks of amazement.

Ulf's fell pony twitched nervously as he guffawed loudly. "Gytha may be a girl, but don't underestimate her, just as you must never underestimate her moder when it comes to planning a battle. Tell us, Bear, what are the lessons here?"

Bear didn't hesitate. He was as pleased as his younger sister to bask in the battle-proven warrior's praise. "The lessons? Well, first, to see the shape of the ground as your enemy sees it, then plan how to use the ground to defeat him. If you think that he can see something you don't want him to see, then conceal it or move it. When you strike, do so quickly and keep moving faster than your enemy can react. Keep beating him to the punch."

"Hah!" Ulf punched Bear playfully in his chest. "There you have it. You've been well schooled by your fader; brother and sister alike." Then he hesitated. "Dai, you ride ahead with Gytha. I need a word with our two young captains."

Agnaar cast a quizzical glance at Bear, then sidled his horse next to Ulf. "Surely my tactics weren't that bad, Ulf?" He joked.

"Hmm...I've heard worse, though your idea wasn't as bad as you think, as you've obviously forgotten the remains of the stone fort and ditch only two hundred paces into the wood." Bear roared with laughter at his friend's very obvious embarrassment, until Ulf's next words sobered his humour. "Laugh not, for this will be your battle to fight. Your moder and I fear that your fader will struggle after that blow to his head. That's why I want to talk to the two of you out of Dai's earshot."

Bear leaned forward in his saddle and gripped his pommel as he listened to Ulf. He knew Ulf was right. The change in his father worried him and he was grateful to Ulf for putting his thoughts and fears into words.

"Aye, Ulf. You're right. I've seen how he's changed. I just couldn't bring myself to speak openly." He glanced at Agnaar, "You've seen it too, haven't you? Remember how he kept pausing to think when he briefed us all yesterday."

Ulf continued as Agnaar nodded. "We must be careful not to take authority away from him. We are all bound to him, and to Lady Ealdgith, but you will invariably be his deputy in the field, Bear, and if not you then Agnaar. If Hravn falls then you must command alongside your moder. That place was once mine, but..." Ulf shrugged, making his withered arm flop helplessly. "My counsel to you is that you must now be alongside your fader all the time, understand what he is thinking and lead should he falter. I can see that, whilst his logic and instincts are as strong as ever, he now lacks the sharpness to react quickly. I've seen the effect of a blow to the head before, and he's going to need your help. Share his thoughts and yours with your moder and heed her counsel, just as your fader always has."

Bear looked up, stern faced, "Thank you, Ulf, I understand. I will speak with Moder when I return."

"And," Ulf raised an eyebrow, "keep Gytha involved too. I see a lot of your moder in her, mayhap more than your fader does. One day she may have to lead in lieu of her moder, and to do that, our people must have faith in her. Let her prove herself where she can."

"Aye..." Bear gave a long sigh. "Everything is changing."

*****

"Don't dawdle, Leo." Gytha shouted over her shoulder, then ran down the muddy track from the long wooden hall at Grassthwaite Howe. The early morning sun gave a luminous green glow to the lichen-covered thatch of its roof. Ulf's hall, on a raised platform atop a high promontory backed by a wood covered hill, was built in the Norse style typical of the Cumbric dales. Leofric laughed and then sprinted after her, his leather boots slipping on the icy mud as he struggled to keep his balance, clutching his bow over his shoulder.

Gytha stopped at the bottom of the hill and waited for Leofric, whilst Loki ran back to meet him.

"Shall we go and shoot some fowl by the lake shore?" Leofric asked, as he caught up with her.

"Hah! Why not? Let's see who's first to hit a duck at a hundred paces, then we can try my sling. But first, I want to show you a new throw that Ada taught me. We can practise under the stand of fir trees. The needles on the ground will be soft and dry after the frost, at least I hope so for your sake." She teased, poking the tip of her tongue at Leofric.

Whilst Gytha unbuckled the sword that was now her prize possession, she surveyed the bed of pine needles. She kicked several fallen cones away and then bent down and flicked the last one at Leofric, catching him on the back of the head. She laughed as he spun around. "Catch me, and I'll show you Ada's throw."

"Feel it as I fall, more like. I know your game." Leofric laughed back as he edged towards Gytha, his arms held wide as he swayed, judging his moment to lunge at her.

Gytha stopped laughing and focused on Leofric's eyes, watching the movement of his body with her peripheral vision, trying to read his intentions and anticipate his next move.

They were evenly matched in height: Gytha, tall for a girl, slim but with muscular arms from practising with bow and sword, moved with fluid agility. Leofric lacked his father's height, but having inherited his strength, was a difficult opponent for Gytha. She relied upon using a man's weight and size against him. Leofric's low centre of gravity made him hard to topple.

When they trained together Leofric usually used a wooden sword, and Gytha could anticipate a move by watching the hand holding the sword. This time it was different. Gytha guessed that Leofric would probably try to catch her out by leading with his other arm.

Ealdgith had long ago drummed into her daughter that if she was to survive as a woman in a man's world, and gain the respect of the men she might one day lead, she must be able to stand against a man, bring him down and if needs be kill him. Gytha was grateful that she had never, as yet, had to fight to protect her honour or defend her life, but she knew that day would come. She had heard her parents' stories about the harrying and their struggle to survive and find a safe haven. Her life in their safe haven was at an end and she now used every spare moment to train and learn the skills needed to fight the sort of war that was to come.

Gytha balanced on the balls of her feet, her knees bent slightly and her hands raised, ready. She danced rhythmically from side to side, watching; then sprang quickly to her right and, turning a full circle, stepped behind Leofric just as he lunged with his left arm.

As Leofric turned and closed the space that she had opened between them, Gytha dropped down and backwards, her downturned palms taking her weight as she kicked forward with her legs into Leofric's shins. The momentum of his turn brought him crashing down as she rolled deftly to one side and stood up, with her foot pressing lightly on Leofric's back.

He laughed, "You always go through my legs, or pull me down over your back. That hurt!" He rolled away, sat up and rubbed his shins. "But it's risky, mind. If your opponent fell on top of you, that would be it."

Gytha grinned. "Yes, I thought of that, but if fighting for real I would have my long knife. Godric showed me just where to use it to kill a man instantly."

Leofric winced, laughing. "Mmm...its best you don't practise that on me." Then he reached for Gytha's hand. "Come, sit by me."

As Gytha sat, with her arms braced behind her, Leofric said. "You're beautiful, Gytha."

He smiled cheekily, watching Gytha blush. "I didn't mean to look at, though of course you are, but when you move. You're not like your moder, or Ada. I've watched them both training with Godric. Ada is like a cat in a fight; swift and vicious. Edie is fast and fluid, like water splashing in a pool. But you. You have a rhythm, like music brought to life. It's like when I play Aunt Frida's lyre, and match it to Moder's singing, and to Adelind's too, now that Moder is training her to sing. I could do the same for you when you move. I can see it, Gytha, but it would be like no dance we've seen before."

Gytha stared at Leofric, speechless, straight faced. She had watched him accompany Cyneburg's singing many times, but she had never heard him talk so beautifully about his music. She smiled slowly, visualising what he meant. "Yes, Leo, I can see it too." She leant forward and kissed him quickly, before rolling away and standing up. "Tell me more as we walk down to the lakeshore."

Gytha took Leofric's hand as they walked and glanced at him from the corner of her eye. They had grown up together, played together and confided in each other as if they were twins. She had assumed that they would always be together as platonic companions, but of late she felt more, and she sensed that Leofric did too.

"I think Bear and Eir must marry soon, and Agnaar and Adelind too, don't you?" Leofric asked suddenly.

"Yes, happen." Gytha was dismissive. "I hadn't really thought of it. Bear and Agnaar have been so busy riding with Fader, and since Dunholm and Fader's injury, there's not been time for a wedding. Bear and Eir live as man and wife already when they can, and I suppose Agnaar and Adelind do too. Why do you ask?" Gytha was suddenly intrigued.

"Because I can see you dancing at their wedding feasts." Leofric squeezed her hand, then released it and slipped his arm around her waist as they continued to walk.

"Now!" As Ulf shouted, Agnaar pulled a cord and stepped back quickly, tugging out the safety pin holding the mangonel's arm in place. The arm sprang forward swinging a long sling behind it.

"Mark where they fall." Bear flinched with surprise as the long wooden arm of the mangonel slapped against a pile of woollen fleeces and the rear end of the wooden frame jerked violently. Ulf's shout drew Bear's attention back to the half dozen fist-sized rocks that had soared into the air from the sling. He almost lost sight of the black dots against the bright winter sky, but kept track until they fell a couple of paces apart at the far side of the field in the broad valley bottom.

Ulf roared with laughter. "I warned you that it had some mean habits. That's only one of them. Right, young Bear, pace out how far the rocks went. Take that sack and gather them up. There's no point in wasting good ammunition. In the meantime, we'll set this up for another throw." He turned to the section of men, "Come on, winch the arm back up."

Bear counted diligently as he paced a direct line across the valley bottom. The power of the mangonel impressed him. It was different to the one at Dunholm and, having seen it work, he understood why Ulf had changed the design. Instead of using a high wooden beam to block the arm's violent swing forward, Ulf allowed the impact of the arm to be cushioned by a great pile of fleece bales. It reduced the chance of a catastrophic break in the arm and the weight of the machine. The addition of the sling had been a good idea too, increasing the range by lengthening the swing of the arm and enabling the point of release to be adjusted. Bear jogged back to Ulf.

"Phew! Just over three hundred paces." Bear panted, grinning.

"Good, good. A furlong and a half. That's all we need."

Agnaar laughed at Bear's questioning frown. "From the bluff below the Dodd to Tethera island."

54

Agnaar referred to the third of the little islands in Patrichesdale bay. "Hasn't fader told you his plan?"

"I was going to let Bear work it out for himself." Ulf chuckled.

"Ah!" Bear's eyes lit up. "I think I know how that devious brain of yours is working. If the Normans attack by boat, they will have to pass the island to get into the bay at the head of the lake. The rocky face of the bluff stops them landing on the north shore so if we block them on land, as we discussed, and block them by water they can't get into the bay," he paused, "and, yes, that island must be a furlong and a half from the bluff. You're a cunning old dog, Ulf."

"There's more," Agnaar interrupted, "from the bluff we can watch the whole of the middle approach along the lake. There's a small shingle landing point just this side of the bluff. We'll base our men there and if the Normans attack down the lake, we can quickly place a section of archers on the island to stop any attempt to get along the south shore, and mayhap another group on the bluff on the south side itself."

"Well done, lads. I'm glad to see that your brains weren't too addled by last night's ale. What we'll do now is practise with different loads of ammunition and different settings on the sling. Once you've mastered how this beast works, I'll have the lads in the section set it up on the bluff. No doubt we'll have to clear trees to give a field of fire. Then we'll work out sling settings for the different ranges. Now, what sort of ammunition do you think we should try?"

Bear was quick to answer. "Not single large rocks. I doubt we could ever have the accuracy to hit a moving boat. We need to straddle an area. Fist sized rocks seemed to work well when I saw them used at Dunholm. They could certainly disable a crewman, but probably not hole a boat."

"How about shingle?" Agnaar interrupted. "Smaller stones might not travel as far but a hail coming down from several hundred feet would deter anyone from sailing into it."

"Or even lead slingshot," Bear continued Agnaar's line of thought, "it would be expensive, given how much work goes into making it, but it has a consistent weight and would give a consistent range."

Ulf beamed at the two young men. "Let's give it a go then, shingle it is. It's lucky I brought a few sacks with me. You can release the action this time, Bear, but be careful. That beast kicks up as bad as any mule I know."

*****

Ulf stood by the hearth, warming his hands whilst his housekeeper tended a large pot of mutton broth. As she lifted it onto the hall's large wooden table Cyneburg called her disparate family to come and eat.

Bear watched Cyneburg ladle the broth into bowls and pass them around, and realised that this might be the last time for quite a while that he and Gytha would share a meal with all their friends together. Very aware that they all needed to understand why the events of 1080 were now, once again, shaping their lives, he plucked up the courage to speak.

"Ulf, can you tell us about the disaster that befell the first time you went to Dunholm. We were all too young then to understand and I fear its legacy is now coming back to change our lives again, my fader's in particular."

The old warrior glanced at Cyneburg who nodded.

"Aye, it is time." He said. "We'll eat first, then I will tell you."

Chapter 5

Ulf wiped his bowl with his last hunk of bread, stroked his lips with the back of his hand and looked around the table at the expectant eyes of his extended family.

"It's time you know everything, young Bear, about what befell us all in the year ten-eighty. It's time you all do, and then you'll understand the feud that Hravn now has with Canmore and Count Alan, and the risk that he faces. I suppose we've never spoken of those days because the pain was just too much. Before that accursed venture to Dunholm we lived in the golden years. Hravn and Edie worked hard to rebuild our lives here. Once we got the lead mines working we had money to develop the lands and employ the men to secure our borders. Hravn and I chose them, and I trained them. They were good, the best, and gold and silver from selling lead funded the best of weapons for them."

Ulf paused to take a swig of ale, then continued, conscious of the eyes upon him. "It was late in seventy-nine, well after haerfest, when we started to hear of refugees from Bernicia arriving in Carleol. Edie was worried. Bernicia is the heartland of her uncle's old lands in Northumberland, and the Bernician fortress of Bebbanburge had been his until his exile. He'd been dead a couple of years by then and the Normans were imposing their own men upon the people, though some of the old nobility still survived. The families of the House of Bebbanburge were there 'til the end. But the Normans weren't grinding the people down like they were in Ghellinges-scir. Bishop Walcher's rule from Dunholm was far from firm."

Bear looked up at the mention of Walcher. "Wasn't it his lands that you raided in seventy-two?"

Ulf chuckled, "Aye lad, but that's another tale, and a happier one."

"Go on, Fader." Leofric urged.

"I went with Edie to Carleol and spoke to some of those who were fleeing. Edie offered them sanctuary on her lands, and some came here."

"I remember them arriving," Adelind interrupted. "They have a farm in Glynrhedyn."

"Aye lass, they were the first to break the ground higher up that dale." Ulf smiled fondly at his adopted daughter. "You've a good memory. Now let me continue, it's a long saga. They told us that the Scots raided just after the haerfest was gathered in, coming across the Tweed and down the valleys from Lothian. They did what all uncontrolled bands of men do. They raped, stole and killed, broke families apart and took the women, girls and elder boys back as slaves. They took much of the haerfest too."

"What? Didn't the Normans who held the land stop them?" Agnaar was aghast.

Ulf shook his head. "It seems that William was away in Normandy quelling his son's rebellion and that Canmore thought that he had a chance to keep the land between the Tweed and the Tinan weak. He didn't hold the land though, just harried it."

"What did the people do? Surely they were outraged?"

"They were that, young Bear. Some of the old Bernician nobility, such as Ligulf, still held positions of power under the Bishop and they stopped cooperating. Ligulf was a distant kinsman of Edie's and when the Earl was pulling the strings of our resistance in Ghellinges-scir, he was at the centre of a network of spies within the Church; that was how the Earl gained intelligence and kept in touch with his cells in the resistance. Brother Patrick, who then still had the church in Morlund, was one of his men. Edie made contact with Ligulf once she heard of the Scots' harrying. In lencten, a man called Gilbert, one of the Bishop's men, attacked Ligulf's hall at night and killed him along with his household. It was Brother Patrick that told Edie of Ligulf's death. Hravn could see immediately how things would unfold; if violence spread into Dunholm our eastern border could become unstable."

Agnaar gave a low whistle, whilst Bear nodded. The others stared at Ulf, open-mouthed, as he continued.

"The people were, as you say, outraged that a member of the House of Bebbanburge had been killed by an agent of the King. They took control of the lands north of the Tinan and agreed to meet Bishop Walcher at Gatesheued. Whether it was a trap or not, I can't say. There was no agreement and Walcher retired to the church there. That was a mistake."

"How so? Surely a church is sanctuary?" Gytha asked, surprised.

"And so it should be, but the people were desperate and starving, and could tell that the Bishop had no interest in their plight. They attacked and killed all outside the church, killed Bishop Walcher and Gilbert too when they tried to flee, then set fire to the church and killed all within."

Ulf took another deep draught whilst studying the shocked faces around him. His face was serious when he spoke. "Hravn and Edie have made a sanctuary here and yours has been a life of peace and goodwill. The world beyond these fells is not like that. It's a world of violence and mistrust, and I fear the fells will no longer keep it at bay."

Bear was beginning to piece together the facts that he already knew. "Was it then that the Normans harried the north again?"

Ulf shook his head. "No, not quite. As soon as we heard about Walcher's death, Hravn led all but four sections over into Dunholm and up towards Gatesheued. He wanted to head off any trouble. He knew that Count Alan would be quick to respond. After all, the King's man in Dunholm had been killed in an uprising. There were more than two score of us. Edie and Godric stayed back to look after our interests here. We met the Northumbrians as they were marching down to Dunholm intent on laying siege to the castle. What a mixed bunch they were. They were led by Eadwulf Rus, a cousin of Earl Gospatric.

There were others of his household with him and a few score men at arms, but most were self-armed freemen with little or no military experience. The freemen had few horses and their only prize weapon was a mangonel. God only knows why the Normans had it in Gatesheued. It was crewed by a bunch of Flemish mercenaries who quickly changed allegiance when Eadwulf offered them a large share of any booty to be had in Dunholm. They were a bunch of rogues, but good company, and we fell in alongside them. Hravn was fascinated with the mangonel and it gave us a chance to see how it was made. We helped them set it up and get it into action. The mangonel we used today was an adaptation of theirs. Anyway, Hravn was having none of the siege and told Eadwulf Rus that his was a lost cause."

Bear laughed disparagingly, "If you could call it that. Surely there were men in the fortress who could break out and clear the siege?"

Ulf shook his head. "I doubt it. You forget that many of Walcher's men had been killed in the church at Gatesheued. There probably weren't enough to deal with an armed mob and that number of men-at-arms. Better to sit tight and wait for Count Alan to relieve them. That's what Hravn thought. He knew that the Count would send his men up the stone road, so he sent us out to the south. We pushed scouts down the road and chose a site for an ambush; and what an ambush it was. We got reports that Eadwulf Rus and his Northumbrians were starting to give up and pull back, and were just about to do so ourselves when the Normans, as arrogant as ever, sent a score of men up the road at the gallop. We took them on both flanks in a hail of cross bow bolts and that was it. Dead and dying horses and men everywhere." As he spoke Ulf glanced around the faces about him. In Adelind and Eir's expressions, he read sadness at the thought of such slaughter, but Gytha's face was alight with excitement as were Leofric and Bear.

"Four of the men were alive. Hravn had us dress any wounds as best we could and then told them that he was Sir Hravn of Bebbanburge. He was desperate that

Count Alan didn't make any connection between us and our lands here. There was one of them who held some seniority and, sadly, he recognised Hravn from his time as a spy in the Count's court. Well, from then on, Hravn was marked as a leader of the rebellion and we, with our red and black shields and green cloaks, were all marked as Hravn's men. We couldn't risk trying to break clean away and get back over Stanmoir in case we were seen and drew the Count's men into our own lands. Instead, Hravn took the Norman into his confidence, explained that he had finally got the people under some sort of control and that they were withdrawing back over the Tinan. He said that rather than provoke more unrest in Dunholm the Count should let them fall back into Northumberland. Surprisingly, that's exactly what happened. As the Northumbrians marched back north we kept a very visible presence on all the points of high ground. Sometimes we threatened the Normans' flanks to make sure that they kept their guard. I'm sure that, because we were so mobile, they thought there were many more of us than just two score. Anyway, it worked. The only trouble was crossing the Tinan. Hravn persuaded Eadwulf Rus to use the crossing that we had used after our raid in seventy-two. They messed around so much getting over the river that the Normans were pressing down the hillside tracks through the woods above the ford and we had to set a series of running ambushes to hold them off. The lads were good, really good, and I was proud to lead them. We didn't lose anyone yet we took down several more Normans. The North was giving a good account of itself; then everything changed."

Cyneburg could see that her husband was beginning to feel the effort of recalling events. She knew the worst was still to come and took a flagon of ale to refill Ulf's cup, gently caressing his shoulder as she did so.

"It must have been late in Thrimilce by then, we were certainly getting close to mid sumor, with hot days and short nights. The Northumbrians had left their women to work the land and were now hard pressed to catch up preparing for the haerfest. People everywhere were starving, and Eadwulf Rus led his household back to Bebbanburge without a care for what was happening around him. It was as if he assumed that the Normans would simply stay at Gatesheued."

"Why didn't you take your leave then? Surely you could have followed the old road along the wall and come back through Carleol? That wouldn't have led the Normans to our lands." Bear asked instinctively, before realising that the decision he was questioning was his father's, not Ulf's.

Ulf gave a sour grunt. "Oh, how I wish that we had, but we didn't. Instead, we held the high ground overlooking the Tinan and watched whilst the Normans built up their forces on the north bank. At first it felt like we were bystanders watching a game play out, then suddenly, we were the game. I think it was the arrival of a new red and gold war banner that persuaded Hravn that he must go to Bebbanburge and warn Eadwulf Rus. He was sure that Count Alan was handing command to someone more senior. He feared that the King might have returned from Normandy. We left after two days and rode hard for Bebbanburge."

"Was it the King?" Gytha asked, awed.

"No, but every bit as bad." Ulf spat sideways into the hearth as he spoke. "It was the bastard king's half-brother, Bishop Odo. Not that he was ever a man of God. We couldn't risk leaving men behind to keep an eye on the Normans in case we lost touch with them, so Hravn led us all to Bebbanburge. What a fortress it was, no doubt still is. Eadwulf took heed of our warning but, fool that he was, decided to stay secure in the fortress rather than re-muster his men."

"Surely you didn't stay, not then?" It was Leofric who spoke, having listened in silence so far.

"Like Hell we did! We took the old road through Alnewich, and rode as fast as we could across country, through Routhebiria, towards the wall. But Wyrd was playing games with us. She spun her web and drew us in. We assumed that Odo would head straight for Bebbanburge and that we could cut around his flank.

Instead, we soon saw a line of smoke from east to west across the horizon. Then, we met the first of those fleeing. The Normans had formed a long front and were steadily harrying northward. Killing those they caught, burning, living off livestock and killing or driving off the rest. We soon realised that they had sent raiding parties ahead of the main front and that we were cut off from the wall. Hravn led us north, along the flank of Hemmel Hill, heading back towards Routhebiria, and around into the dales to the west. That's when we first hit them. We were riding hard along a forest track, two score of us strung out but close behind each other, when we burst into the open and right into a dozen or more ravaging a farmstead. Most of the buildings were in flames. They'd heard us coming and were prepared. It was sudden and vicious fighting. Snorri led the first section and our lads were cut down as they left the cover of the wood, but numbers told and we slew all, or mayhap most of them, for the loss of five."

"I remember Snorri, do you too Agnaar?" asked Adelind. "I would have been nine at the time. He was fun, he used to tease us a lot."

Agnaar shook his head, his eyes sad as he thought of his father and uncle who would also have been there.

"Snorri was a good man. He'd been with us from the start, and when we raided Dunholm in seventy-two. Anyway, it was late in the day and Hravn didn't want to blunder into more Normans in the dark, so we stayed at the farm and posted guards. Normans were out there though, sure enough, and they knew their stuff. They attacked at first light, just as we were rousing the men. The first we knew was when we were rushed. They came on foot and had got close before the guards saw them. Hravn got us into a shield wall between the still-burning barns. At least that protected our flanks. We were in two ranks and managed to take down a couple of them with crossbow bolts. That stopped them, but then they tried to work around our back, so we were reduced to two ranks, facing in opposite directions. It was desperate. Our horses were still where we had tethered them and it was impossible to break out and get to them. Furthermore, we

63

only had the weapons we had grabbed when they attacked, nor had we water or food. Our only chance was to face them down and beat them."

"How many were there?" Bear asked.

"A score, at least. Mayhap more. We had the advantage of numbers, but not training. We were horsemen, skilled in the art of the ambush and sudden attack. Although we had practised the shield wall, we had never seriously expected to fight in one. These Normans had, they were heavy infantry: solid, slow and bloody strong. Our only strength was our desperation. Our charge took them by surprise, but they soon held, their weight and experience told against us and it was hard to use our advantage in numbers to get past their flanks. It became a brutal stabbing match and men on both sides began to fall."

Ulf glanced at Cyneburg, then reached across the table and grasped Agnaar's wrist. "That's when your fader fell, and your Uncle Ole, within moments of each other. I'm sorry." Ulf squeezed Agnaar's wrist, then let go as he saw his foster son clench his jaw tightly, trying to fight tears.

"But you won in the end. How?" Bear wanted to spare his friend further distress and tried to move the story on.

"Your fader broke the stalemate, or rather his hound did. Hravn fell out of the wall, took Sköll to our flank, then sent him around to attack their centre from behind, just as he would if hunting a deer. He brought one man down with his jaws around the back of his neck then, as he went for another, that broke their line. We got between them and slowly our numbers told." Ulf paused, then shrugged his withered arm, "But not before I got this. My bicep was sliced through in almost the last blow of the fight. I was bleeding like a boar stabbed in the hunt. I was going to bind it with a cord to stem the flow, but Hravn said it would be better if he cauterised it with a hot blade."

Ulf gave a deep sigh, followed by a sheepish grin. "By the gods! It hurt. But at least I kept the arm, even if it's bugger all use now." Then, seeing the tears in

Cyneburg's eyes, he stood and moved to her, hugging her with his good arm. "I only ever needed one arm to hug you, my love, so what's there to worry over?" Kissing the top of her head, he sat down.

"There were mayhap a dozen and a half of us still standing, me included. Two or three of the men, I forget how many, were too wounded to be moved, let alone able to get onto a horse." Ulf's eyes held the stares of those around the table. "We couldn't stay with them, nor could we leave them to the Normans. Hravn said that he alone would see to it, and he did. I saw the pain in his eyes afterwards."

Ulf looked at Bear, then at Gytha. "He's a good man, your fader. It takes courage to lead, and he is the best of leaders, believe me. What he did next was just as difficult. We agreed to burn our dead in the Norse fashion. We didn't have the tools to bury them and we couldn't leave them to be scavenged. Some of the lads wanted to leave the Norman dead untouched, but Hravn insisted that all would share the same funeral pyre. He said that they were all soldiers and deserved to meet their maker recognised as such. He was right, even if it wasn't a popular move."

"He was right." Eir spoke quietly. The others nodded, silent.

"We left after that. We were broken as a war band but we still held our heads up. Hravn insisted on taking all the horses, even though most were without riders. We needed remounts to help us ride for longer, and we had to gather and carry all the arms and armour from our dead, and the Norman dead too. Hravn knew, even then, that he would have to rebuild us and that we could not afford to replace many weapons. He took us up into the western dales then down towards the wall. This time we rode overnight and, in the dawn, we rode into a small vill that had been destroyed. Women and children were sitting on the ground and, from the piles of fresh earth, we could tell that they had just buried their menfolk. We didn't ask the women what else had befallen them, there was no need. They shied away as we rode towards them, then rallied slowly when they realised we meant no harm. Hravn explained who we were and then asked them to ride with us. Most did, and their need for protection gave us a sense of purpose. They stayed with us when we reached Carleol, and Edie accepted them into her household."

"What happened after that?" Bear was asking most of the questions.

"It was the end of things for us as far as Hravn was concerned, but not the Normans. The King sent his son, Robert, north after haerfest. He crossed the Tweed and made a show of force up into Lothian. Canmore refused to give battle and once again submitted to the Norman crown. On their way south, Prince Robert ordered the building of a new castle on the north bank of the Tinan. He called it Novem Castellum and installed Robert de Mowbray as Earl there. That was the end of the House of Bebbanburge in Northumberland. Any nobility that hadn't been slaughtered fled into exile. Dolfin and the rump of the family in Cumbraland are all that survive now."

Cynburg then spoke for the first time. "But it was the start of further disaster for our wider family." She made a wide gesture to imply that it involved everyone in the room and, looking at her children, said, "I know you remember, Adelind, but the rest of you will have been too young. Nightmares about the final battle plagued your fader for months, and I know they plagued Hravn too. The shock and stress of violence can last for a long time, as I'd already found out for myself long ago in the past. The men may have recovered, outwardly at least, but it was different for us women. Your moder's heart was broken, Agnaar. Her love for your fader was all embracing, as was his for her. She had already lost several babies before young Osberht was born and her inner strength had been weakened. Orme's death broke her, and she died within months."

Agnaar nodded, looking down at a tear that had dripped on to the table. "I know, I remember."

Cyneburg bit her lip before continuing. "You may not know, but it was your fader and Hravn who rescued

Ada from abuse by a Norman when she was still a girl. It was the day that the same man had killed Ole and Frida's parents. Ole and Ada were of the same age and for a long time Ole was the only male that Ada would really talk to. His death could so easily have broken her too. Instead, it drove her into a black mood of revenge. It was only Godric and Edie that brought her out of it."

Bear spoke absentmindedly, his question surprising them all. "Why was it that Godric had never married by then?"

Ulf was about to reply, when Cynburg lifted her fingers to stop him. She smiled at Bear and Gytha. "Mayhap you don't know, but when your moder first went to Bebbanburge she was hard pressed, as a woman of sixteen, to gain the respect of the men she was determined to lead. Godric was one of the most capable men-at-arms in the war band that her uncle had transferred to Hravn's command. He was so impressed by Edie that he immediately and publically swore loyalty to her. His oath helped persuade the other men, and it is an oath in which he has never faltered. I'm sure it's fair to say that your fader is well aware, as is your moder, that Godric's respect for her is akin to love. Godric always had a close bond with Ada too. He carefully, and very maturely, nurtured her and Ole together as they grew up. It was Godric who suggested that he and Ada should adopt Osberht after Frida died. He wanted to give her a focus in life and it did work. You know just how they are together. Ada is unswervingly loyal to Edie and Godric, but she is very vulnerable too. That's why Hravn didn't take Godric to Dunholm."

"And that is really it." Ulf resumed. "We rebuilt the war band. Some of the survivors became the new section leaders, Tófi for one, but it was never as large as it had been. As you know, we've trained you hard to fight in a shield wall, but promise me, never get into the situation where you have to."

"Thank you, Ulf. I understand a lot more now, we all do." Bear glanced around the table." I understand, too, why Fader is struggling after the blow to his head. Wyrd is still playing with his mind."

Ulf leant forward and tapped the table sharply with his forefinger. "Good, I'm glad you understand. The burden of the struggle ahead is going to fall on all your shoulders. Bear, you and Agnaar should return to Crosebi Raveneswart tomorrow and work with Hravn. Leofric and Gytha, it will be better if you stay here for the time being. I want you to get to know every nook and cranny along these lake shores. I see you working with the teams of slingers and archers I'm training, and planning where to set ambushes. I'll tell you more tomorrow and in the coming days."

As Gytha gasped with surprise, his face relaxed and he smiled reassuringly, "Don't worry, lass. Your moder and I have agreed this. She, like me, has great faith in you. You're ready now to take a lead just as she did at your age." He chuckled, to their surprise, "After all, it was at your age that she first tumbled me in a fair fight."

"Now, Eir, and you Adelind, Edie wants you to turn part of the hall, here, into a place where we can treat our wounded. She says you will know what herbs to gather and how to prepare a clean place to work."

Cyneburg added, "I will help and I know just where we can make a start."

Ulf turned to Bear and Agnaar, "I want to get our three heads together now and talk through the detail of what Hravn has in mind to hinder the Normans when their invasion comes. Fill your cups with ale and join me by the hearth."

Chapter 6

"Ship oars!" Leofric called to Gytha as he judged the moment to stop rowing. They lifted the oars from between the peg-like tholes that held them in place on the gunwhales, and let their boat glide onto the shingle shore. Thin ice cracked and pebbles scrunched under the bow. They flexed their shoulders and stretched their fingers, neither wanting to admit that the half-morning's row along the length of the lake had been more challenging than anticipated. Both blamed the light north-easterly head wind. The boat was a very small version of the revered Norse snekkja, or longship, and Leofric was proud to have been entrusted with it. He was pleased too, that he and Gytha were able to sail, row and manoeuvre it so skilfully as its shallow draught rendered its balance particularly challenging when sailing in anything other than a following wind.

When Ealdgith had first taken charge of her lands around Ulueswater, Hravn had ordered the building of a fleet of boats funded by the revenue from their newly opened lead mines. Working with Patrichesdale's boat builder, Ragnaar the Young, he had concentrated on building a fleet of two specific types of vessel, naming them after Norse Valkyries: the first called a Kára, a larger tub shaped boat with a crew of four capable of carrying two sections or cargo and livestock, and the smaller Svanmeyja, or swan maiden, named for her graceful S-shaped bow and stern posts. The Svanmeyja had been designed to carry a section of four men and a fifth as helmsman when needed. It had no crew and the section rowed themselves. Although Patrichesdale's Norse settlers had generations of experience of boat building they were hampered by the quality of their tools and resources. The wooden planks of all the vessels' clinker sides were roughly finished and held together by wooden pins rather than iron nails. All had a central mast with a yardarm supporting a grey sail, made from finely spun Herdwick wool.

Leofric grabbed the carved dragon's head at the top of the bow post and, jumping from the gunwhale, almost cleared the water's edge. Gytha laughed at the splash as she vaulted lithely over the bow. Loki followed. "You should learn to keep your feet dry, Leo. Here, I'll give you a hand." She took hold of the boat's painter and helped haul the Svanmeyja higher up the shingle beach.

"Isn't Brynhildr beautiful? So fast and sleek, even when rowing, and with a following wind we can outpace any Normans on the shore. She glides over the water just like her namesake." Gytha admired the boat as she helped pull the rope.

"Yes, everything else at this end of the lake is in her shadow." Leofric grunted as he heaved on the rope and nodded towards the middle of the wide bay. "There are a few of the first Káras, and those tubs out there were built by Ragnaar before your fader and he came up with the idea of the Kára." He chuckled, "They're even older than Bear and are pretty leaky, so I hear. Otherwise the folk hereabouts still use coracles and rafts. They don't have the same need as us to carry goods up and down the lake. They just use them to fish the deeper stretches."

"Well, for as long as I can remember, Ragnaar and Alv have just built Svanmeyjas, and they've got another two on the stocks." Gytha said, appreciatively.

"Yes, and Fader's now got one for each of the sling and archer sections, so we really will be able to harass and ambush any Normans when they do come. I just hope we get enough of a warning."

"That's why we need to speak to Thorkel Akison. Where do we find him?"

"His fader, Aki, is the headman at Bartun but we should find Thorkel here, in Pulhoue. He's head of the pool fishers. Come, let's track him down." Leofric leant over the gunwhale into Brynhildr's bow, and unwrapped the deerskin cover from their bows. "Here." He passed Gytha's bow across to her then, hoisting his on his shoulder, led the way up the shingle beach.

"Is that him there?" Gytha pointed to a man in early middle age, standing at the apex of a V-shaped line of large stepping stones linking the two banks of the wide River Eamont.

Leofric whistled appreciatively, "That takes real skill and balance. I'd be thrashing about in the water if I tried casting a net that size."

"We'll give him a few moments before we call him. He will be in the water if you startle him." Gytha knelt down on the river bank as they watched the fisherman slowly haul his net in, then quickly seize a fish by its tail and deftly strike its head sharply on the rock by his feet before dropping it into a bag hanging from his waist.

Leofric chose his moment, then called. "Thorkel?"

"Aye. Who..."

"I'm Leofric from Patrichesdale, Ulf's son. May we talk?"

Leofric accepted Thorkel's nodded grunt as confirmation, and waited whilst he stepped carefully along the line of rocks.

As Thorkel neared the end of the stepping stones he looked up, his eyes upon Leofric and then Gytha. "And you must be our Lady's daughter." It was a statement, rather than a question.

"How...?" Gytha's look of surprise gave way to a shy smile. "Yes. Who else would dress like this? I'm Gytha." She held her hand out in greeting, and was surprised by the warmth of the fisherman's gnarled, water-scarred hand.

"Thorkel, my fader has sent me, us, to ask for your help." Leofric could see that Thorkel was a man of few words, and he came straight to the point. "We all know that the Normans are going to take these lands sometime soon. We can't stop them here, but we can stop them getting to the head of the lake. My fader's invitation to everyone in the vills hereabouts still stands; you are all welcome to join us at Patrichesdale. If we are to fight them we need forewarning. We have men ready to harry their flanks all along the lakeshore track, but it will take time to get in position. Ulf wants a beacon on top of Dunmallard." He gestured with his thumb to the top of the rounded hill behind them. "He asks that you place it in the old fort on the top and clear away any trees that might hide it from view from Wethermeloc. We'll have a chain of beacons on prominent points along the lake; high enough to be seen and low enough not to be shrouded in mist. They'll be above Skelly Neb at Wethermeloc, on the bluff at the foot of Glencoyne and on Keldas, above our faders' halls."

"Hah!" Leofric watched Thorkel's dour, weather-creased face slowly come to life as it broke into a thin smile. "Aye, happen that could work."

Gytha took over the conversation. "Thank you, Thorkel. You should know that my fader intends to slow the Normans when they do come and will fire beacons on the east fellside to warn us all. Keep your eyes towards Stanmoir. My moder and brother will be here by then too. That will give you some warning."

"Aye, Lady. It will suffice. I will speak to the head men, and as soon as any foreigners come near the vills of Bartun or Dacor, we will fire the beacon. I can't speak for them, but I plan to take my family by boat to Haugr-tun. Firing the beacon on Dunmallard will be the last thing I do here."

Gytha knew that she was growing up very quickly. Ever since her meeting with Urgust she had felt that the three Norns, the spinners that weighed a man's life and spun his fate, were thrusting her forward into adulthood. She had gradually realised that the people of her parents' lands were looking to her for leadership too. At times, she felt as if she was suffocating under the pressure, at others she felt herself floating free, buoyed by self-confidence. She shook Thorkel's hand again and held his eyes with hers. "Before we go, Thorkel, you should know that my moder has gifted her lands south of here to my elder sister, Lord William's wife, in the hope that he will retain them when the Normans come. His moder is Norman. My fader, though, is a marked man. Count Alan of Richemund sent men to kill him last haerfest and, though they failed, we know they will try to hunt him down. This does put the vills and people around the lake at risk. Can you make sure that the people understand this? If they don't want to join us then Lord William's lands might be a safer refuge."

Thorkel nodded appreciatively, "Aye, my Lady, I will."

"You're a good man, Thorkel, and you have my fader's thanks too." Leofric shook hands, then added, "I'll tell Bjarni at Haugr-tun to look out for you."

*****

Gytha held her arms wide and spun round and round, laughing as she looked at the views around her. Loki, bemused, ran around her, barking. "What a place! We can see everything from here: the lake from Pulhoue to the old fort Ulf showed us, across the vale of the Eden to Stanmoir, the black crags of Helvellyn and all the high fell tops etched in white by snow, all these secret valleys behind us. No wonder Ulf chose to settle moder's people there."

Leofric stopped her spinning, pulled her to him, and then turned her around, holding her close. "Look." He pointed, as Gytha lay back against his chest enjoying his warmth. "Up yon right-hand valley. That's Boredale; there's a pass at the top that leads down to Patrichesdale. It's the way out for all the people here if the Normans do threaten, but it's also how we can get our own men here too. We could have men on ponies here in the time it would take to row down the lake. We should return here and spend time getting to know where we might best lay an ambush."

"I agree, but for now we've spoken to Bjarni and he knows what he has to do about the beacon yon side of the lake at Wethermeloc. Let's get back home, I want to see what Alv was working on. I'll race you down to the boat." Gytha twisted out of Leofric's embrace and ran down the hill. Leofric followed at a steady jog as he watched Gytha ahead of him, enraptured by her lithe beauty and grace, and a little envious of her natural agility. Loki galloped ahead of them both, glancing back playfully at his mistress.

73

Gytha loved to run on the broad fellside slopes. The speed thrilled her, and she had learned long ago how to use low hillocks to slow her speed and guide her route. Reading the ground a dozen paces ahead, she adjusted her long-legged pace to the terrain and almost bounced down Hallin's long turf-clad slopes. She slowed as she neared the lakeshore. Once, in earlier childhood, she had run so fast that she tumbled over the edge into the lake. Thankfully it had been deep enough to break her fall but not so deep that she had drowned. She had learned two lessons that day; to control how she ran, and that she must learn to swim. She had mastered both.

*****

"Ready!" Leofric shouted as he pushed Brynhildr off the pebble beach and swung past her stern post onto the rear thwart. As he did so, Gytha pulled on the oars and rowed out into the centre of Haugr-tun's sheltered bay.

"When you're ready, Gytha, ship oars and raise the yardarm. I'll take charge of the sail."

As the wind caught the grey sail, Brynhildr swung around to her left and surged forward, accompanied by two whoops of joy.

Gytha stayed in the bow to keep an eye open for any part submerged rocks whilst Leofric guided the svanmeyja swiftly past the steep boulder strewn slopes of Place Fell's northern flank. He was confident that this was one route the Normans would never choose. As they neared Tethera Island, Leofric aimed for the centre of the gap between the island and the southern shore. "Gytha, see how a boat in the middle of the channel is within a bow-shot of the island and the crags on the shore. Two sections could block any attack."

Gytha looked at the fast-approaching island. Its low rocks and solitary pine tree offered little protection. "Surely men-at-arms protected by a boat's gunwhale and their own shields would have the advantage?" She shouted to Leofric.

"Ah! That's why Fader has got the sections making thick man-high wicker screens. When the time comes, we'll secure them with stakes and they'll give all the cover and protection the men will need. And..." he paused for effect, "Fader's been training them to use arrows wrapped in pine-tar soaked cloth. One thing that boats hate, is fire."

Gytha's eyes widened as she laughed back. "It's the men in them, not the boats, that will hate them. Woollen sails won't burn, and it will take quite a few to set a boat alight. But, pine tar is hard to put out when it's burning. Think what the wounds would be like...and if the flames catch on clothing, well..." Gytha left the thought hanging.

"Mmm, you're right. It will certainly make them keep their distance, that's for sure. What's more, it will make it easier for us to track the arrow's flight across water, especially at a distance. We can then adjust our aim more easily."

Gytha moved the discussion on. "Let's land by Ragnaar's boat stocks. Didn't you say that he has Alv making something special?"

"Ah, yes." Leofric said, with a conspiratorial wink.

Brynhildr's headway dropped off quickly as she sailed into Patrichesdale Bay and Leofric turned her into the wind whilst Gytha furled the sail and dropped the yard arm.

They beached Brynhildr on the shingle beach at the lake's head, next to the boat-builder's two nausts. The wooden boathouses built just above the shoreline were Ragnaar's pride and joy, enabling him to work on boats in all weathers.

"Ugh! What's that smell?" Gytha pinched her nose as acrid oily smoke wafted towards them.

Leofric laughed. "You said you wanted more pine-tar. Ragnaar's been making it. He's dug a conical pit over yonder, lined it with birch bark, filled it with pine roots, turfed it over and set fire to it. The sap is boiled out of the roots and runs to the bottom of the hole, where it can be collected as tar. I thought you knew that." He teased Gytha, poking the tip of his tongue at her.

"And I know where my first fire arrow is going." Gytha laughed back whilst they walked towards a group of men, two of whom were standing thigh-high in the lake.

"What is that? It looks like a body in the water between them. Surely not?"

Gytha's puzzlement amused Leofric. "Well, that's one way of stopping a boat. Though it's a cruel way to treat your prisoners."

Gytha gave a bemused look in return, then kicked Leofric sharply on his ankle.

"Ow!" He flinched and twisted quickly away from her, laughing.

"It's a log! Alv's making a chain of logs!" Gytha gasped in sudden realisation. "How are they connected together? I can't..."

Leofric grasped Gytha by the hand, "Come, I'll show you. Fader was puzzling over how to slow any Norman boats so that the mangonel would have a chance of hitting them, when Ragnaar suggested this."

"Welcome Gy... My Lady." Alv realised that Gytha was no longer the girl that he had teased as they grew up.

Gytha smiled. "It's good to see you, Alv. Just call me Gytha, as you always have. Now, I've heard that you've got something that can stop a Norman war-boat dead in the water."

"We have that. Two chains of logs, between Tethera Island and the shores on either side. They're simple to make but a bit more of a challenge to fit together and move."

Gytha gave a low whistle.

Leofric stood back as Alv led Gytha to a section of newly cut pine a man's height in length and a hand's span wide. "It's been no small task to get the timber. We felled a whole stand of pine on the edge of the Dodd. They're in various lengths and widths, depending on the tree; from a man's height to three times that. Anything longer is a challenge to tow when rowing. If we hammer a spike with an eyelet into each end of a long log we can then link them together to form a floating barrier."

Gytha crouched down and tugged the spike at the end of the log, then stood and looked at the one floating in the water. "That is so clever, Alv. I can see that it floats low in the water, but I doubt if they would sink a boat."

She glanced around as Leofric spoke. "The idea is to buy time. The chain of logs should stop a boat long enough for Fader's mangonel or an archer to strike it."

"Yes, a shower of fire arrows would soon finish the crew off." Gytha was enthusiastic, then, with a note of uncertainty, she asked Alv, "Will the spikes hold?"

"Aye they will, and as the wood swells they will be held in place even more firmly."

"But won't the logs get water logged and sink?"

Alv understood Gytha's concern. "Doubtless they will, but that will take months. Anyhow, we plan to keep them on a beach until we need them. Fastening them together and moving them is the problem that I haven't solved. Here, Tosti, throw me a link." He called to one of his men.

Leofric joined Gytha and leaned in as Alv explained. "Look, we could join them together with a single O-link between each of the eyes, but it would mean a four-furlong chain of logs. There is no way anyone could tow that in the water. Or, we could use an open C-link and fix them together in the water."

"Mmm." Leofric pulled a face. "But wouldn't that risk the C-links coming apart in choppy water? The eye at the end of the spike is bound to find the gap in the C-link."

"Aye, that's the problem. I've figured out that we can tow short chains of logs in a relay of Káras or Svanmeyjas, and use a second Svanmeyja to link them together and keep the last log in the chain in position until it's anchored by the island, but the open links risk coming apart..."

"But..." Gytha interrupted. "Why not use two C-links? You could have one facing up and the other facing down. That would stop the eye slipping out. If you flatten them a little then they won't spin around either. You will just need to make twice as many links."

"What! Of course," Alv roared with laughter, "Gytha, you really are 'My Lady'!" He threw the link back to Tosti. "Here, give it a go. I'm sure it'll work."

Gytha had a 'floating moment' as she flushed with confidence. "How long will it take to put the barriers in place?"

Alv scratched his teeth with his thumbnail, thinking. "Two days, mayhap less. We're planning on storing the logs on beaches opposite Tethera island, close to the anchor points." Then he shrugged, "Worry not, we'll have time. Ulf's sure the Normans will come by land before they make an attempt on water. I'm sure that you will buy us the time we need."

Lencten 1092

Chapter 7

Bear was only half watching Tófi's section as it led a line of laden ponies ahead of him along the track from Kircabi Stephan to Burc. His mind kept going over the details of the last few weeks. They had been full of long days spent with Agnaar and Hravn, whilst Hravn explained the skills needed to plan and command a battle: how to hold a bird's eye picture of the ground in the mind, model the picture on the ground so that men could understand it, to see the ground as the enemy would, and to evolve a plan to wrong-foot the enemy. Bear understood what he had to do, but the time and effort it took was, at times, mind-numbing. Hravn had drummed into them the importance of planning for food, fodder, ammunition, all contingencies of weather and the relationship between speed and distance. Bear appreciated his father's confidence in him, and he seized the opportunity to take responsibility for setting up their new base in the wooded valleys above Burc, towards the top of the Stanmoir pass. Agnaar's voice jerked his attention.

"They say that if Hrēðmonath comes in like a wolf, then it will go out like a lamb, don't they?" Agnaar referred to the third month in the year.

"Err...yes, they do. I hope it does. This nor'easterly is bitter, and there's fine snow in it too. At least it should keep Count Alan's men at bay." Bear blew warm breath onto his bare hands and rubbed his numbed finger tips against his slightly warmer palms whilst he guided his horse with his knees.

"Hey! What's happening up front? Tófi's stopped. We'd best check." Agnaar shouted, spurring forwards.

Bear could see Tófi leaning sideways out of his saddle, talking to a sokeman who was pointing vigorously towards Burc. Tófi turned as Bear rode up, touched his right temple with his fingertips in a salute of respect, then said, "It seems we have Norman company, Lord. This man saw us riding up and ran to warn us. There's mayhap a half dozen men-at-arms in the old Roman fort whilst another two are outside, standing guard mounted, holding the others' horses. My guess is that they are checking if the fort will provide a suitable base."

"I agree, Tófi." Bear turned to the sokeman. "Your warning was timely. How long have they been there?"

"Only moments before I saw your men on the track, Lord." The sokeman spoke breathlessly. He pointed. "The old fort is on that low rise, the men still mounted are on the other side, beyond the north gate. They left the road and cut around the edge of the vill to enter the fort."

Bear looked at the fort and thanked the gods for the warning. The old Roman building was barely three furlongs away on a low spur, from where it dominated the small vill to the east. Now, they had a chance. He could revenge the Count's attempt on his father's life and, if he could gain a prisoner, discover something of the Count's intentions. He thought quickly. "You say there're six in the fort and two on yon side of it, with all the horses?"

"Yes, Lord, from what I could see. They all seemed very purposeful, as if they owned the land and didn't feel threatened." The sokeman spoke in the lilting Gallo-Norse accent common in parts of the vale of Eden.

"Tell me about the fort. Do all the walls still stand and are the gates open?"

"Yes and no, Lord. The walls stand, as do the buildings inside, though none have roofs. The tower over the south gate has collapsed, closing the entrance. You can see that from here. The other gates are open, east and west where the road runs through, and the north one overlooking the river."

"Good...good." Bear spoke half to himself as he quickly mulled over his options. "Agnaar. Call the sections in and have them hobble the pack ponies." Agnaar signalled to the three section leaders as Bear returned his attention to the sokeman. "What's your name?"

"Olaf, Lord."

Bear opened a pouch at his belt and took out a handful of hack silver. "Well, Olaf, you deserve this. Your quick thinking has doubtless saved my men and given us the chance to fettle the Normans' plans. Stay and mind our ponies, then we will speak again once this business is over."

"Close in!" Bear called the three section commanders to him. The sun's glint on his eyes gave Bear a slightly demonic look as he looked at their confident questioning faces. "We have a chance to kill Normans, and we're going to seize it, now. If the arrogant bastards think they can ride into our lands without a care, then we will teach then a hard lesson. There are, we think, six over there in the old fort and two more guarding their horses by the beck on the far side. Olaf, here, saw them only moments ago. I would not normally risk an engagement with mounted Normans, but we outnumber them, just, and we know that most are dismounted. We need to keep it that way. Which of you has crossbows in his section?"

"I've two." Tófi spoke first.

"Only one with me." Wulf added.

Ranald shook his head.

"That decides it. Tófi, you are to kill the two guards. Approach through the vill. Get your bowmen into a covered position from where they can hit the two mounted horses, not the riders, we can't risk missing one and letting him escape. They are to wait for the sound of my horn, then shoot. When they shoot, you and your fourth man are to charge the two men down. With luck, they will have been thrown by then; at the very least their horses will be spooked and hard to control. Have your bowmen reload and remount, then ride directly to the north gate. They are to hold it to prevent escape. If the Normans form a shield wall your bowmen are to take them from behind. Understood?"

Tófi acknowledged Bear's orders with a nod. "Lord."

"Wulf, you are with Agnaar. Get into position outside the west gate, but keep out of sight. Have you anyone that can mimic a fox's bark?"

"Aye, Lord." Wulf gave an amused grin.

"Good. He is to bark twice when you are in position. Wait until you hear my horn, then enter and clear the south side of the fort. I want to force the Normans back towards the north gate. They will either run or form a shield wall. Clear?"

As Wulf nodded, Bear turned to Ranald, "You are with me. We will enter through the east gate and take the north side of the fort. I want two prisoners to interrogate later. Agnaar and I will choose them. The rest are to be killed, even any wounded. Understood?"

"Aye, Lord." The three spoke in unison, as Bear caught sight of Agnaar's frown at the mention of prisoners.

"Good. When we are done, we will strip the bodies and take their arms and armour. Now, you've three minutes to brief your men. It's vital we strike quickly." Bear jerked his head at Agnaar, ushering him to one side, "I mean what I say about prisoners. Fader needs to know what the Count's intending. He can then deal with them as he likes. There're plenty of us who want them all dead, but it's more important we get what we can out of them. Agreed?"

"Aye, so be it." Agnaar spoke curtly.

Bear led two sections at a trot into the cluster of small wattle, daub and thatch cottages. Villagers stood gawping, then fell away at the sudden arrival of armed horsemen wearing green cloaks and carrying red and black shields emblazoned with a raven soaring above a screaming wildcat. Most recognized the device of Sir Hravn and Lady Ealdgith; it engendered respect, not fear, but they sensed that today it heralded violence and death.

Tófi peeled away, leading his three men around to the edge of the vill and dismounted behind a cottage. "Bran, Cunon, with me. Rhun, tether their mounts and guard mine." He crept along the side of the cottage, then froze. "There's only one guard." He whispered to Bran.

"No, look. Down by the beck. The other's watering the horses."

Tófi judged that the mounted guard was at least a hundred paces away whilst the one watering the horses was less than half that distance from a byre at the very edge of the vill. He edged himself backwards then turned to Cunon. "You can take a man at fifty paces, can't you?"

Cunon laughed under his breath, "Double that, on a good day."

"Good, choose a position down by the byre. Crawl in and for all the gods' sakes, don't make a noise."

As Cunon sidled away, Tófi tapped Bran's shoulder. "You should be able to hit the other guard's horse from here. Rhun and I will then ride in from where we left the horses and ensure both men are slain. Happy?"

Rhun's deep grunt was all the confirmation he needed. Tófi, a jovial Dane, had great faith in the three taciturn Cumbrians in his section.

Returning to the horses, Tófi mounted and edged his horse backwards until he had a clear line of sight to Bear, then raised his fist and extended his thumb. Bear acknowledged with a wave and rode to the side of the arch in the fort's stone wall, waiting for the bark of a fox.

The innocent bark of a fox was followed by the shattering blast of a horn echoing around the stone walls inside the fort. Bear blew it as he charged, wanting to gain every advantage from the surprise and speed of his attack. He was immediately surprised by how confined the fort was. Seeing four men-at-arms at the central crossroads, Bear led Ranald's section towards them, the five charging men filling the width of the paved road.

The startled Normans turned then fled, running to Bear's right towards the north gate. As the section swerved around in the central junction, Bear saw the men-at-arms gather shields from a stack and form a shield wall across the paved road. "Halt!" He yelled to Ranald and reined back harshly, the five horses skidding to a halt in front of a wall of shields and four spears. Helmet shrouded eyes glowered above the shields. Bear leant towards Ranald, speaking from the side of his mouth as he kept his eyes on the glowering eyes. "Keep pressure on them and edge them slowly back towards the gate. The shield wall will collapse when Tófi's bowmen take them from behind. See if you can take two as prisoners, but don't risk your men. I'll check where the rest of them are."

Bear wheeled his horse around and froze. A man-at-arms, fleeing down the road from the west gate, burst into the cross roads just as two of Wulf's men galloped onto him from the south road. Simultaneous sword blows half severed his head and an arm. His body was still falling as the riders halted in front of Bear.

"He's the last one, Lord. Agnaar and Wulf have killed two others and we are just clearing the buildings. Agnaar's by the west gate."

"Well done..." He wheeled his horse around again as the double thwack of crossbow bolts ripping into mail-clad flesh, and screams of pain and confusion, told him that the shield wall had been broken.

"Yield! Yield!" He yelled in Norman, then Cumbric, unsure if the two remaining men-at-arms were Norman or Bretton.

One of the men-at-arms slumped to his knees, his head bowed, whilst the other, wearing a cloak in the chequered blue and yellow of Count Alan's colours, stood facing Bear with his sword point lowered. He spoke in Brythonic, with a heavy Bretton accent that Bear strove to understand.

"I am Felix de Kiberen, to whom do I yield?"

Bear, remaining mounted, waved his arm around in an expansive gesture, then smiled thinly before he spoke. "These are my family's lands. My father, Sir Hravn, will speak to you. Mayhap you have heard of him?" He leant forward in his saddle, "Your sword."

Felix hesitated, then nodded slightly and reversed his grip on his sword, handing the hilt to Bear. As he did so, Tófi stepped up behind the other man-at-arms, gripped the collar of his hauberk and yanked him to his feet. "Your sword too," the powerful Dane barked gruffly in the man's ear.

Speaking in Cumbric so that the two Bretons might understand, Bear shouted orders. "Tófi, gather their horses and slay any that are injured. Wulf, strip the dead of their arms and armour, then load it onto their horses. Ranald, take charge of the prisoners. Get them mounted then bind them to their saddles." Bear looked around for Agnaar, "Take Wulf and Tófi and finish setting up the new camp. Ranald and I will take these two back to Fader. I'll meet you back at the ponies. I want to make arrangements with Olaf before we move on."

Leaving Agnaar to oversee the work, Bear urged his horse to a trot and stopped on the edge of the vill, where he signalled to Olaf to join him. He dismounted and offered his hand to Olaf in appreciation as he ran up.

"Who is the headman here? I must speak with him."

"He's in the fields, Lord, though I can speak for him."

"Good, thank you. There are five dead Normans in the fort and at least one dead horse. We've stripped them of their weapons and we will take their horses with us."

Olaf nodded, then his face froze as Bear spoke again.

"Olaf, you must tell the people here that the Normans will return. I don't know when, but I do know that the Scots' king has forsaken these lands and that the Norman king will take them, soon. There is nothing we can do to stop them, at least not in the open vale, though my fader intends to make them pay a price. We do intend to deny the fells and lakes to them. My moder, Lady Ealdgith, has opened her lands around Ulueswater to all who want to take sanctuary there."

Bear smiled reassuringly as Olaf's mouth dropped. "Make sure the people here understand all of this. If any want to escape the Norman yoke they will be welcome at Patrichesdale. My moder will give them land and shelter. Now, though, you must bury the Norman dead and mayhap use the horse for meat. For the sake of those who remain behind, there must be no sign of what happened today. That fort..." Bear pointed, "...is one place you can be sure the bastards will base themselves when they come."

Olaf was momentarily speechless as he stared questioningly into Bear's eyes. "How, Lord? How will we know when they are coming?"

Bear chuckled soberly. "You'll know, Olaf. We are about to make a camp at the head of the pass from where we will hit them as soon as they cross into my family's lands. Mayhap I'll see you again before then, we will no doubt call on you for food."

Bear swung himself back into his saddle as Agnaar rode up to take charge of the pack-ponies. "Now, I think you must find your head man and warn him."

*****

Bear slid from his saddle and walked towards the hall at Crosebi Raveneswart. Hati sensed his arrival and was scratching at the door as he pushed it open. She nuzzled his hand then returned to lie by the hearth.

Having galloped ahead Bear wanted to give Hravn warning of the prisoners' arrival. His father looked up from his seat by the hearth fire as Bear entered.

"I didn't expect you back 'til nightfall. What's happened?"

"Normans, Fader. That's what happened. We got warning that they were checking inside the old fort at Burc. We attacked, slew five and I have two prisoners following behind. Agnaar's gone on to set up the new base."

"What! Well done!" Hravn slapped the long table with his hand and called to Wassa, "Fetch mulled beer for Bear and call all the huscarles to me now, Lady Ealdgith too."

Hravn directed everyone to sit round the long table as they came in. "Bear and Agnaar have claimed first blood in our coming fight. Count Alan thought he could walk in and claim the fort at Burc as a forward base. Bear's men slew five and he has two prisoners arriving here momentarily. None escaped and the Count will now be confounded as to what's happened to his men."

Bear felt a surge of pride at the housecarls' cries of appreciation. They quietened as Hravn continued. "This means that the Count's move is close. We have to assume that only foul weather will delay him. Bear, once Agnaar returns, take a fourth section and get men into two of the towers up on Stanmoir. I want a watch kept on the road to Bogas, and get a plan in place for our first ambush. I'll join you with more men once I've dealt with the prisoners. Who are they?"

Bear shrugged. "Both are Bretons. One appears to be just a man-at-arms; he yielded readily enough. The other, though, is a knight of your age. He appears to be of some status. Felix de Kiberen is what he calls himself."

Hravn glanced at Ealdgith, "Hmm... Bretons might be easier to deal with than Normans, though, as the Count's a Breton, they will doubtless be very much his men. Edie, what do you think?"

Ealdgith looked at the huscarles before answering. "We can either use violence and try and break them, or lull them into talking freely." She paused deliberately, "I favour the latter. A man under duress can say anything to satisfy his torturer, whereas if he is speaking freely and heady with ale, he may be more honest. What do you think?" The housecarls exchanged glances, shrugged and looked to Godric to speak for them. "We agree, My Lady. That's how any one of us would act in their place." He glanced at Ada at the end of the table, her face was clouded by a dark frown. "I'm sorry, my love, but that's the truth of it. This is not a time for vindictive torture."

"We must keep them apart, though. That will add to their insecurity." Hravn came to a decision. "Godric, work with Dai and Brandr and take the man-at-arms. Use the central hall. Edie, Bear and I will deal with de Kiberen. Wealmaer, I want you to move between us and keep Godric and me informed about anything that either lets slip. Ada, I know that this isn't to your liking so I won't ask you to pretend to be hospitable, but please help Wassa and prepare food and ale aplenty."

Ealdgith placed her hand on her husband's arm. "You know what this means? It is time for me to lead the rest of our household to the lake."

There was a note of sadness in Hravn's voice as he replied. "I know. Make arrangements tomorrow. Be ready to leave when I ride for Stanmoir."

*****

Hravn pushed his trencher aside and gestured to Wassa to top up de Kiberen's ale.

"So, Felix, where is Kiberen? I assume that is from where you hail?"

Felix felt uncomfortable at the hospitality he had been shown; it was not how he would have treated a prisoner. Even his man-at-arms was, he had been assured, being well looked after by his social peers. "Kiberen, yes, it is a port on the Atlantic coast. My family seat is there, and it is from there that generations of my family have served Count Alan and his family."

"And you? How long have you served the Count?" Felix was nonplussed by Ealdgith's question. The influence of this woman, any woman, in a warrior's household was as unsettling as her hospitality. He answered courteously.

"Mayhap twenty years, My Lady. I joined him as soon as I aspired to manhood. I served as an esquire to one of his knights until I was knighted myself."

"Does your father serve the Count too?" Hravn asked conversationally.

Felix shook his head and spoke matter-of-factly. "No longer, for he is dead. I was nine when he sailed to Hastings with the Count and Duke William. I didn't see him again until I was esquired to another of the Count's knights, just after the Count was first granted the Honour of Richemund. He was slain by silvatici in a cowardly ambush, not long after we had rebonded."

Ealdgith glanced quickly at Hravn, then smiled gently at Felix, "I'm sorry to hear that, I understand that the green men were something of a curse in those days. Those were certainly hard times for all of us in the North. But what of life in Ghel.., err, Richemund-scir now?" Ealdgith refrained just in time from using the pre-Norman name for her homeland.

"The land is settled and safe, and more productive by the year." He laughed, "Those English nobles that the Count let retain their lands are now almost French in their ways." Felix's pride in Norman domination of English life was very evident.

"English nobles? Who might they be?" Ealdgith's question was innocence personified.

"There are several, my Lady, Gospatric for one holds many manors from the Count."

"Indeed." Ealdgith said simply, omitting to add that she considered her father's brother to be a traitor to the family and disgraced the name 'Gospatric'.

"I heard that the Scots caused trouble for the Count last year?" Hravn subtly changed the subject, adding, "Over the border in Dunholm."

If Felix was surprised, he didn't show it. "Yes, they're a hot-headed bunch, the Scots, or at least their king is. One moment we were riding hard to try and break their siege on Dunholm and regain the lands north of the Tinan, then the next we heard there was an agreement with my Lord King and peace in Northumberland."

"I've heard something of that agreement." Hravn leant forward conspiratorially. "Though the Scots claim these lands, they've never held them. I've heard that King Malcolm may have swapped a tenuous hold on Cumbraland for a stronger hold on Lothian."

Felix frowned with surprise, then smiled slowly. "Mmm…that's not quite as I've heard, but you can certainly expect King William to have an influence here quite soon. The Kings have agreed that William is to secure the border south of the Solway, and Malcolm the border along the Tweed."

"Would that have something to do with why you were at Burc today?" Ealdgith asked conversationally."

Before Felix could answer, Hravn added, "If I'd known that the Count had a legitimate interest here then my son would have been less brutal. I hold the passes into Cumbraland for Lord Dolfin, so any armed men will be dealt with if they are not here with his authority. Should I expect to see your King's men any time soon? I would like to ensure that they are properly received."

Ealdgith flashed a sharp look at Bear as he smirked at the thought of the reception his father had in mind, then she nodded towards the door at the back of the hall where Wealmaer hovered in the shadows. Bear understood her meaning and, taking his leave, went to Wealmaer who spoke quietly in his ear, "The Frenchie couldn't hold his ale, he's out cold, but not before he gave us their whole line of march." Returning moments later and, standing behind Felix, Bear gave his father a meaningful smile.

Felix continued, unaware of the conversation behind him, "The Count plans to march as soon as this bad weather breaks. He'll establish himself in the fort and at another near a place called Penrith. We were due to reconnoitre it next."

"Reconnoitre? It's a word I don't know." Hravn questioned.

"We were to investigate to see what shelter the forts offered."

"Ah, I see. What will the Count do now?"

Felix shook his head glumly, "I've failed in my duty to him. I assume he will send others in my place." He turned to Hravn. "Now you understand, will you allow me to complete my mission, or assist whoever is sent?"

Hravn's cold look was answer enough. Ealdgith spoke. "Your coming into these lands armed and uninvited was an act of war. You must know that."

Hravn continued, "I will take you to Lord Dolfin. Only he can decide your fate."

Chapter 8

Cerdik shivered, cursed, then pulled his cloak tight around his body and stamped his feet in an attempt to keep warm. He stopped suddenly, feeling the ancient rotting beams beneath him shift alarmingly. "Keep to the edges and move slowly," he cautioned Nudd who worked alongside.

With one eye on the distant Norman castle at Bogas, three leagues to the east and lower down the Greta valley, and his other eye on his men, Cerdik was feeling very exposed behind the low parapet on the roof of the ancient signal tower. Two of his men led ponies laden with dry wood up from the woods along the River Greta, and through the layer of thin snow that blanketed the high moors, whilst Nudd hauled bundles of wood up the side of the stone tower.

Cerdik didn't trust the strength of the floors and stairs within the Roman signal tower and was uncertain whether the top floor would hold the weight of the beacon he was building. The two things he was certain of were that the Normans would never spot the beacon as they rode along the adjacent stone road, and that once it was alight, the dry timbers within the old tower would explode into flame with a column of smoke that could be seen right across the vale of the Eden.

He turned and looked to the west, reassured that he could see the top of the second tower two leagues away. That tower stood on a high spur, almost a league south of the stone road, from where it dominated the high pass and had a clear view across to their camp in the Borrowdale woods. The high moorland in-between the two towers was covered with decaying remains from the Roman days. A sprawling fort embraced the stone road at the top of the pass. Although its decrepit walls were no longer defensible, Cerdik was sure that the fort would be a focus for Norman attention. He hoped it would keep inquisitive eyes away from the two towers. He knew that Godfrid was building a similar beacon on top of the second tower and wondered why they had drawn the short straws. Life in the cold towers, with their leaking roofs and no prospect of a warm fire, was not going to be fun. The only thing he was thankful for was Bear's promise to rotate the sections every three days.

*****

"Riders are coming! Six of them." Nudd shouted down to Cerdik from the top of the tower.

"It'll be our reliefs, along with Bear or Agnaar and one of the huscarles." Cerdik called back, before kicking the feet of the two men sleeping just inside the tower's entrance. "Wake up, you two. Get the place tidy before they get here."

Bear nodded approval as he walked into the tower, then asked, "Show us up to the beacon, Cerdik."

"Take care, Lord, and keep close to the wall. The timbers are riddled with rot." Cerdik led the way up two flights of steps within the dingy age-blackened walls.

Bear blinked in the bright daylight as he clambered onto the top platform, then grimaced as he felt the old boards flex under his feet.

"It must be your weight, Lord." Cerdik joked.

Bear grunted, unimpressed by Cerdik's over familiarity, but accepting that the youngest of their section commanders still had more to learn. "You've done well, Cerdik. Green wood layered over dry brushwood should burn slowly and give a thick smoke. Whoever lights it had better get away quickly, these floors will burn through within minutes." He turned and studied the view towards Bogas. The road formed a faint etched line through the white wilderness of the snow-covered moor.

"I can see the castle, just. But could you see when men ride out from it?"

"No, Lord." Cerdik shook his head, then, realising the reason for Bear's concern, added, "There's a long stretch of road in dead ground that we can't see. We can't be sure of seeing a Norman force until they are a league away, mayhap a little more."

"Mmm..." Bear glanced across to Dai. "It's what I thought. We need an observation post right down by Bogas, and another beacon."

"Aye," Dai nodded, "and that means two men committed further forward. We're going to need at least a section and a half here."

Bear came to a quick decision. "Cerdik, select two men to leave with Ari. They'll stay here with him until the Normans come. I can no longer spare the manpower to keep relieving those here every three days. Dai, we'll take Ari and find a suitable forward post." He tugged his beard, thinking. "How long would laden ox carts take to reach here from Bogas?"

Both men shrugged, Dai spoke. "Two hours, mayhap. It's a long uphill haul for them. They'd need a rest too."

"Good." Bear looked suddenly pleased with himself. "I do love it when a plan comes together. We know that their line of march will be mounted men-at-arms first, followed by archers and infantry on foot, then the baggage train. We can assume that the Count will want to get his men-at-arms into the fort at Burc as quickly as he can. That means the rest of his men are going to become very strung out. I think it will take getting on for an hour and a half for the cavalry to reach the ambush point, by which time those on foot will be just past here, and the baggage train still well down the slope. The main ambush will only last moments, which means that the group attacking the baggage train should have time to get from the first ambush to here at about the same time as the ox carts arrive. The smoke from the beacon will be a good reference point for them. If we keep Ari and his men here, they can track the baggage train and direct Fader and Agnaar onto them. Ye gods! I wish I was attacking with them, instead of heading to Ulueswater."

Dai laughed then spoke, whilst Cerdik looked bemused. "Aye, Lord. The way Hravn is using the sections, it will still give us thirty-two men for the first ambush and twenty-four here. That's two good bloody noses we can give the Count and his men." He pointed, "See how the road slowly drops to the right of the ridge we are on. I think we could observe Bogas from the ridge and use the dead ground to the left of it to come and go from here. I'll get Ari ready."

Bear explained his plan to Ari whilst they rode their ponies over to the far side of the ridge. "You'll need to stick to dedicated tracks, Ari, we can't risk your presence being discovered. You are only to light the beacons when the main force moves. If a small party attempts to ride up the road again, vacate the tower quickly, leave no sign of your presence and pull back over the ridge. Then get word to me. Hopefully the tower is far enough away from the road for them to ignore it. Though I can't see them moving whilst there is snow on the ground, I'm sure the attack will come as soon as it has thawed."

"Aye, Lord, and I'll scout out the best points from which to attack the baggage train in the next couple of days." Ari was one of the few survivors from Hravn's original war band. Bear appreciated his experience and counsel.

The land behind the ridge was easy to ride upon and was obviously now waste, having not been grazed or farmed since the harrying twenty years earlier. Large tracts had reverted to scrub and it was open and firm under the thin snow. Dai chose a route just below the ridge line and periodically rode cautiously up to check their position in relation to Bogas.

Dai checked for the fourth time, dismounted and waved for the others to join him. Crouching just below the skyline he pointed to a small conical hut a furlong away, just over the crest of the ridge. "An old shepherd's hut, I would think. Ari, your lads could keep watch from there and build a beacon just this side of the ridge. There's woodland for fuel further down the valley behind us."

Ari nodded, "Looks good to me. I'll rotate the lads twice a day; it'll stop them getting too cold and they can tether their ponies behind it. I'll get them to build the beacon first then keep watch from tomorrow."

Bear tapped Dai on the shoulder. "Let's get back. I want to check out the main ambush site next. Ari, I'll send Agnaar to have a look at the ground tomorrow. I'm sure Fader will come too, once he's joined us."

*****

Hravn was agitated as he drove his horse hard on the ride back from Carleol. Wealmaer and the section who had escorted the prisoners were pushed to keep up with him, and their horses suffered. He knew he was acting out of character, and he knew the cause was the persistent fuzziness in his head and his sudden inability to remember words and incidents from the past. His body had recovered from the blow, and he was fine physically, but his head was a different matter. His ability to cope with the demands of the coming conflict worried him and, for the first time, he couldn't bring himself to talk to Ealdgith about it.

He was depressed too by his visit to Carleol. Dolfin had been uncharacteristically dismissive. He had ordered that the prisoners be locked in a cell in the guard tower, saying that they could rot until de Mowbray arrived and released them, and had then turned his attention back to stripping the fort and hall of anything of value, overseeing it being loaded onto a line of ox carts. "I want it all safe in Dunbar before ever the Normans arrive," he had said matter-of-factly, adding, "now, Sir Hravn, if you've nothing else for me I suggest we go our separate ways. My family's historic lands here are being taken from me and there is nothing I can do for those who remain. As I said to your son, I recommend you look to the protection of de Taillebois, for you will get none from Count Alan."

Hravn dismounted outside the stables, handed the reins to a groom and strode to the entrance to the hall. It had been a cold ride and he clapped his hands to get the circulation going, then stopped in the doorway, surprised. "William! Is something amiss?"

William and Ealdgith turned. Ealdgith walked over to give her husband a welcoming kiss whilst William waited for Hravn to join him by the warmth of the hearth. He gave Hravn a reassuring smile as they shook hands.

"Fear not, nothing is amiss. Aebbe and Gunilda are well, the little one has a thankful gift for suckling and sleeping."

"Other news, then?" Hravn grabbed a stool and sat, indicating that William should take another.

"Yes. As I was telling Edie, I've had word from my man in Ivo's court. His men haven't been reinforced yet, which means that you face little threat from Amounderness or any of the other lands to your south."

Hravn puffed out his cheeks and blew a sigh of relief. "Good, though I am sure Ivo will seize our fort at Tibeia. I would in his place."

William grunted in agreement. "Aye. He will certainly come north, in his own time, once Carleol and the middle vale have been secured."

"Has he said as much?"

William nodded. "He has. My man heard it from his lips. He sees no benefit in moving men-at-arms from his lands in Lincolia-scir when Count Alan and de Mowbray have enough to hand already, but he certainly intends to reap his share of what's to be had. He was also heard to say that the vale is so fertile that it should be a lot more productive than it is."

"And we can all draw our own conclusions about what that means." Ealdgith summed up their feelings.

"Aye, Edie, but I will strive to keep my promise to you. Ivo may do what he wants on any lands he seizes, but he won't take those that you have entrusted to Aebbe and me."

Ealdgith placed her hand on her son-in-law's knee, "I know, William. Now!" She strove to brighten their mood, "Join us for a meal before you return. You and Hravn will be in want of food after your respective rides."

Later, William having left, and with an early spring sun unexpectedly warming the day, Ealdgith took Hravn by the hand.

"Come, we can't leave this place for good without one last visit to the place where Bear was conceived." She laughed at the sudden confusion and consternation on Hravn's face and reached up to kiss him. "No. It is too cold for that and I am too old to face more child birth...but let us just walk up to our special place above the escarpment and take a last look at our lands at peace."

*****

"Go, my love, and don't look back. Keep your eyes fixed on the road to Patrichesdale and our future there. I'll see the last of the waggons away from here before I ride to join Bear." Hravn pulled Ealdgith to him in a very tight embrace, then released her slowly before helping her into the saddle of her bay mare.

"Keep your promise to me." Ealdgith looked sternly at Hravn. "Once you've done enough to keep the Count's attention well away from Ulueswater, break away and get all the men safely back to me. I know Agnaar, he'll want to keep taking Norman blood."

Hravn smiled with more reassurance than he felt. "I will, Edie, now go." He stood watching, breathing deeply to try and stem the emotion rising within, whilst Ealdgith flanked by Godric and Ada led a long line of carts down the track from the hall. Osric's section rode alongside her whilst Wulf brought up the rear. He knew that she was in safe hands, both men had served them since their days at Bebbanburge.

He turned away at last and called to Wealmaer, "Have the men mount. We ride to fight for our lands!"

*****

"This is it, Fader. What do you think?" Bear stood on the upper edge of a furlong-wide limestone escarpment. The old Roman road ran along the foot of the crags as it began to dip down from the top of the pass. "See how it dominates the road. We can get all the men within fifty paces of it, yet they will be protected by the rocks and the Normans won't be able to get up to them."

Hravn turned to his son. He felt happier, thankful to be free of the strain and responsibility of planning and relieved to be committed to action at last. "It's good, Bear. Very good. Now, tell me how you see the fight unfolding."

Agnaar watched with a wry smile whilst Bear enthused about his plan. "If you look closely you can see a natural way between the limestone blocks. It starts on our right and follows the contour across the middle of the scarp, down to the bottom left corner. That will be our way in and out. We'll tether the ponies up here in dead ground that can't be seen from the road. Godfrid will be here by then, as his is a shorter ride from the second signal tower." He paused, allowing Hravn to study the ground, then continued as Hravn nodded.

"I'm planning on three groups. As I'm going to leave and join Moder after the attack I'm going to put my three sections on the right. We'll spread out and cover you and Agnaar as you pull back and ride to ambush the baggage train. I suggest that you put Agnaar and two sections on the left and have the rest with you in the centre. That way we can protect the flanks if they do try and push around, but I can't see horses coping with this rough ground, and men-at-arms clad in mail will struggle to move uphill quickly."

"Exactly when do you intend to hit them?" Hravn interrupted.

"We know that they will have a large leading conroi, or a couple of conrois, to secure the road, followed by the Count and his commanders, then the rest of the conrois. The archers will be next, followed by the infantry on foot, some distance behind. We have to assume that some of the archers will be mounted. We need to break clear before they can get engaged, or strike as soon as they are in range, otherwise they could start to pick us off."

Bear continued, as Hravn nodded his approval, impressed by his son's battle planning and the clarity of his presentation. "I, that is Agnaar and I, think that we should wait until the Count is in front of you before we all let loose our first volley. That will cause the maximum confusion. We should go for the horses first. They are a bigger target and are likely to throw their riders or bolt downhill. There is a very steep slope down to Argill Beck, so any that do bolt are likely to throw their riders. We can give the men mayhap three minutes to shoot at will, until those outside the killing ground rally some sort of counter attack. You choose the moment, Fader, and pull back up through the crags. Agnaar will follow and I'll hold them off until you use your horn to signal that you are clear. Agnaar has found a covered way that will enable you to get over the ridge without being seen. I'll break clear quickly and we'll keep ourselves in clear sight until we are over the ridge someway to the west of here. That way, the Normans will think that we are withdrawing further down the valley and certainly not towards the baggage train. After that we'll give warning to any villagers left at Burc."

Hravn clasped Bear on the shoulder. "Well done, son. Well done, both of you. This will be your battle to lead, Bear, just as the attack on the baggage train will be yours, Agnaar. Now, before we finish here, I want to go down onto the road and see how the ground will look to the Normans as they ride into the killing area, and what it will look like to those who have already gone past when we launch the ambush."

As they rode around the escarpment and down to the road Hravn called across to Agnaar. "Where do you think we should base ourselves after the attack?"

"Bear and I thought Mallerstang. It's remote and wooded. We could raid from there for months. After all, from what you've told us, the Pendragons were nigh on untouchable there."

"Aye, they were." Hravn agreed.

"I sense that you are about to say 'but'," Bear interrupted.

"Hah! I am." Hravn laughed back. "It would be my choice too if it wasn't now land that we have passed to William and Aebbe. I don't want to draw attention to them, and it is a half day's ride from any Norman targets we will need to attack. No, I think we need somewhere closer to the road between Burc and Penrith. The hall would be ideal, but Count Alan will doubtless send men to look for me there."

Bear was quick to reply. "How about Morlund? Tyr was very concerned about the future when Moder sent me to warn him."

"My thoughts exactly, though I didn't know that you had given him warning. That could make things easier for us. Go and see him tomorrow. If he is agreeable, tell him that you will warn him after the first attack, when you go to Patrichesdale, and that he should expect Agnaar and me shortly after."

"Lord?" Agnaar sounded hesitant. "Surely we could be raiding for a month or two before we go back to Patrichesdale. Isn't Morlund too close to where we think the Normans will base themselves?"

Hravn cursed himself under his breath. His judgement had erred again. He came to a firm decision. "Aye, you're right. Bear, ask Tyr if I can base Agnaar with Brandr and two sections in his barn. Agnaar, you will determine when and where we should attack and then call forward men as and when needed. I will be with Wealmaer and three sections in Mallerstang. We will train men from the vill to work with us and keep you supplied from there. That way you won't be a burden on Tyr. I will see you every few days and we'll plan the detail of the attacks together."

"I agree, Lord." Agnaar sounded relieved. "I can fall back on Mallerstang if we are under pressure or become cut off from Ulueswater, and you can also raid onto the pass at Stainmoii more easily from there."

Agnaar's next question surprised Hravn. "Lord, did Adelind give you a message for me before you left the hall?"

Hravn halted his pony and turned to face both young men. "Sadly, no. She has been with Eir at Patrichesdale for some time now. Edie sent them both back there to train some of the women in the vill in the art of healing. I know how you both feel, and you're not alone, many of your men have left their women and families too. It's easiest if you put all thoughts of family behind you now and just focus on what we have to do. It was a hard lesson that I too had to learn many years ago." He rode on for another hundred paces, then stopped and turned.

"This is probably the first that the Normans will see of our ambush site, assuming it's not shrouded in mist and rain. What do you see?"

Bear's focus was on the escarpment. He had checked already from this position and was quick to reply. "Nothing, and the Normans will see nothing so long as the men keep their heads below the rocks until we are given your order, Fader."

Agnaar, understanding the probable mind-set of the invaders gave a different answer. "Well, if the tops were in the clouds I doubt they would risk the pass anyway. Assuming the weather is fair they would see a land of opportunity, a broad fertile valley ripe for taking, and a smoking beacon on a watch tower in the near distance. They won't even look at the rocks. They'll think that the warning will be for the people in the valley beyond."

Hravn looked surprised at Agnaar's insight, then gave him a gratifying smile. "I hope so, I do hope so."

Chapter 9

Agnaar lazed against a tree, chewing a birch twig to clean his teeth, whilst Bear lay back against a broad boulder and gently stroked the blade of his sword with a honing stone. The edge was already so sharp that the slightest pressure would slice through skin, as the cuts in his thick leather gauntlet testified, but the activity steadied his mind and gave the illusion of activity. He shifted his back against the cold rock, thankful for the warmth from the over-night fires that had been kept stoked by the guard. They had been burning wood at a phenomenal rate, but he wasn't worried, they would soon leave the camp, never to return.

The last of the sections was eating close to the cooks' fire as the first clear light of dawn lit the far side of the valley. Bear had tasked each section to cook for the whole camp in turn, and encouraged them to obtain food from those who remained at Burc. Over the past couple of weeks many of the villagers had taken heed of his warning and left on the long trek to Ulueswater. Some remained, several younger women amongst them, and were becoming increasingly dependent upon the thirty men in the camp. He knew that he had a duty to take them with him when he led his three sections away after the forthcoming battle; and was checking mentally that he would have sufficient spare ponies to carry them, when he heard a shout.

"The beacon's lit!"

Bear glanced at Hravn as he sheathed his sword. Hravn nodded and yelled, "This is it, lads. Leave the fires, check you've left nothing, and then mount up in your sections. Section leaders, report when ready."

They had all anticipated the Norman advance since a sudden thaw two days earlier, when Hrēðmonath's grasp on winter gave way to Eostremonath, the bringer of spring.

Their stomach-tightening dread of the uncertainty of battle lifted quickly as the prospect of the imminent fight focussed their minds. Bear, reinvigorated, was thankful when his father checked him with a quiet, "Don't rush, we've time enough yet. Take Agnaar and inspect the men once they've formed up. I'll talk to them once you're ready. Remember, words of encouragement will be worth a lot now. When we go, lead at a steady trot. Many a battle has been lost by a rush to fight."

Bear caught his father's eye and nodded with a quick smile, "I will, Fader, thanks."

Hravn turned to Wealmaer, "Check the men and make sure that they have used charcoal from the fires to break up the outline of their faces." He had learned many years ago the benefit of smudging the face with charcoal to disguise its shape and reduce reflection. It was one of the simple measures that could help conceal men lying in wait in an ambush.

Low morning sun cast long shadows across the high moorland as the troop halted in a broad hollow just above the escarpment, and tethered their ponies so that they couldn't stray. Patches of snow clung to the northern slopes, making a stark contrast to the dead winter grass, brown heather and patches of glutinous black peat. The men's mottled green cloaks blended well as they followed Bear along the track between the rocks.

Hravn settled into position in the centre of the forward edge of the rocks then called Cerdik and Godfrid to him. He knew that neither of the two section leaders, nor their men, had previous battle experience.

"How many of your men have crossbows?"

"Three, Lord." Godfrid answered for them both, "The rest have bows."

Hravn was deliberately reassuringly calm. "Good. Wealmaer and I will fight alongside you, Cerdik, and make up for the two men you lost to Ari."

Wealmaer squatted on the rocks watching the road, estimating distances whilst listening to Hravn talking to the two section leaders. "I'm sure you've already told your men, but make sure they lay a dozen arrows or six bolts to hand on the rock in front of them. The archers will have a much faster rate of fire. Now, make sure the men gauge the speed of the horses and aim off directly in front of the lower throat. That way, they are bound to hit the horse somewhere along its body, or take the rider in his leg. Don't aim for the men until they are on the ground. Oh, and tell them to leave the Count for me." He added, with a wink.

"Yes, Lord. I'm sure there'll be targets aplenty." Cerdik was his usual cocky self.

"There will, Cerdik. Now, make sure that the men don't rush. They will be nervous, most haven't killed before. Remind them of the first principles: control their breathing, steady their aim, then loose and watch the effect in case they need to adjust their aim for their next shot. You've a few minutes yet, so go."

Hravn half crouched with his back to the rock, an arrow notched to his bow string and his head turned so that he could watch the road from the corner of his eye. He took a deep breath to slow his own heartbeat; it was a long time since he had killed, and it never got any easier. He could hear the Normans coming moments before he saw them. As expected, the leading horsemen appeared more interested in the view down the valley, one even pointed to it. He let them go by at the trot, then waited for the next group, hoping that it would be the Count with his commanders; their blue and yellow chequered livery and pennants suggested it was.

"Loose!" Hravn's action was swift and fluid. He stood, turned and drew the bow in one quick movement, then tracked a horse in the second row hoping that it was Count Alan's. It was hard to miss at fifty paces and his arrow ripped into the horse's chest, piercing a lung. It reared and staggered, its rider clung skilfully to its back and then urged it to the ground as he rolled from the saddle to shelter behind its left side. Hravn cursed as he drew his bow again and chose the next horse in line. He knew that if that had been the Count he would stay behind the shelter of his dying horse until the ambush was stopped.

Smiling thinly, Hravn picked off horse after horse methodically as the arrogant pride of the invading Normans was shattered. Horses squealed, reared and collapsed, throwing their riders to the ground whilst others bolted. Some dragged men with their feet caught in the stirrups, others plunged in panic down the steep bank beyond the road. Then, as the onrush of cavalry stopped, the green-clad men began to aim at the men on the ground below.

"To your right, to your right!" Bear screamed at the three sections alongside him as the leading cavalry returned at the gallop. With their lances lowered, the riders urged their mounts off the road and up the steep grass bank below the rocks. One horse stumbled, and then another, their feet catching on the rough ground and hidden rocks. Two men-at-arms recovered and ran forward clumsily trying to draw their swords as they clambered up the increasingly steep slope. Both fell backwards when crossbow bolts thumped into them.

The remaining riders wheeled, then tried to force their way around the edge of the rocks, only to find their horses stumbling as their knees collapsed on the steep broken ground. Man after man fell. Each was hit as he tried to clamber forward to engage with the archers and crossbow men.

Hravn lowered his bow and took stock of the situation. The road to his front was a sea of dead, wounded and sheltering men and horses. Bear had broken the counter attack from their right and he could see the first men-at-arms on foot trying to work their way around the edge of the hill to their left. He raised his horn to his lips and blew. As the horn's sharp blast cut through the noise of battle and drew his men's attention, Hravn gestured to Agnaar to start their withdrawal.

"We're next." Wealmaer tapped Godfrid on the shoulder as the last of Agnaar's men filed behind them.

Bear took charge of the rear guard. "Ivar, cover the left flank and kill any archers you see coming within range. Tófi, keep the right flank. Ranald, with me, we'll cover the centre."

Seeing his father preparing to follow behind Wealmaer, Bear tapped his right temple in a casual salute and was reassured by Hravn's salute in return. "Stay safe, Fader. We'll meet again in Patrichesdale."

Bear's eye was drawn by a movement in the middle of the road below. Catching sight of a man with a blue and yellow chequered cloak kneeling up from behind a dead horse, then beginning to stand, Bear whipped an arrow from the quiver on his shoulder and, swiftly notching it to his bow string, drew, took aim and loosed the arrow. He cursed as the man dropped down, the arrow striking the edge of the road immediately behind. "Sorry, Fader," he muttered.

Hravn's horn blast cut through the noise of the battle below.

"Ivar! Fall back to the ponies. Tófi, move when he is past me." Bear yelled orders, striving to be heard at a distance. As soon as Ivar's men were clear of Ranald's line of sight, he ordered his section to keep a fast stream of arrows falling on the Normans to their left; their higher position gave his men the advantage of longer range. Bear winced as Norman arrows flew back in return, landing just short of their position. "Ranald, move back now. We can't delay any longer." Bear turned and followed the last of Ranald's men, running up the track between the rocks.

Reaching the ponies, Bear briefed his section leaders. "We've time, it'll take them a while to clear their way through the rocks. Let the men catch their breath then follow me up the spur to our left. I want everyone down there to see us ride onto the ridge and then follow it towards Burc. Hopefully they will assume Hravn and Agnaar went that way too."

When they reached the ridge, Bear turned to look down upon the carnage on the road. A semblance of order was returning. Bodies had been pulled to one side, doubtless awaiting collection by the baggage train, and dead horses were being rolled over the bank. A huddle of men-at-arms by a blue and yellow chequered banner indicated that the Count was giving orders. He turned to Dai, "Take Tófi's and Ivar's sections. Make sure that we have left nothing at the camp, then gather the spare ponies and collect the people from Burc. I'll speak to Olaf and warn them to be ready as I ride past, but I won't wait. I'm going to Morlund to warn Tyr. We'll meet at nightfall at Pulhoue and claim hospitality from the people there."

*****

Ari lay on his stomach on a patch of turf within the heather. As he watched the waggon train grind its way up the steep straight road on the slope below, his eyes were drawn back constantly to the abandoned signal tower. He was fascinated at how the stone walls were slowly turning pink, and supposed that it was due to the heat of the fire within. The tower still burned, but not as fiercely as it had. The beacon, burning through the planks of the old floor within minutes, had suddenly set light to the ancient dust-dry timbers within the tower and, drawing air through the entrance below, had created an inferno that threw flames and burning debris out of the top. It was a display of the power of fire that the men had never seen before. His attention jerked back to the present as he felt the tremble of pounding hooves before he heard them.

"Bran!" He rolled over and shouted to one of his men sitting in the lee of the ridge twenty paces away, "Our Lord is coming. Ride and meet him, then lead him here."

The rest of his section mounted and waited whilst Ari continued to watch the long line of ox carts. The first were already level with him, but the line stretched on and on. He couldn't believe their luck. He had watched for half the morning, first as scores of horsemen had passed and then, after a gap, men-at-arms on foot had marched steadily and determinedly up the hill. Finally, after a much longer interval, the first elements of the waggon train were passing. Ari mounted and rode to meet Hravn as the war band arrived.

"Lord, your timing is perfect." Ari saluted then wheeled his pony next to Hravn. "The ox carts are passing now. Most have only a driver and they are strung out down the road. We can pick them off almost one by one. The infantry are half a league ahead and, even if they get wind of our attack, it will be a while before they can return at the double and reach the carts."

Hravn turned to Agnaar. "I said that this was to be your battle. What's your plan?"

Agnaar felt his blood surge. This was his chance at last. He could start to take revenge for the death of so many of his family. "Lord, I rode over the ground here two days ago. We'll work in two groups. I'll take two sections and you take three. Keep Ari with you, whilst I ride several furlongs further down. Once I turn and cross the ridge, attack from here. The road is little more than a furlong beyond the crest of the ridge. Then, we'll work towards each other, slaying the carters and driving the oxen down into the valley beyond. Many will break their traces, others will persist in dragging the carts and no doubt break axles and wheels as they go."

Hravn nodded, smiling as he appreciated the simplicity of Agnaar's plan. The carters weren't men-at-arms. Many might have been pressed into service for the task. He assumed that they might well run once they saw their comrades being slaughtered. He hoped so.

"Good, Agnaar, good. A simple plan is always the best."

Agnaar breathed deeply, relieved and gratified at Hravn's praise.

"Do you want to plunder, Lord?" He asked.

Hravn shook his head. "No, there is nothing we want here other than to disrupt as much of the bastard Count's supplies as we can. It will be many a day before they can recover what is here. Rather, let us regroup when we meet in the middle, then repeat the attack at the rear of the waggon train." He held up his hand to attract the attention of all the section leaders. "Remember, many of the carters will be English, they are our kith forced to work for the Count. Kill them if you must but let those that run live. Save your arrows for the real enemy. We've slain many of those already today, and we'll slay many more in the days to come."

Agnaar acknowledged his orders with a quick nod and turned to his section leaders. "Toudwal, Ewen, with me. Let's go."

Agnaar's spirits soared as he led the nine horsemen at a gallop across the turf and heather clad moorland. The pent-up frustration from weeks of waiting cleared; he knew that he was born to do this. Brandr kept close on his heels, sensing his young lord's renewed vigour. Agnaar aimed for a point at which to cross the ridge, slowed and shouted to Brandr. "Stay with Toudwal's section, I'll take Ewen's. We'll leapfrog our way along the line of carts." He drew and wavedhis sword towards the line of slowly moving carts and yelled, "Charge!"

Brandr adjusted his line of attack to his right, towards the next cart in line. The men followed, screaming, battle-lust upon them.

Agnaar laughed into the wind as he caught sight of the terrified faces of the cart drivers, and glanced sideways at his men. The carters were right to be frightened at the sight of charging warriors: faces streaked with charcoal, hair flailing wildly behind steel helms, mail glinting under green cloaks that concealed them against the winter moorland, and the bright glisten of spear tips pointing directly towards them. They were terrifying.

There was little the first two cart drivers could do. One was disembowelled by a spear thrust, the other fell sideways from the lumbering cart, his hands clutching at a blood-spurting slash along the length of his thigh. Their carts veered slowly to the left as the green-cloaked men grabbed the traces and pulled the oxen around towards the rough moorland slopes and the River Greta. The oxen bellowed in pain and anger as spear jabs goaded them further from the road, then a leather trace broke as a wheel jammed against a boulder and the first ox broke free.

Months of hard training paid dividends as the green men worked their way methodically from cart to cart. There was little need for shouted orders. They worked in pairs, turning the oxen down the slope, driving them until the waggons broke, then cutting them free from the traces to wander towards the valley bottom. There was no need to kill the cart drivers; they fled ahead of the advancing riders.

Moments after their attack Agnaar heard a horn further up the line of carts. Its call was picked up by another, and then another. He knew that the alarm had been given and infantry, and then cavalry, would soon return down the road.

Pausing momentarily, he saw Hravn's group working their way quickly towards him, the three sections moving along the line of waggons quicker than his two. As they came together he called to

112

Hravn, "The alarm's been given, we should leave and ride for the end of the waggons."

Hravn raised his hand to quell Agnaar's haste. "No, we've time yet. Do you see what's in the waggons?" He asked, with a sudden glint in his eyes.

"Aye, fodder for the horses in some, tentage and piles of long stakes in others. What are the stakes for?" Agnaar was perplexed.

"Hah! A stake-wall, of course. With those they can quickly put a defensive perimeter around any camp they make. I've seen it before." Hravn recalled watching the building of Richemund castle twenty years earlier. "Quick, call the men together. Have them take some of the fodder and stuff it around the tents and stakes, then set light to them all. It will distract the Normans when they do come and will help cover our next attack and escape."

Hravn sat on his pony, alongside Agnaar and the two housecarls, watching whilst the men in the sections worked quickly, methodically setting alight one waggon after another along the long line. The burning carts terrified the oxen as they dragged their flaming burdens further away from the road. The sound of a distant horn drew his attention to the head of the pass. Sunlight glinted on spear tips as the first men galloped over the top of pass. They were at least half a league away.

"That's it. Reform and ride." Hravn shouted across to Agnaar, then sounded his own horn as a signal to his men. "Go now. Work your way along the rest of the line. I'll watch with Wealmaer and warn you when we need to make our escape."

As Agnaar led off at a gallop, Hravn followed at a more sedate pace, glancing repeatedly over his shoulder. As well as cavalry, he could now see mail-clad infantry marching at a forced pace back down the road. He felt better than he had done for months. Clarity of thought was returning and he realised suddenly that he hadn't felt the dull nagging pain in his head since their early morning call to arms. He chuckled and called across to Wealmaer, "What a wasted panic that is. We'll be gone before ever they get down here, and for what? We've burnt the lot. They'll be knackered by the time they have to march back up the hill. Hah! I'm sure the Count will have someone's head for all their efforts. Come, it's time to call Agnaar to heel and make our escape across the Greta. We've five leagues hard riding ahead of us to get to Mallerstang."

"Aye, and we can salute the Normans with two fingers from the far ridge as we go." Wealmaer laughed back.

*****

"Moder! Moder! Warriors are here!" A blonde girl of maybe eight years ran shouting up the track to the hall. Bear chuckled, laughing to himself as he recalled how his mother once described Gunnar's daughter, Aebbe, to him. This girl must surely be Aebbe's daughter. The hall always impressed him. Built in the Norse style of Tyr's forebears, it dominated the low ridge that overlooked the surrounding fields. A stone foundation wall was topped by an ancient, broad, steeply sloped shingle-clad roof. The ends of a large beam extending beyond the edge of the long roof had been carved to give the appearance of a large dragon's head staring down on those below. The two cross beams above the gabled entrance on the side of the longhouse were smaller, but similarly carved.

Ranald whistled, then said under his breath, "She is beautiful!"

"Aye, and married, so keep your thoughts to yourself." Bear cautioned him with a grin whilst he appreciated Ranald's point. The woman in the gabled entrance had the full rounded body of one entering early middle age. The sun caught the gold in her hair as she bent to pick up the little girl, "Aebbe is like a sister to my moder."

"Æsc," Aebbe used Bear's given name, "it seems that Wyrd has woven our families' threads together once again. Come inside and meet my husband. Tyr and he are planning how we should move to join you at Patrichesdale." Whilst her smile was welcoming, Bear read sadness and annoyance in her eyes.

Bear dismounted and passed his pony's reins to Ranald. "You can water the ponies from a trough behind the hall, and I'm sure Tyr won't begrudge them some fodder. I'll be as quick as I can." He followed Aebbe and blinked as his eyes adjusted to the smoky gloom inside the hall.

A stocky balding man with long flaxen hair and ruddy cheeks stood up, hand outstretched. He was the image of his father. "I'm glad to see you again, Tyr." Bear clasped Tyr's hand and then turned to an equally broad man with thinning hair and a thick, salt and pepper beard.

"Rhun, we met at Gunnar's funeral." The man introduced himself without standing or offering his hand.

Bear sensed tension as Aebbe stood behind her husband and glowered at Rhun. He raised a questioning eyebrow, then turned back to Tyr.

"Rhun is here to discuss the Norman threat you warned of. He is minded not to heed you, though I, we..." Tyr glanced at his sister, "...fear that there is much truth in what you said. We remember well the strife the Normans brought your parents many years ago."

Bear sighed. His huge frame dominated the table. "Ignore my warning at your peril, Rhun. I have come to warn Tyr that this morning we slew a couple of score or more of the bastards as they crossed over the Stanmoir pass, and as we speak, my fader will be destroying Count Alan's baggage train. By nightfall he will have hundreds of his men in the old fort at Burc. Even now my men are leading the last of the villagers there to join my moder at Ulueswater. I urge you to do likewise."

Rhun's jaw dropped. "But this is Cumbric land, under the protection of the Scots King. How..."

They flinched as Bear smote the table with his fist. "No, Rhun. It's as I told Tyr. The Scots have forsaken Cumbraland for Norman guarantees over their border in Lothian. Dolfin has already left Carleol, my fader saw him go." He shrugged, "The choice is yours. Take a chance on Red William letting your overlord keep his lands; though, even if he does, can you be sure that he won't take your lands into his desmesne? Or, you can join us in the dales around Ulueswater. It'll mean a new start, a hard start. You will be given land, though not as much as you hold now. I'm sure we may have to fight to keep the Normans at bay, but at least you will have your freedom and will save your family. My fader is, with Tyr's help, going to harry the Norman lines and keep their eyes away from Ulueswater until we build our defences there." Bear leant forward on impulse and offered Rhun his hand, "Join us."

"We will." Aebbe shocked them by speaking first.

Her husband turned, caught her cold stare, then stood and shook Bear's hand.

Reaching behind for a stool, Bear sat. "Thank you. I will warn my moder to expect you, and Aebbe." He smiled up at the woman. "You can expect the warmest of welcomes from her." He could see that Rhun was fazed by the impact of it all. "Rhun, I suggest that you use ox-carts to move all that you can to Pulhoue. I will arrange for the loads to be taken to Patrichesdale from there by boat. It will be easier than struggling on the old road. Then try and drive as many of your livestock along the lake road as you can. We need to gather as much food as possible." He could see that the simple plan helped to reassure Rhun, so he turned to Tyr.

"I have to leave for Pulhoue now. Agnaar will

be here within a couple of days, once he and Fader have re-grouped in Mallerstang. I suggest that you start to empty your hall and move as much as you can to Pulhoue along with Rhun. Rest assured, once there you'll be in good hands."

*****

Bear rode ahead of his men. They had left Pulhoue not long after the early morning sun cast a pink glow over the lake. As he cantered across the flat land of the lower Glynrhedyn valley, he felt as if the chapters of his story were being rewritten. He reined to a halt outside his parents' hall, threw the reins to Dai and strode in. He found Ealdgith in the entrance and embraced her warmly. Her sense of relief was palpable as her body relaxed.

Ealdgith pulled back and smiled. "Your arrival tells me that the Normans have come and that the Count's nose has been bloodied. Come and tell me how it is whilst we eat. We will discuss the future in my council after we have all broken fast."

Chapter 10

Godric stood and pulled back the chair at the head of the long table. Ealdgith took her seat and looked gravely at those around her. Bear, Dai, Eir and Leofric to her right, Ulf, Godric, Ada and Gytha to her left. The empty chair at the far end of the table signified Hravn's absence very clearly.

"Yesterday, all our lives changed. How they change is now in God's hands and ours. The Normans, once again, have come to threaten our very existence. Bear's already told you how we bloodied their nose, and Hravn and Agnaar are now buying us the time we need to turn the lake and fells into our sanctuary and fortress. You, all of you, will be my council. Hravn and I have a firm idea of what we must do, but it is through you that we will turn that idea into a plan."

Ealdgith turned to Ulf, "You have more battle experience than any of us, though Godric runs you a close second." She flashed a quick smile at her housecarl. "Keep working with Bear and Dai to prepare our men and our defence until such time as Hravn can rejoin us."

As the three men nodded Ealdgith looked to her right. "Eir, you now know as much as me about the arts of healing, and Adelind is learning fast. The care of our injured, for injured we will have, is down to you. Choose whomsoever you want to help and take whatever you need. Remember, it will help you a lot if you have some of the older men to assist carrying the wounded for you. I know Cyneburg has already readied a building for you to use." Reading concern in the young woman's eyes, she added, "You cannot rely on me to be there to direct you, and nor need I be. You are our 'wise-woman' now."

"Godric, Ada, I want you to stand behind me at all times. Protect my back and give orders on my behalf when you need to. And Ada, that includes to all our womenfolk too."

Ealdgith's tone softened as she looked from Gytha to Bear. "Gytha, your fader has already taken the fight to our foe and we do not know whether any of us will fall in the days to come. It will be as God or Wyrd wills. But one day Bear and you will lead our people, and now is the day when you must start. I have tasks for you both."

Gytha's stomach churned and she strove to stop worry from reflecting in her face.

"Of course, Moder." Bear spoke with confidence.

"Gytha, Ulf has already set you to work with Leofric to plan ambushes along the road from Pulhoue. Speak with Ulf afterwards. You are to lead and Leofric is to be your deputy. I want you to do two things: take charge of the teams of archers and slingers and, with them, provide my eyes and ears along the lake shore approaches from Pulhoue. The beacons will tell us when the Normans reach Pulhoue. Warn me when they move past Pulhoue, then fight our first battle to slow their approach."

Gytha gasped.

"You have my complete trust, Gytha." Ealdgith spoke reassuringly, although there was a stern undertone in her voice. "I was your age when I faced the reality that to lead men, a woman must prove that she can fight. Now is your time. You are as much a Valkyrie as I was, and remember that Queen Aethelflaed's blood is in your veins as much as it is in mine."

Gytha took a deep breath, then relaxed, feeling sudden confidence surge within as Bear winked at her across the table. "Thank you, Moder," she mouthed with a slight smile.

"Good. Now, Bear, it's vital that the forge can keep casting weapons and horse shoes. We have to get lead to Rengles to trade for iron. The road has only just reopened after the snows, so tomorrow lead our jaggers with a section as escort to Rengles. Ulf sent warning to our agent there many weeks ago and the iron ingots have been ordered from the Eskdale mines. You've been there before?" Ealdgith was suddenly uncertain.

"Yes, Moder, with Fader two years ago, and several times since. I know the way and I know Aedan, our agent."

"Thank you. The lead is ready to be loaded, you just need to warn the jaggers and prepare your supplies for a week."

Ealdgith tapped her fingers onto the thumb of her right hand, mentally ticking off the points she wanted to raise. "With so many families joining us, and Bear having brought more with him with more to follow, I'm concerned that we will have to strip our woodland in order to build houses. We can't risk using the trees we need to build our boats, fuel the ore furnaces and provide for all our domestic needs. Therefore, I propose that we should start building with stone." Ealdgith gave a low laugh, "After all, we have fellsides littered with it." She paused, seeing realisation and agreement on the faces around the table.

Ulf laughed. "And why not? The people hereabouts have built small drystone structures for generations. They just haven't built anything as big as a house. Leave it with me," he chuckled.

"Thanks, Ulf, that leads to my last couple of points. I don't want all the new arrivals to split into little groups based on where they have fled from. I want them as one big community, blended as quickly as possible with those already living in Glynrhedyn. Godric, muster all the new men and choose those whom you think can hold a spear and shield. I want them to train every other day. They can clear land and build shelters for their families on alternate days. I don't see them fighting in a shield wall, but the Normans must think that they can. Talk to Ulf afterwards, he knows just how they are going to be used."

"Aye, my Lady, how..." Godric was interrupted.

"And make sure they are good at digging." Ulf's conspiratorial wink reassured Godric.

Ealdgith looked from Godric to Ada. "I don't want the women just looking after their families. Ada, form them into groups. One group is to do the daily cooking for all of the families, the other groups are to get temporary shelters built as quickly as possible. They can live communally until the houses are built. Once that's done, there will be more land to clear and ground to break. We need to get them sowing barley and oats as soon as they can."

Ulf interjected, raising his hand. "If there are any single girls with nimble fingers Cyneburg could do with extra hands in the spinning gallery. The women she has working in there are hard pushed with the extra spinning and weaving tasks, particularly those extra green cloaks you asked for."

"Ah, yes. I should have thought." Ealdgith clicked her fingers in frustration. "How about help with dyeing the fabric?"

Ulf chuckled. "I'm glad you asked, Edie. The lass that Cyneburg trained a couple of years ago could do with more help too. I forget her name."

"That would be Asta, Ragnaar's daughter." Ada said quietly.

"Aye, that's the lass. Well, it seems she's turned the task of blending the blue from woad and the yellow from dyers' greenweed into something of an art. The mottling on the latest green cloaks is really good. When I saw her yesterday she was experimenting with using the ink from oak galls and adding stripes of grey and brown into the green. She'll render our green men well-nigh invisible at this rate. I was thinking of calling it Glynrhedyn Green. Anyway, I'm sure that one or two of the older men that I can't train to stand in line can help her out. It's a pretty wet and heavy task, and hard on her hands."

Ealdgith laughed, "That's good, Ulf, a colour that reflects how our mottled and diverse people come together."

"Where's Leo?" Gytha asked Ulf, as Ealdgith wound up the meeting.

"His moder had a task for him in the spinning gallery. He'll be there, if he's not shirking. Don't you be distracting him." Ulf said, with a wink.

Gytha jogged along the track to Ulf's hall, then paused to gather her breath before walking up to the spinning gallery. It was a long, narrow, open-fronted structure butting against a south facing crag. Gytha was always struck by its simple effectiveness. The overhanging roof kept rain off those inside, whilst the open southerly aspect let in as much light as possible without it being too exposed to the prevailing wind. A floor of roughly hewn wooden planks saved the feet of the half dozen young women working there from getting too cold and wet. Supervising the spinners was one of Cyneburg's many responsibilities, and it was not one that Gytha envied. She spotted Leofric talking to his mother and called across to him.

"Hey! Leo. I know you're a dab hand with a spindle and distaff, but Moder has a task for us both." Gytha fretted as she spoke that Cyneburg might be irritated by the interruption.

"Are you volunteering your services then?" Cyneburg answered, good humouredly.

"You know me, Cyneburg. When it comes to spinning I've ten thumbs and no fingers. Moder has just told Ada to send some of the refugee girls your way. They'll be much better than me." Gytha spoke quickly, suddenly aware that the girls in the gallery were staring. She didn't want to demean their work, nor did she want to belittle herself. With a surge of pride, she added, "Moder wants Leo and me to lead the sections of slingers and archers, and to start training them tomorrow. That's why I need to steal him away from you."

Cyneburg stood, smiling, with her hands on her broad hips. "I guessed as much. You're your moder's daughter, right enough. She was never one for needle work either. As for Leo, he's too much of a distraction here. Now get along, both of you."

*****

Gytha had spent a sleepless night dwelling on how she could win round the six sections of archers and slingers. She still couldn't quite believe that her mother trusted her to fight the battle that would slow the Normans' advance up the lakeshore. But now that she had come to a decision, and buoyed by the warm spring sun and Loki's playful mood, she felt reassured.

Leofric followed a pace behind as they walked down the track to the clearing by the shore where Ulf had told the sections to meet her. Gytha scanned the group that lounged against trees or lay on the beds of pine needles, waiting. All appeared young, some her age and others a few years older. One tall dark-haired man was older, possibly ten years her senior. Ulf had told her that he had deliberately chosen those who were fit, nimble on the fells and skilled in poaching, fowling and hunting. She knew that their field craft would be instinctive. She was surprised, though, to see two girls. Twin sisters she surmised, as tall as her, lithe, with long black hair. Both stared at her impassively.

Gytha stood in the middle of the clearing, her hands on her hips, and looked at the half circle of faces. Some smiled, most just looked at her, a couple scowled. "I'm Gytha and this is Leofric." She gestured behind her. "Oh, and this is Loki," she added with a smile, trying to break the ice. "He hunts as well as he plays. Don't be put off by his size."

One of the two girls spoke, interrupting what Gytha was about to say next. "Why you?"

Gytha was taken aback. She had expected some push-back from the group, Ulf had told her to expect as much, but not before she had had a chance to speak.

"Why you?" the girl asked again. "We thought your brother would lead us. We all know he is a warrior now. But what can you do that I can't?"

Gytha heard Leofric growl behind her. She had to act quickly to grip the situation before her credibility was snatched from her.

"And you are?" Gytha's voice was icy, cutting through the warm air like an arrow.

The girl hesitated, sounding truculent. "Neven."

"Wrong!" Gytha snapped back, then stared at each person in turn, holding their eyes before moving on to the next. "It's Neven, Gytha...or Neven, my Lady. But it's not just Neven. Understood?"

The girl was mute.

"Do you understand, Neven?" Gytha made her point coldly.

"Yes...Gytha." Neven accentuated the pause in her reply.

"Thank you." Gytha stared at Neven momentarily, then turned to the group with a smile. "That wasn't the start that I had expected. You should know that my brother is to lead the rest of my fader's men in the main battle that is doubtless to come. They will stand shield to shield, sword to sword, against those Norman bastards." She paused, letting her words sink in. "Ours is to be a different fight, which is why my Moder has chosen us," Gytha gestured behind her, "because Leofric will lead under me, to lead in a different sort of battle. A battle for which I have a very clear plan. That is why I lead you."

Some of the young people in front of her nodded, most remained expressionless. Gytha knew she must say and do more. She shrugged, with an open smile.

"Neven is right. Am I any different to her? I am a girl after all. What can I do that she can't?"

Pausing for effect, Gytha then stepped forward and paced up and down in front of the sections. She spoke clearly, firmly, but with a smile. "I've grown up around this lake, just as you have. I can take a deer with an arrow, or a bird with a stone, just as you can. I can sail, swim or run as fast as anyone here and," she chopped the air with her hand and pointed to all around her, "I'm happy for you to choose a champion to challenge me to do any of those. But, before you do, I challenge anyone of you to fight me, now, with a seax."

Gytha grinned as the impassive faces turned to looks of shock. "Wooden ones, of course. I don't want to hurt anyone more than I must. The rules of the holmganga are simple. Leofric will explain them if you don't know them. So, choose your champion. Call me when you are ready." Gytha turned away deliberately and went to sit at the far side of the clearing. She was confident that few, if any, of them could handle a seax. Not that they need worry, she intended to fight unarmed.

A few moments later Leofric called across to her. "Gytha, they have chosen Owst."

Gytha stood up, rolled her shoulders, and called out. "Owst, step forward. Leo, give him a seax. I will fight without. And hold Loki for me. I can't risk him attacking Owst if I should fall."

Gasps of surprise sounded around the clearing. Gytha knew that she was beginning to win support; but that had been easy, the hard part was to come. She wasn't surprised as the tall dark-haired man stepped forward; who else could they have chosen?

Leofric handed Owst a wooden seax, then turned to Gytha with a quizzical look. "Are you sure?" he mouthed.

Gytha nodded, focussing all her attention on Owst. She faced him, shifting slowly round in a circle. "Come on, Owst. Strike me three times and you win, it's that easy."

Owst began to look confident. He tossed the seax from hand to hand, waved it dramatically with an outstretched arm, then settled down to face Gytha. He advanced on her slowly, intending to strike her with the flat of the blade. He knew full well that she was their Lady's daughter. This was not what he wanted, but he would put her in her place. Gytha goaded him, talking loudly so that all could hear.

"Come on, Owst, you're wasting time. Think of yourself as a Norman man-at-arms. Think what one would do to me. Come on. What would a Norman bastard do to anyone of us here?"

Owst's eyes narrowed. Gytha read his rising embarrassment and growing annoyance. She judged the moment of his lunge and spun away, twisting behind him, and landed a high kick in the small of his back before she danced outside of the range of his flailing sword arm. A titter of laughter ran around the clearing.

"That's one to me, Owst." Gytha laughed. She felt a confidence that surprised her, experiencing once again that floating feeling. All the staring eyes stimulated her; it was as if she was one of those itinerant performers who entertained at her parents' hall. Those months of hard training with Ada and Godric had been worth the pain, the bruises and the aches. Moving nearer to the crowd at the edge of the clearing, she continued to project her voice whilst goading Owst.

"So, you're their chosen leader, are you, Owst? And how will you do that, eh? Do you know our battle plans? Will you sit in my moder's council? I think not! Well? Come on, take me down if you can, or maybe let Neven have a go. She seems so full of herself. I bet she could do a better job." Gytha teased Owst with her fingers, waving for him to come closer. She skipped lightly forward and shrugged again.

Owst roared, enraged, and ran bull-like at her, all thought of sword play gone. Gytha jerked her body as if she was about to move sideways, then suddenly dropped down, curling into a ball on her knees, her arms protecting her head and neck. Owst's shins hit her hard as he fell over her body, grinding his hands across the hard, bare earth. She stood quickly, smiling at the outbreak of laughter around her. "That's twice, Owst. One more fall to go."

Gytha could tell that Owst lacked experience with a sword and she knew that it was unfair to continue to humiliate him, but he was the group's champion. If she beat him she would win their confidence. She decided to end the match quickly and stood her ground, swaying gently as she balanced on the balls of her feet. Owst held his arms wide. It was obvious to Gytha that he intended to feint with his left arm, pretending to grab her and force her to move to her left, whilst he swept his sword arm across to strike her. She held his eyes, watching the position of Owst's legs in her lower vision.

Owst gave his attack away by breaking eye contact. His grasp towards Gytha's right arm clasped at thin air, then, as Gytha dived under his legs, he felt her feet snagging his ankles and knew that he couldn't stop himself falling flat on his chest and face. His cry of shock, then pain, was choked off by the weight of a foot on the back of his neck. He lay still, panting for air.

Gytha lifted her foot and, as Owst rolled onto his back, she leant forward and grasped his hands to help him stand up. As he stood, she raised his right hand above his shoulder and turned to the crowd. "Well fought, Owst. I'm sorry if I hurt you, though I sense it's your pride that's taken the beating. You are a worthy champion but, as with all of you, you have a lot to learn about how to really fight."

As Owst shook his head and smiled, Gytha bent and picked up the wooden seax by its tip. She pointed the hilt towards Neven. "Can you do that, Neven? Do you want to fight me now?"

The girl's reply was prompt and respectful. "No, my Lady."

Gytha turned to face her new command. "Know me as Gytha. Now, introduce yourselves and tell me your skills. I will then group you into three large sections and explain how we will train and work. Ulf has given me the names of those who should command the combined sections. They are Kali, Gufa and, of course, Owst. I'll wait to see how you all perform before I choose their deputies."

Later, after a period of introductions and grouping the sections, Gytha set them to demonstrate their individual ability with the bow. Turning towards a gruff cough behind her, she saw Ulf watching. He stepped forward and hugged her shoulder with his one arm. "Well done, Gytha. I've watched from afar all morning. Your fader would have been proud to see you."

Ulf led her to one side. "I'll leave you now. I suggest that after you've tested their ability with bow and sling you should break to eat, then see what their water craft is like. Tomorrow, get them working in sections and competing against each other. There's no better way to build their teamwork." He lowered his voice. "Those two sisters, Neven and Duwe, are as canny a couple of vixen as you'll ever meet. Use them, push them, and make the lads want to beat them. You'll have their loyalty soon enough."

Gytha beamed at him. "Thank you, Ulf." She continued watching him, smiling, as he stomped back up the track. The thought of her father's pride in her meant more than anything. She wished he was there to watch her too.

Chapter 11

Bear smiled as he watched Gytha lead Leofric down the track to the clearing. The lightness in her step betrayed her confidence. He was proud of the way his younger sister had grown up. He sensed that there was something about Gytha that would inspire others to follow. Turning, he walked back into the hall; there was a lot to do before they could leave for Rengles.

"How are we doing, Tofi?" Bear called to the giant Dane. He was leaving Dai behind to assist Ulf and relying on the experienced section commander as his deputy.

"Almost ready, Lord. The jaggers have all the ponies laden and the men are just collecting our rations for the week. It'll take us three days each way, with a day in hand when we get there."

"Remounts?" Bear asked about spare ponies.

"Four for us, Lord, to carry the rations. Plus four for the jaggers. Some are bound to go lame carrying a load both ways."

Bear nodded approval. It was a long journey. Twenty-five leagues over three high mountain passes would take its toll on the laden pack ponies; not to mention the toll the weather could take on all of them. He took his leave and walked through the back of the hall to the stables where he saddled and loaded his fell pony. Whilst walking the pony around to the front of the hall Bear paused, distracted by a shepherd's whistle. He watched, as fascinated as always, whilst the shepherd worked his two dogs, driving a flock of sheep up the far side of the valley and onto the high summer pasture beyond.

Mounted at last, Bear signalled for the lead jagger to move on. The score of pack ponies, with a jagger riding alongside every fourth one, began its slow grind up the semi-paved road from Patrichesdale over the pass called Kirkstein, then down the steep descent to the old town of Ameleseta. Bear knew it was slow, but at least it was much easier than the alternative route up onto Brethstrett and along the high fell tops. Bear had ridden it once and heard how his father's first jagger train had almost been blown over the steep crags in the mist and rain. He looked at the sky and thanked the gods that it looked set fair for the next few days.

Although the Eostremonath days were lengthening, the sun was dipping towards the western fells as they descended towards the clustered cottages of Ameleseta. Shadows darkened their way through the narrow streets and alleys as they threaded their way between the buildings to the old fort by the lakeshore.

Leaving the jaggers to water, feed and pen the ponies, Toki set his section to work building a fire and preparing a meal. Later, Bear took two jaggers and two of his green men to the ale house, with the promise that they could swap with those standing guard upon their return journey. The ale house was in an old, stone-walled Roman building on the edge of the vill, its tiled roof long since replaced with thick slabs of turf. Bear coughed and blinked as the acrid smoke of the blazing hearth fire stung his eyes. At least the fire lit the large, otherwise windowless, room. He led the way to a trestle table at the edge of the room, away from the over-powering heat of the fire, and sat with his men, gesturing to the landlord to serve them.

"Well, Lord, you'll be heading to Rengles, no doubt?" The pot-bellied landlord seated himself at the table whilst two serving women placed large cups of ale on the rough, ale-stained wood. He spoke in Cumbric, but with a Gallo-Norse accent.

"Aye, Grimr. The passes are open at last, or so I'm told." Bear replied, remembering the landlord, "Now, tell me, have you heard anything about the

Normans showing interest hereabouts, or mayhap down at yon end of the lake?"

"No," Grimr tugged his unkempt beard, "not here, but there's talk of disquiet further south and there have been men passing through of late, young men mostly, and some women amongst them. They're hesitant to say where they're headed but some talked of joining a Jarl Buthar."

Bear's interest was pricked, but he suppressed any reaction. "Mmm...at Wythburndale perhaps?" he referred to the long steep-sided valley to their north, over the high pass where the king of Strathclyde, Dyfnwal ab Owain, had been killed in battle a hundred years earlier.

Grimr shook his head. "There's no one of that name up there. Further west, mayhap. The dales over yon side of the fells are remote. I've never heard tell of who holds them."

Bear took a swig of ale and, placing his cup down, said, "That's good to know, Grimr. You'd best be aware that Red William is set to seize Cumbraland and by all accounts, the Scots' King won't oppose him. The bastard Normans have already crossed to the Eden and we are set to lose our lands there. My fader's going to fight to keep a hold on Ulueswater, but we need to be sure our back is safe. If you hear anything be sure to send word. We're leaving for Rengles in the morn, but will be back in four days with a load of iron ore. I'd be interested in word of where Jarl Buthar is to be found. See what you can glean."

Grimr's jaw dropped in surprise and concern as he began to understand Bear's interest in the enigmatic Jarl, "Aye, I will that, Lord."

*****

Their second day was a long, slow grind over one high pass and then another, with the night spent in the shelter of an old stone fort on a high plateau just beyond the second summit. Many years earlier, Hravn had overseen the reroofing of some of the derelict buildings in order to shelter the regular pony-trains.

The next morning's descent to the coast was easy and uneventful as the rocky moorland gave way to woods and then strips of fields, some of which were being worked by men still sowing in preparation for a late harvest. They kept a close eye on the land to the south, across the valley of the Esk, but saw nothing. Bear knew that although those lands had long been under Norman control, they were very much a backwater. It was one reason his parents had chosen to ship their lead through Rengles rather than the more accessible port of Carleol.

As they approached Rengles, Bear could see more detail. The small port was tucked close by the shore of a wide, enclosed bay from which the sea drained completely at low water. It was a natural, not man-made, harbour and it was always busy. Two large tub-like boats that Bear recognised as knörrs were getting under way to catch the ebb tide, as a third nosed its way in. The still rising sun highlighted it against the dark grey sea beyond. A series of low jetties stretched into the water and were connected above the high-water line by a hard-packed earth track, bordered on the landward side by a series of large stone buildings. These were warehouses that Bear had long surmised had been built by the long-gone Romans.

"Yo, Aedan!" Bear spurred his pony forward, waving at a plump black-bearded balding man in a dark blue tunic. He could tell that the fabric was expensive. Everything about Aedan's attire suggested success, not least the heavy gold rings on his fingers. Bear chuckled to himself. Aedan was the living image of his father, Finán, with whom Hravn had first traded in the year Bear was born.

Aedan waved back. "Well met, young Bear," he called, "I was thinking it was time you came. I see you have the lead Ulf promised. If you get your men to line the ponies up my men will give a hand to carry the ingots into the sheds." Bear grinned, "Thanks,

Aedan." Aedan had long since given up weighing the ingots, knowing that they were produced to a consistent high quality and weight.

"What of the iron ingots, Aedan? Do we collect them from the Eskdale mines on our way back?" Bear assumed that the lead would have been left at the fellside smelt house.

Gesturing with a nod of his head, Aedan led Bear away from the men. "It's here, in the sheds. I was going to leave it up there for you, knowing it would be easier on the ponies, but having secured it at a good price, I heard that Jarl Buthar was sniffing around buying up as much iron as he could get his hands on. I thought it would be safer down here." Aedan mistook Bear's look of surprise for concern that the price had risen, and added with a teasing smile. "Hah! Don't worry, I haven't charged for storage."

Bear grasped Aedan's shoulder and looked at him earnestly. "No, Aedan. You mistake me, I wasn't thinking that. Surely, our families have traded together for so long that I trust you implicitly, as you do me. But, your mention of Jarl Buthar concerns me. His name was mentioned in Ameleseta too. Who is he?"

Aedan sighed deeply. "I'm not entirely sure. I know of no Earl by that name but, by calling himself a Jarl, he is obviously Norse. By all accounts, he lives in a dale somewhere north or northeast of here." After a pause, Aedan said, "My best bet is that he is a local chief, self-appointed as a Jarl, who has taken advantage of the gap between Dolfin's departure and the Normans' arrival to seize power and guard his own, and his people's, interests."

"Aye, and who could blame him for that?" Bear nodded agreement. "Mayhap he, like us, needs iron ingots to forge weapons." Still grasping Aedan's shoulder, Bear said, "Promise me you'll let me know if you hear more about where this Buthar lives. We are going to need all the allies we can get if we are to keep the Normans at bay."

Aedan tried to lighten the mood. "You're right there, and you might find that you have more allies than you know. I only found out a while back that we are kin, of sorts."   "What!" Bear's sudden broad grin gave away his surprise and pleasure. "How?"

"My wife's fader is Jarl of the Sheading of Garth." Aedan referred to one of the six Manx districts.

Bear gave a low whistle. "That was a good marriage."

"Hah! I think my fader's wealth had something to do with it." Aedan gave a wry smile. "But it has worked out for us both. Anyway, my wife was talking to her moder about yours. Word of a strong woman whom men will follow spreads far and wide, especially amongst women. When her fader heard that Lady Ealdgith is kin to Gospatric he realised that she must be distant kin, and so must you."

Aedan laughed at Bear's confusion. "I'm being unfair, why would you know?" He continued, "Gospatric's fader was the Cumbric Prince Maldred. His sister was my wife's fader's ealdmoder. We're cousins of a sort, it seems."

*****

With a nod and a wave to Tófi, Bear spurred his pony forward down the long descent from the Kirkstein towards Ulueswater. He was buoyed with the news he had gleaned from Grimr the previous evening. Jarl Buthar's lands were in a long valley with two lakes, and bounded by high steep-sided fells, somewhere in the far northwest. He wasn't sure where exactly, but as he rode his mind formed a bird's-eye view of the mass of fells and lakes. If the Jarl was prepared to stand and fight he was an ally that must be cultivated, and Buthar's mere was a place he had to find.

As he cantered past the track leading towards Ulf's hall, Bear's heart suddenly skipped. A slim figure with braided fair hair crowning her head was walking towards him through the trees, down the path from his parents' hall. He reined his pony to a skittered halt that sent a shower of dirt and pebbles from beneath its hooves.

Eir beamed widely. His arms open, Bear strode towards her and lifted her clear of the ground in a tight hug. Eir's lips sought his then, as he set her slowly down, Eir spoke first. "It's been too long, my love."

Bear looked into the clear blue of her eyes as Eir lay back in his arms. He knew what she meant. "Come, before anyone tries to steal me away again. We'll ride up to the tarn above the hall."

"Yes, and I know just the place when we get there. There's a shaded glade with bluebells in bloom." Eir let Bear lift her onto the pony.

Chapter 12

As he slowed his pony to a walk, Hravn wiped sweat from his brow. The late Eostremonath weather had warmed his long, fast ride from Morlund and he needed to gather his thoughts before briefing his men. He looked at the great wooden hall of Mallerstang in the distance. Despite all the years that had passed since he and Ealdgith had been held captive there, he always felt a sense of awe and foreboding when he saw it. Maybe it was the way the great Norse-style longhouse with its steep turf-clad roof was surrounded by a high stake-wall, embraced by dense woods. These swept up into the craggy slopes of the high fells that enclosed the long, permanently gloomy, valley. He always felt that Mallerstang belonged to a different place and an older time. It would be his home again now, for a while, and whilst it would be hard for Normans to find, he knew that it would be difficult to escape once they did.

Hravn pushed that thought to the back of his mind and forced himself to concentrate on the outcome of his visit to Morlund, and Agnaar's plans to further harass Count Alan. He was impressed by his young deputy. Agnaar had certainly been busy in the couple of weeks after their first ambush. He had established that the Normans were nervous of further attacks on the high pass, manning all ox carts with infantry and providing a cavalry escort. Hravn had agreed with Agnaar that it would be too risky to return to Stanmoir in the foreseeable future. He had also agreed that an attack on the road from Burc to Brougham, where the Count had set his men to work building another wooden castle, would risk drawing Norman attention towards Morlund. Agnaar had a different plan in mind; one that Hravn readily endorsed.

As he drew closer to the high wooden gate and guard tower Hravn could hear curses, the thud of wood on wood, grunting and shouts of encouragement. Wealmaer was training the men hard. The heavy gates swung open as he approached and, dismounting after he had entered, he tossed the reins to the guard whilst signalling for Wealmaer to join him. "Call the section leaders together," he shouted.

Wealmaer motioned for the three section commanders to sit on the steps to the hall whilst Hravn used a spear tip to sketch in the earth in front of them. They were used to his use of diagrams and models to describe his battle plans. Hravn spoke as he sketched.

"This line is the stone road from Burc to Brougham. You can see where it crosses the rivers Eden and Eamont here and here. It then continues through Penrith towards Carleol. Morlund is just west of the road, here."

Hravn placed a fist sized rock beside Brougham and Penrith. "This represents the prominent rounded hill known as Rhudd Hill. It's named after its red stone and dominates the ground around there. Agnaar has found another stone road that is overgrown and little used. It splits from the main road here, near Sourebi, then fords the Eamont here before passing north of the hill and joining the Carleol road a few leagues north of Penrith, here, by another old fort. This road is the key to our next attack." He glanced up at the men. Their eyes were all fixed on the sketch in the dirt below them.

"Whilst you've been training, Agnaar's had his lads out observing. What they have seen is that the further the Normans are from Stanmoir the more relaxed they become. So, we are going to ambush them here, where they will least expect it, at the northern junction on the Carleol road. We'll hit them with all five sections then, whilst any survivors are scrambling to get back to Brougham, we'll be away down the hidden road and back to Morland."

Wealmaer gave a low chuckle whilst Ari glanced up at Hravn, his eyes twinkling. "I like it, Lord. It reminds me of the good old days."

"Hah! I'm pleased you do, Ari, because we'll leave first thing tomorrow, rest briefly at Morlund, then move again tomorrow night and snatch a couple of hours' sleep in the northern fort. That fort lies right next to the road and that is where we'll strike. Let's get the men ready."

*****

Agnaar took Hravn's advice and decided to move at last light, just as the sun dipped below Helvellyn's distant high ridge. The sight distracted him momentarily as he thought of Adelind in the hall at the foot of the great mountain. He had chosen their route carefully, taking the track north through the small vill of Clibbrun to its junction with the ancient half-hidden stone road. The gloom darkened quickly as they rode along the straight line of moss-covered pavings, down towards the ford over the Eden. The first moonbeam glinted off Hravn's helmet, casting his ash-smudged face into shadow, as the half-moon rose over the Stanmoir ridge behind them.

Hravn let Agnaar take the lead, impressed by his competence. Although Agnaar struck a more formal relationship with the men than he would himself, Hravn could see that they followed him loyally, out of respect rather than duty.

The hidden road cut a straight line through the wild woodland north of Rhudd Hill. It joined the main Penrith to Carleol road by a cluster of collapsed grass-covered mounds of rubble known as Old Penrith. Instead of riding directly to the ruined fort, Agnaar led the troop across the road, along a shallow dip in the ground and around the back of a small

138

wood. He then swung east and approached the crumbling buildings from behind, keen not to leave any sign of their arrival upon the long grass between the road and the fort.

Agnaar was confident that although the fort was small its frontage of one hundred paces was enough to conceal four sections. He split the fifth, Cerdik's, in half and tasked the two pairs to take up positions a furlong away on the road either side of the fort. They were to keep watch and ride back quickly using the cover of the roadside trees to give warning of any approach. Agnaar checked with Hravn and decided they must shift some rubble and build a barricade across the fort's roadside entrance to block it. He didn't like altering the fort's external appearance, but couldn't risk Normans forcing their way in whilst his men fought from the battlements above. Wealmaer detailed a guard roster then left the men to prepare their weapons before huddling in the inner rooms, to shelter from the stiffening breeze. It was to be a long night, with no fires to give warmth or cook on.

A pale pre-dawn glow silhouetted the line of peaks south of Cross Fell when Agnaar roused Hravn. Agnaar had slept badly. Each scenario for the forthcoming attack had jostled for his attention and, as he fretted, the discomfort of cold flags had further hindered sleep. It had been a relief to rise, stretch and motivate the men. The road had been busy when he had watched it a few days ago, but would it be busy now? He thought that the first movement would come from the direction of Brougham, but would it? What if travellers had been benighted to their north? What if there were just a couple of riders, or a single cart? Should he let them pass? Would an attack be wasted and give their position away? Worry continued to gnaw at his mind.

Hravn sensed his concern and called him to one side. "Let the men get a good breakfast, we've bread and cheese enough. We're unlikely to see any traffic for a couple of hours or more, so call the men in, talk them through how you see the ambush happening and make sure that you control the timing of our attack yourself. Don't waste our efforts on just a couple of men. Let them pass, unless they take a close interest in the fort. If we are patient we will be rewarded, I'm sure."

Agnaar nodded his thanks, relieved that it echoed his own final decision.

Both men were right. Two hours after dawn a single horseman galloped past travelling north, riding so quickly that the flank guards let him pass, confident that Agnaar would not want them to risk being caught out and seen. Next, not long afterwards, a single cart passed hauling the last of the previous harvest's hay. As he watched the slow jolting cart disappear into the distance, Agnaar's attention shifted to Cerdik and Nudd as they galloped through the side entrance.

Cerdik reported, "Lord, ox-carts with an escort. Mayhap ten minutes away. We counted four carts, but I'm sure there are more. The escorts are riding in front and alongside."

Agnaar thought quickly, glanced at Hravn, then shouted final orders. "This is it! Ari, cover the left flank and front, signal when the last man is level with you. I want to trap the enemy front and rear along the frontage of the fort. Godfrid, cover the right flank and front, kill those on the lead cart, then their escorts, that should block the road. Brandr, take Cerdik and Nudd, stay down below and be prepared to cover either side entrance in case we get outflanked. Toudwal, you're left centre. Ewen, right centre. Both of you, be prepared to reinforce Hravn and Wealmaer blocking the roadside entrance. All of you, have spare arrows and bolts to hand, and keep your heads behind the battlements until my order. Watch for my signal...and good luck!"

With his back to the parapet wall, Agnaar watched the road below from the corner of his eye.

He heard the rumble of the ox carts before he saw the first one. Drawn by two lumbering beasts, it moved at a man's walking pace, the driver goading the oxen onward with a long rod and lash. A bored looking man-at-arms rode alongside, seemingly lost in his own world. Agnaar smiled thinly, pleased, then flicked his eyes to Ari, watching for his signal. As Ari nodded, Agnaar yelled "Now!", then stepped into a gap between the battlements, braced his bow and aimed at the horse of an escort. The man-at-arms, hearing or sensing the threat, turned in his saddle. Agnaar saw his jaw drop in surprise, then he was pitched backwards as his horse reared up, wounded, as Agnaar's arrow drove into its neck.

Agnaar paused, staggered by the immediate impact of the ambush. The lead cart had stopped, one ox having collapsed in its traces with two crossbow bolts embedded in its skull. The driver was dead too. All but one of the escorts' horses had been hit in the first onslaught of a score of arrows and crossbow bolts. More cart drivers fell as a second wave of arrows was unleashed, and then crossbow bolts began to pick off dismounted men-at-arms. The swift, mind-numbing carnage stunned him momentarily. He watched, holding his breath, as the last mounted man-at-arms wheeled his horse and started to gallop northward, out of the killing zone. Barely three paces later he fell, the back of his mail hauberk pierced by a bolt, with two more paralysing his mount's rear quarters.

"Hold! Hold!" Agnaar yelled to his section leaders. "Kill any survivors then prepare to leave. I don't want any witnesses to who we are, or whence we go."

Agnaar shook his head in mock disbelief and called to Hravn as he ran down the stone steps from the parapet, "That was quicker and easier than I expected."

"Aye," Hravn agreed, "a good ambush has to be sudden, swift and totally shattering for the enemy.

If it isn't, and they gain the initiative, then we'll struggle to match them one for one. It's why we must fight as we do."

"Well, we had the better of them today, the bastards!" Hravn shrugged at Agnaar's harsh words. He disliked killing, but accepted its necessity. He knew, however, that Agnaar was drawn to kill for revenge.

"Section leaders, get the men mounted. Cerdik, call the southern guards in." Agnaar turned to Hravn, "Lord, can you lead the way out whilst I finish here? I'll use Ari's section to cover our withdrawal."

Within moments the men had mounted and trotted from the fort, past the devastated convoy of carts. The sound of their ponies' hooves drowned out by the panicked bellowing of distressed oxen still attached to the carts.

Leaving Ari's section as the rear guard, Agnaar galloped forward to catch up with the next one, just before it turned onto the hidden track. He cursed, dismayed. A crowd of horsemen were galloping northward on the stone road. They would be on them within minutes.

"Ewen!" Agnaar yelled at the section leader as he pointed towards the looming threat. "Get into position a hundred paces ahead and prepare to cover Ari." He wheeled his pony around and gestured frantically for Ari to close in.

"Keep the men mounted, just inside the track junction. We'll hit them with a volley of bolts then fall back to Ewen. Then reload whilst his men cover us."

With barely moments to spare Ari lined the section across the old road, just inside the junction. They could judge the moment to shoot by the increasing clatter of hooves galloping on stone pavings.

"Ready!" Agnaar called, cautioning the men as he glimpsed the outline of the first rider through the edge of the trees. "Now!" He yelled, as the men-at-arms swept around the corner in a tight turn, their horses' hooves skittering on the hard surface.

It was hard to miss bodies closing head-on at ten paces. As the first five Normans were pitched backwards by the impact of crossbow bolts ripping through mail vests, the riders behind collided with the uncontrolled horses. It gave the green men just enough time to wheel and gallop back to where Ewen's men waited, mounted, blocking the Roman road.

Moments later the remaining five men-at-arms were upon them. Wise now to the threat, hunched low over their mounts and with spears couched underarm, they posed very hard targets. "Loose!" Ewen screamed. The four hastily aimed crossbow bolts slashed through the air. One missed its target. Another sent a man flying backwards whilst his horse galloped onward, and two more hit horses. One man fell heavily, pinned screaming under his collapsing mount, whilst another still swept forward. The horse tore through the line of ponies and staggered towards Ari's men as they knelt, trying frantically to reload their crossbows. Oswin fumbled and looked up, terror-stricken. His scream went unheard as the rider thrust down with his spear. As Oswin fell backwards clutching at the spear projecting from his chest, the horse collapsed and rolled onto its rider. Weight and momentum crushed the man instantly.

The two remaining men-at-arms continued through Ari's section. Bran flung himself sideways, away from flailing hooves then gasped in pain as a spear tip slashed along the length of his forearm. He continued to roll, grasping the sliced flesh in a vain attempt to staunch the bleeding.

The Normans, knowing that the size and power of their horses gave them a distinct advantage over the pony-mounted men, wheeled around intending to even the odds against them. As they did so, they saw the rest of the green men galloping towards them. Closing together to escape, they powered through Ewen's dismounted men who scattered to avoid Bran's fate.

Agnaar had rallied the men by the time Hravn closed in with the other three sections. He shouted to Ari. "There's clean linen in my saddlebag, and some mead. Souse Bran's wound then bind it tightly." Agnaar feared infection and regretted that Adelind or Eir hadn't been kept with them to look after any wounded.

"Worry not, Agnaar. There's a woman at Mallerstang who Edie trained years ago. We'll get Bran to her." Hravn had sensed Agnaar's concern. They knew all too well what would happen to an infected limb. He continued, "Those two Normans will doubtless warn the garrison at Brougham within the hour. They won't make a connection with Morlund yet. But once they find this road and follow it back to Sourebi they will start to search all the woods and vills thereabouts. It's only a matter of time."

"Aye," Agnaar nodded, "that was my first thought too." He paused, then added enthusiastically, "Lord, can you take the men back to Morlund and warn Tye that he must leave. I'll take Toudwal's men up onto the east fellside and light fires in the woods there. Come nightfall we'll have the Normans looking for our camp in the middle of nowhere."

Hravn laughed, "That's as good a ploy as any I've heard in a while."

*****

Hravn was surprised when Tyr accepted his warning with a resigned shrug, "It feels that this day has been a long time coming. I've been mourning the loss of these lands since your first warning. But there're only a few of us here now, the women and children left for the lake days ago."

"We'll be safe here tonight, Tyr. Tomorrow's when the Count's men will start combing the vills and woods hereabouts."

Tyr nodded, slow to speak. "We'll go in the morning. There's little of value left, and the few goats we kept for milk can be slaughtered for your men tonight."

Hravn clasped Tyr's shoulder, "It's not the end, my friend. I'm determined we'll hold the lands around the lake, and you'll build a new hall there. Of that I'm sure; a good Norse one of which Gunnar would have been proud, and we'll drink ale there together."

"What'll you do now?" Tyr seemed slightly less sombre.

Hravn stroked his bearded chin and a slight twinkle lit his eyes. "We'll be gone by first light, though I want to discuss things first with Agnaar, when he returns. I think the bastards will be expecting us to harry them along the Stanmoir road again, but I know these lands better than most men. We'll ambush them as they move between vills, from the moment they leave Brougham all the way to the head of the valley, if that's what it takes." He paused in thought, "You must excuse me whilst I see to a wounded man, and bury another."

"Wealmaer, Ari!" Hravn shouted to his housecarl and section leader, gesturing for them to join him. He looked Ari in the eye as he walked across. "I'm sorry about Oswin, he was a good man and it was Wryd's wish that he fell. There was nothing you could have done. Wealmaer, can you have the men bury him in the churchyard before the day is done? There's no priest there since Brother Patrick died, so just say a few words for him. As to Bran, I want him to get back to Mallerstang as soon as he can. We can't risk his wound becoming elf-shot." Hravn used the old slang to refer to the risk of gangrene setting in. "Is he up to the ride by himself?"

"Aye, Lord." Ari nodded.

"Good, get him on his way now. Make sure he has water and some food."

Hravn stopped Ari as he turned to leave. "Ari, you're one of the original few, and one of the most experienced soldiers amongst us. Now that your section has been halved I want you to join Wealmaer as his deputy and send Mungo to assist Brandr and Agnaar. I see us working as two groups of two sections from now on."

Hravn was reassured as Ari's sober frown cracked slowly into a grin.

*****

Agnaar arrived back late in the afternoon having left three well-stocked and slow-burning fires dispersed amongst the woods on the east fellside. Hravn watched the thin spirals of blue smoke twisting in the still air and hoped that they would draw the Normans' attention well to their north. The rest of the day was spent in discussion with the huscarles and section leaders as they devised a new way to fight.

"Good, that's decided." Hravn looked at the faces clustered around the long table in Tyr's hall. "I'll work with Godfrid and Cerdik, keeping to this side of the Eden. Agnaar will take Toudwal and Ewen, and cover yon side. We'll meet at the crossing at Aplebi on the second night. I want us out at first light, and in position on Whinfell well before the Normans appear. We'll be able to see their routes from there and Agnaar can plan when to cross the Eden at Sourebi. Tell the men, then get an early night."

Hravn sat on his pony at the edge of the forest on the side of Whinfell. Although it seemed only moments since he had concluded the previous night's planning, he felt more rested than he had done for a long time. The fug that had clogged his mind had lifted. Nervous energy and the focus of battle had been like a wind blowing mist from the fells and from

146

his head. Smoke rose from the camp fires in and around the old stone fort at Brougham, and he thought that he could make out the thin line of stakes circling the perimeter. The Normans were there to stay.

He saw the low easterly sun glint off a dozen clustered points, then moments later the faint sound of a horn carried towards him on the breeze. "Stand by!" He called across to Agnaar. "At least one group is moving." As he watched, Hravn could see that the line of glinting reflections was moving along the far side of the river Eamont. "They're heading towards the hidden road. I think they'll work their way back along it, then move across the Eden. See if you can take them at the ford, Agnaar, then keep falling back. Good luck."

Hravn continued to peer intently, then called Ari to him. "Do you see that shadow moving just this side of the river? That's a body of men, for certain."

"Aye, Lord, would you not say that they are heading towards Clifton?" Ari glanced questioningly at Hravn.

"I agree." Hravn chuckled. "Warn the men, we ride now. I want us in position between Clifton and Melcanetorp. Cerdik is to lead and observe from outside Clifton. We'll set the ambush where the track enters the wood on the top of the hill."

Hravn led at a canter down the southern slope of Whinfell and then swept around to his right, keeping a low ridge between him and the Norman soldiers. He regained the track and approached the ambush point through the wood. Hravn held up his hand to halt the section, then rode forward with Wealmaer and Ari. "Just like the old days in Ghellinges-scir, eh! Ari?" He quipped as he quickly chose the ambush site. "We'll tether the ponies north of the wood and then take the bastards from here, where the undergrowth is too dense for their horses, and far enough in from the edge to prevent any escaping and circling around the wood. I want you

147

both as cut-offs to stop the last men into the wood fleeing when they see the trap. Now, let's position Godfrid's men."

With time to spare, they placed the ambush and then Hravn went forward to inspect it from the Normans' perspective. He walked slowly along the track scrutinising the thickets on his left. Satisfied at last, he laughed loudly then called out, "If there is anyone there then I can't see you. Well done. Stay as you are and I will shout when I get warning from Cerdik. When I return, I'll take up position behind the base of the oak, five paces back from the track. Shoot upon my signal."

Moments later Nudd galloped up the hill and bent over towards Hravn. "Six Normans, Lord. They went through the houses in Clifton, threw a few blows, but didn't appear to kill anyone. They'll be heading up the hill in a few minutes. Cerdik has gone around the back so as not to be seen. He'll be a bit longer."

"Thanks, Nudd. That's good. Get yourself to yon end of the wood. When Cerdik joins you, tell him to hold it in case any break through from here."

Hravn shouted a warning then stepped carefully around the undergrowth in front of the oak and, pulling the cowl of his green cloak over his head, unslung his bow and chose three arrows.

The six Norman men-at-arms rode purposefully along the track into the wood. Glancing around with brisk efficiency, they appeared satisfied that the wood showed no sign of occupation, then spurred their mounts forward into a trot. The swiftly moving horses made hard targets and Hravn quickly readjusted his plan. Switching his aim to the leading horse after it had passed, he yelled, "Now!" then loosed his arrow into the rump of the animal. It shied and then its right leg collapsed. A crossbow bolt simultaneously punched through the rider's mail hauberk and flung him sideways out of his saddle. He fell, grievously wounded, trapped under the kicking horse.

The second rider urged his horse to the left in an attempt to cut past, but was thrown from the saddle as his horse reared, kicking, dying from the impact of a bolt into its chest that pierced through a lung and into its heart. Arni half watched the fallen man whilst he re-cocked his crossbow. As the man pushed himself up slowly, Arni aimed again and sent a bolt directly into the side of his helmet.

Their way forward along the narrow track blocked, the following men-at-arms wheeled around only to find that the sixth man was already down, with his horse running amok with fright.

Hravn realised suddenly that, as his men were still reloading their crossbows, there was a good chance that the remaining Normans could escape. He doubted that Wealmaer and Ari could stop more than one fast moving rider. Hoping that Godfrid's men would understand what he was doing, he stood up quickly, drawing his sword. Natr's blade reflected the dappled light under the trees. "Freûler ou bâtards Normand!" he yelled in Norman French. His challenge to fight was clear. Unable to move their horses into the undergrowth the three men-at-arms flung themselves from their saddles and, drawing their swords, moved towards Hravn. Their anger was their undoing. Crossbow bolts cut into them from left and right. One was left standing but dazed.

In no mood to be encumbered with a prisoner, Hravn stepped forward and thrust Nadr swiftly into the Norman's stomach.

Cerdik stepped onto the track, and Wealmaer and Ari ran up as Hravn wiped his blade clean on the dead Norman's cloak. "Recover the ponies. I want to get back onto Whinfell to see where else they are searching. We still have work to do." Hravn grinned, elated by the thrill of action.

Sumor 1092

Chapter 13

Ealdgith woke with a start. The day's first light was filtering through the shutters as a blackbird trilled his dawn chorus. Nothing was amiss outside, but she felt a sense of dread, panic almost. She opened the creaking shutter slowly, lest she wake others, and breathed deeply in the still, early-summer air. It was cool, almost cold. She shivered, as she looked across the mirror-like lake and the black-grey reflection of Place Fell's broad summit. Light was already creeping over its northern shoulder. Hravn was out there somewhere. Somewhere beyond the fell and the wide valley of the Eden; somewhere where she knew he was in danger.

*****

Hravn lay back against a giant oak on top of a low hill overlooking the ford in the river bend at Aplebi. As he watched Agnaar approach the far bank with his two sections he mused that one day soon the Normans would no doubt build another of their castles on the hill top. It was a perfect place to dominate the valley, the vill and the river crossing. He was enjoying reaping his revenge, but he knew that it couldn't last. Although the Normans seemed to have a more delicate touch upon the community than he had expected, harsh experience had taught him how brutal they could be. He knew too that the more he harassed them the harder their revenge upon the communities would eventually be.

As Agnaar's ponies splashed their way across the ford, Hravn stood and hollered.

Hearing the shout, Agnaar looked up, caught sight of Hravn's wave and saluted back. Leaving the ford and urging his pony up the bank, Agnaar swung to his right, up the hill to the oak.

Later, refreshed by a meal, the two men sat by the fire in the centre of their small camp whilst their men continued to attend to the ponies' needs and checked the state of their weapons after two days of ambushes. Agnaar turned to Hravn, "Lord, I haven't seen any of the Count's men since our third ambush. It's as if they have run out of men, or courage."

Hravn laughed. "The former, I would think. It was much the same for us. They've taken a lot of casualties very quickly and I doubt they have a clear idea of who or where we are, having been hit from so many directions."

Agnaar nodded agreement, thinking. "It seems to prove what I've been mulling over in my mind. We can't be seen to be fighting for a specific piece of land. Land is no longer as important as killing Normans."

"No, Agnaar," Hravn shook his head, "it's not that simple. You're right in that we must not be identified with one area, because we could never stand against the Count if he concentrated his forces, but we can't fight for too long. To do so will invite harsh retribution against the people. Some of these lands are now William's and Aebbe's, and the people are ours to protect. Anyway, we will at some point need to defend Ulueswater. For now, we must just keep his attention well away from the lake." He changed the subject. "How about casualties? Have you any? I saw Toudwal limping."

"Hah! He twisted his ankle in a rabbit hole when he leapt off his pony. Bada, though, does need to see the wise woman in Mallerstang. He took a hard sword blow to his shield when one of them broke through, before he was hit. The blow almost shattered the shield boards. I don't think his wrist is broken but it is swollen."

"Mmm, that decides it, we'll need to get him back there." Hravn was just about to tell Agnaar his next plan when the thought of Mallerstang jagged at a worry at the back of his mind.

"Ye gods!" Hravn sat upright so quickly that Agnaar jumped.

"What!"

"Aebbe's lands. She and William can't prove ownership if the Normans pressure them to do so. Edie always insisted that everything is written down, witnessed and sealed. She said that it is the only way we can prove what is ours by right. Everything: our wedding, the Earl's grants of lands to Edie and me, my knighthood, our grant to Aebbe. It's all been written into charters, and those are all still hidden at our hall. Edie didn't take them when she left and I forgot. Hel!"

Agnaar looked aghast. "But the Normans can't just take lands off you."

"The bastards might. Red William could certainly try. But these lands were granted by Earl Gospatric in the name of the Scots' king. Although the Earl was a vassal to William in Northumberland, he was Canmor's man in Cumbraland and Westmoringaland. But William and Aebbe would need to prove that."

Hravn glanced up at the sun. "There's time yet this evening. You sort things out here. I'll take Wealmaer and Ari. We'll be back not long after dark." He jumped up, calling for his housecarl and assistant.

They covered the three leagues to Crosebi Raveneswart at a quick pace, following the main track that cut across the low rolling hills of the upper Eden valley. The sun was just dipping behind the western fells as Hravn reined to a halt on top of the hill just south of the hall and ford, recalling as he did so, Ealdgith's fight and the first Norman attempt to seize their hall twenty years earlier.

"I don't like the look of that, Lord." Ari pointed to blue smoke, tinged pink by the setting sun, rising beyond the trees that screened the hall from sight.

Hravn's heart jumped and he cursed, fearful suddenly that he had been caught out. "I fear you're right, Ari. We'll ride down slowly, keeping in the shadows."

They moved cautiously, the ponies taking the opportunity to gather their wind. Hravn missed Sköll, the hound had a nose and instinct for a hidden threat.

They dismounted then moved through the wood. "Look!" Wealmaer stopped them with a whisper and a hand gesture. "The fire is in the courtyard between the wings of the hall. There're six, no seven, of them sitting around it. They don't seem to have an interest in the hall itself." The seventh threw a couple of large logs on to the fire, sending sparks flying up into the darkening sky.

Hravn looked puzzled. "Those are Count Ivo's colours on the pennants. See where their spears are stacked in a stand."

"Mayhap they have a message for you, Lord." Wealmaer suggested.

"Aye, but what sort of message? Though he's Williams's grandfather, Ivo's long had an interest in these lands and is renowned for taking what he wants by force."

"Mmm, and I doubt he will want Count Alan holding sway across the whole of Eden." Ari's shrewd observation persuaded Hravn.

"You're right. Whilst this may be as innocent as it looks, we can't risk finding out. Seven to three is poor odds. If we work our way around to the other side I could slip in unnoticed. The charters are under a loose stone in the wall in our bed chamber," he said, adding, "we might need to distract them though. We can't risk someone coming inside whilst I'm there."

They moved quickly once they were out of sight of the men by the fire, and were tethering their ponies at the back of the hall when a startled shout broke the calm late-evening air.

"Skita!" Wealmaer cursed, "that's all the distraction we need. Sparks from that bloody fire have set the roof alight. Look."

Hravn looked up and saw smoke rising from the far side of the hall. Frantic shouts and the neighing of panicking horses indicated that the Normans were about to leave in a hurry.

"We've not long until this side catches. Wealmaer, guard the door; Ari, with me." Hravn spoke urgently, keeping his voice low, and ran to the hall's great oak door. The gloom and dust inside surprised him, and he bumped into half-seen furniture as he made his way to the bed chamber.

Hravn ran his fingers along the top of the stone foundation wall, searching for the loose stone.

"Here, Lord." Ari passed Hravn a short seax to help him ease the stone out of the wall. He wiggled it forward, then lifted it clear. A sudden loud crack caused them both to flinch.

"That's the master beam in the old hall. The roof must be collapsing." Ari looked at Hravn with wide eyes. His unease was clear. The room suddenly seemed lighter. Hravn looked up and saw flames and tendrils of smoke creeping out of the thatch directly above.

"Ari, get back to the door. Now!" Hravn yelled, feeling very vulnerable. He reached into the cavity below the stone and pulled out a leather roll. Then, reaching down a full arm's length, he found a second. As he stood up he rammed both rolls down the front of his leather jerkin. "That's it, Ari. I'm..."

Hravn's words faltered as he looked up. Flames, igniting then exploding the clouds of disturbed and rising dust, shot across the underside of the thatch above the bedchamber. Within seconds the dry beams had caught.

Ari glanced over his shoulder then yanked the oak door open. As he escaped, air rushed in, sucked by the air-thirsty fire in the old hall and equally demanding flames in the roof above. Hravn tried to run forward, but the in-rushing blast of air knocked him backwards. He stumbled on a stool and fell sideways, ramming his head against an oak post. He passed out as his recently fractured skull yielded for the last time.

As Ari stumbled out of the hall, Wealmaer rushed in. He looked around, then flung himself forward towards the slumped body.

"No! Lord?" Wealmaer yelled, then coughed as the hot acrid wood smoke caught in his throat. He grabbed Hravn's collar, got both his hands under Hravn's armpits then staggered backwards, dragging Hravn with him. Ari took over as Wealmaer collapsed, choking, in the doorway, then both men pulled Hravn away from the blazing hall to cooler air.

Wealmaer laid Hravn down gently, loosened the clothes around his neck and felt for a pulse. There was none. There was no need for him to shake his head. As he looked up, the runnels of tears down Ari's smoke stained cheeks confirmed what he knew, that their lord was dead.

*****

Agnaar fretted as he watched the dull glow of a large fire towards the west. He was sure that it was somewhere near Crosebi Raveneswart. As the fire flared, then dimmed, Agnaar knew something was amiss. He went in search of Brandr and found him counting arrows with Mungo.

"Something has happened to Hravn. He's late and that fire towards Crosebi Raveneswart worries me. Keep charge here. Mungo, come with me." Agnaar spoke more curtly than usual.

He knew the track well, they all did, and in the light of the half-moon it was easy for the sure footed fell ponies to pick their way. Just as he forded Asby Beck he caught sight of movement coming down the track ahead. Three ponies, but two riders. He urged his pony into a trot, desperate to find out what had happened. "No!" Moments later Agnaar's anguished cry rent the night air.

They rode in silence, lost in their own thoughts, as they retraced the route to Aplebi. At last, Wealmaer rode up alongside Agnaar. The gruff urgency of his voice jerked Agnaar out of his despair. "Lord, we need to decide what to do next, before we get back to the men."

Agnaar slowed his pony to a walk. "You're right." He said nothing further for a moment, then added, "What do you suggest?"

"I must take Hravn back to our Lady at first light. His death is a grievous blow and risks unsettling our ability to hold the Normans away from the lake. I think Edie would want you back with her, but for all our sakes, I think you need to keep Norman eyes away from her for a while longer. I know the Ulueswater defences won't be ready yet."

"I agree. It's much as Hravn and I were talking about before..." Agnaar's voice tailed off.

Wealmaer continued. "I'll take Cerdik and his section back with me; he's the least experienced of the section commanders here. Keep the other three, plus you've got Brandr, Mungo and Bran, when he's fit again. That'll be more than enough for you to keep the Normans entertained for a month or so more. I suggest you work out of Mallerstang, take the fight some distance away from there, and plan on re-joining us by Æfteralida. That'll give you two months."

Agnaar's expression relaxed, relieved that the decision had been made for him and, Wealmaer sensed, thankful that he could keep fighting.

Chapter 14

Bear stood, wiped his brow and stretched his back and shoulders to ease the stiffness at the base of his spine. It was hard work shifting rocks and boulders. From his vantage point at the top of Martindale Hause, the pass over the eastern shoulder of Hallin, he surveyed the morning's work. Bear knew that if the Normans tried to force their way along the lake's southern shore they couldn't be stopped from reaching Haugr-tun, but they could be prevented from crossing the hause to Sandrwic. For the last few days he had supervised the building of defences along the earthen track that wound its way up and over the hause, to pass under and around craggy outcrops. Bear had selected the best places to use the crags to dominate the route and then chosen where to place tracts of rocks and small boulders that would render the ground impassable to horses or armoured men trying to move in formation. Any that did would doubtless trip, stumble and, with luck, break an ankle, or be forced to lower their guard and open themselves to attack by a slinger. Baskets of rocks for throwing or slinging had been positioned on top of the craggy outcrops so that defenders could bring a constant hail to bear on any attackers.

Pleased with what he saw, Bear raised his eyes to take in the wider aspect of the lake, then he turned to look back at the fells to the south. He froze, his attention taken by a line of ponies winding their way down the flank of the fell opposite, following the old track down from Brethstrett. The early afternoon sun reflected from the riders' steel helms. He shielded his eyes, stared hard and then shouted to the men below him. "Dai, get our men together and mounted. We've company coming. It looks like a section or more of our men are coming in the backway. Something must be amiss."

Bear continued to watch. He couldn't make out faces, but he could see that a body lay across the back of one of the ponies.

Mounted at last, Bear led off at a gallop down the pass and along the flat valley bottom of Martindale. As he neared the riders he began to recognised grim faces: Wealmaer, Ari, Cerdik...but not his fader. Wealmaer urged his pony forward. They met by a large yew tree.

Wealmaer took a deep breath as he felt the intense questioning stare of Bear's eyes. As he shook his head he said, "I'm sorry. Hravn was killed last night." He dismounted and walked towards Bear, holding out his hand as Bear leapt from his pony. "Come, let's walk over by the yew and talk."

Bear's eyes glistened as he listened to Wealmaer's account. He refused to shed a tear in front of his men. There would be time enough in the days to come. For now, he knew that he must lead them, and keep their resolve firm.

Rather than borrow a boat in Sandr-wic and then a long tedious row up the lake, Bear decided that it would be just as quick to keep all the men together and take the pass over Boredale into Patrichesdale. They rode as quickly as the rough ground permitted and arrived just as the sun dipped and cast the houses around the head of the lake into shadow. Wealmaer mused that it was a portent of the gloom that was about to fall over all in the little communities, but he kept his thoughts to himself.

Ealdgith's sense of unease had stayed with her, nagging at her mind since the previous morning. She stood outside the hall watching boats on the lake below practise manoeuvring the log barrier, just as the sun dipped below Helvellyn's jagged ridge behind her. As the light dimmed in the valley, she caught sight of a line of dull glints of light on the track cutting down across Place Fell's broad flank on the opposite side of the lake. A cold dread settled upon her.

Bear felt guilty as he realised with some relief that he didn't need to break the news to his mother. Ealdgith stood in front of the hall, an ashen-faced statue with tears trickling down her cheeks. He dismounted slowly, passed the reins to Wealmaer, then walked steadily towards her, clasped her shoulders gently with his hands and pulled her slowly against his chest. He held her as he felt her pent-up sobs break within.

Wealmaer gestured quietly for the men to disperse and sent Ari to find Godric and Ada. He would find Gytha and break the news himself.

*****

"No, Cedd." Ealdgith leant forward and placed her hands over those of her priest as they sat knee to knee in front of the hearth. She spoke gently. "I understand that you want Hravn to be buried in the Christian way, but we must respect Hravn's beliefs. In so much as he followed any god, it was the old Norse gods. He felt that his life was always in the hands of the three Norns and that they would weave his fate as they wished. And that, I think, is what has come to pass."

"Yes, but a cremation is not how we treat a God-given body. It must be respected and buried."

Ealdgith looked up at Cedd's face. She read the compassion in his eyes and knew that, whilst he was telling her what he must, he would also bend to her will. "Is it not the spirit rather than the body that matters? It is Hravn's spirit that must endure and inspire. Remember, not all here are yet committed to The One God, some still think as Hravn did. Please?"

As he looked at Ealdgith, Cedd saw the sorrow in her dark-rimmed green eyes, but also the determination in her clenched jaw. When he spoke, it was with a gentle softness, "Very well, Edie. I am sure

The Lord will understand. We will lay Hravn in the chapel and I will say a mass over him, then, when you are ready, take him to the beach and let the people say their farewells before you row him to the island. God will take his spirit in his own way." He paused, before adding, "I know what you have both achieved here, over the years. You've brought together all the communities: Cumbric, Norse, Angle and those of the One God, no god or the old gods. I've always accepted that their harmony is all important and that is why I haven't striven to convert non-believers as my brothers might. Let Hravn's passing cement that harmony."

Ealdgith smiled weakly, "Thank you, Cedd. That is all I can ask from you." She turned as she heard movement in the unlit part of the hall, then held out her hand as she saw Gytha in the shadows. "You've been crying, my love. Come." Ealdgith squeezed Gytha's hand, then said, "Find Bear for me, Ada and Godric too. I want us to decide how we will say farewell to your fader."

Although Ealdgith didn't say as much, she was sure that her family understood the reason for her haste in arranging Hravn's funeral: the warming weather would not be kind to a body already two days dead.

*****

Ealdgith had been grateful for the support of the women in her wider family to help bathe and prepare Hravn's body. She was thankful too for their presence as they took turns to kneel beside her whilst she watched over his body in front of the altar within the small lakeshore chapel. Her grief gave her the strength to overcome tiredness during the eternity of the short early-summer night. Memories of their life together flooded her mind in a random assault of images and emotions, then she gradually found herself in conversation with Hravn, with each asking

160

and answering their unspoken questions. As the sound of birdsong outside the still-dark chapel heralded dawn, Ealdgith finally felt at peace. She knew what she must do in the days and weeks ahead, and she knew too that Hravn's spirit would guide her way.

Cyneburg sensed Ealdgith stir next to her. "Come, Edie, let us eat a little, and you must lay your head down for a wee while. It's been a long night and will be an even longer day for you."

Later, a little rested, Ealdgith led her extended family along the lakeshore to the chapel. It stood on a rocky ledge by a natural spring, above the track from Patrichesdale to Glynrhedyn and was barely big enough to accommodate the family mourners, let alone the many villagers clustered outside straining to hear Father Cedd's mass. The quiet reassurance of his words buoyed Ealdgith for the more difficult moments that were yet to come.

Ealdgith gave Cedd a tight-lipped smile of thanks then waited whilst Bear and the three housecarls lifted the wooden board upon which Hravn's body lay. With Ulf leading, the four men carried the board from the chapel whilst Ealdgith turned and led the way for her people, following the bearers from the chapel down onto the pebble beach of the lakeshore.

Ulf stopped by two broad knee-high boulders and watched whilst the bearers laid Hravn's body down gently. He waited as they bowed their heads and stepped back then, clearing his throat, he spoke. His voice, hoarse at first, softened as his nervousness left him. It carried clearly through the still air. "Hravn was our lord. He was the greatest of leaders and, for me, the closest of friends. We all know how he strove hard to create the peace and wealth that has given us the best of lives. Some of you know what it was to fight with him in battle, but none of you know who he really was and what made him the very special man that he became. Listen whilst Lady Ealdgith tells us."

Ealdgith took Ulf's place by Hravn's head. "Hravn was my cousin by marriage. We grew up together, played and hunted in the woods and hills of Ghellinges-scir. Hravn's fader, Æsc, looked upon me as a daughter and with that acceptance into his family I knew that I would never be parted from Hravn..." she hesitated, words catching in her throat, "...not until now." With a deep breath, Ealdgith continued. "Ours was a life of peace until it was shattered over night when the Normans came." She continued speaking, recounting her life disguised as a boy whilst held hostage by the Pendragons, and then talked of the time of their resistance in Ghellinges-scir, before introducing Ada to talk about how Hravn spirited them away from the woodland settlements and all the way to Bebbanburge, where he was knighted and gifted his Westmoringaland estates.

Godric and Cyneburg spoke too. Whilst they did, Ulf slipped away to find Neven. She caught sight of his warning nod and tapped Duwe and Owst on their shoulders. They left the crowd surreptitiously and made their way along the shore to their svanmeyja. The twins climbed on board and Duwe took the oars whilst Owst pushed the boat clear of the shore and hopped over the bow.

Neven kept a close eye on Ulf, watching him move back around the crowd to regain his place behind the speaker. She smiled to herself; Ulf had timed things perfectly. Owst had just dropped anchor in the middle of the wide shallow bay at the head of the lake when she saw Ulf raise his good arm.

She caught her sister's eye, "Ready? Remember what we practised. Take my lead then join in."

Duwe nodded, gently tapping her hand over the drum between her knees as she picked up the timing of Neven's drumbeat.

Gytha, standing by her mother, nodded slowly in time to the beat, appreciating how cleverly Neven had chosen where to anchor the boat. The sound echoed from the three valleys at the head of the lake, its sombre, but mellow sound magnifying, resounding, dying away, then resurging as if the fells were talking together in their own way. As suddenly as it had started the tone and tempo changed, as a faster, lighter and gentler drum took over.

Gytha took her cue and stepped forward to stand at her father's feet. She leant forward with her eyes shut and began to sway in time with the beat, her golden hair hanging loose in front of her body. She listened as the plink of a lyre's string echoed the rhythm and, counting in time, she intensified the swing of her body as Cyneburg knelt by Hravn's head and began to keen in a high clear voice.

The crowded mourners stood frozen-faced whilst the sad beauty of Cyneburg's voice hung in the air. Ulf bit down on the inside of his lip as he strove to fight back tears. He had never loved Cyneburg more than at this moment and, in knowing the pain he would feel in losing her, he knew the pain with which Ealdgith must now be living.

On Ulf's nod, the four bearers stepped forward, took hold of the board, and lifted Hravn gently from between Gytha and Cyneburg. It was the signal for them to stop and regain their composure before walking, hand in hand, behind Ealdgith as she followed the bearers to the waiting kára.

Ealdgith stood and watched patiently whilst the men hoisted Hravn's board above their shoulders and lifted it across onto the Kára, before pulling themselves over the gunwales. As the boat was rowed slowly across the lake she led the six women of her extended family to two waiting svanmeyjas for their own journey to Yan Island, the first of the lake's three small islands.

Gytha sat alongside her mother and took her hand, dreading what was to come. She knew that the day before, Bear had worked with his men to build a pyre on the rock at the edge of the small island. They had first made a wind-driven stone furnace around a low flat boulder large enough for a body, and then stacked the space between the boulder and the furnace wall with dry branches around a core of charcoal and a top layer of green wood. Ulf had assured Bear that this would give the intensity of heat and hot smoke needed for an effective cremation, leaving charred fragments of bone, but no wood ash, on the surface of the boulder. Gytha strove to keep images of what would happen out of her mind. She was worried too about what Father Cedd had said. Ealdgith looked across at her and squeezed her hand. "Don't fret, Gytha, it's what Hravn wanted and that is all that matters. His spirit is with us now. Whether it is buried or burned, his body must leave us."

Gytha nodded. Her tears mirrored those in her mother's eyes.

The oarsman held the svanmeyja close to the island whilst the men in the kára grounded their boat on the small pebble beach then manoeuvred Hravn's body carefully out of the boat and onto the boulder at the centre of the pyre. Their task done, they returned to the boat and pulled away from the shore, leaving Bear by the pyre. He waved discreetly to his mother, then walked down to the beach to help her and Gytha from the svanmeyja as it ground gently on the pebbles.

Both women nodded as Bear looked them directly in the eye. There was no need to speak. Then, leading the way, he returned to the pyre and bent down to strike a spark from flint and steel, and ignited a small pile of tinder. Bear then took a pine-tar soaked torch lying beside the tinder and lit it. He stood and turned.

"Moder, Gytha, please hold this with me. The burden of what we must now do is too much for any one of us." They stood facing the funeral pyre, and lowered the torch slowly until it caught the dry wood in the entrance to the furnace. A small flame danced, barely visible, from twig to twig, then branch to branch. Suddenly, caught by the wind, flames flared and the dry logs inside the furnace exploded with a whoosh.

Ealdgith stepped back and pulled Bear and Gytha with her. Rising heat seared their faces as she said, "Farewell, my love. Your spirit lives within me, within all of us. Now we must leave you." As she turned away, Ealdgith called Bear and Gytha after her. "Say farewell then come to the boat, before the fire consumes us too." Blinking away smoke-filled tears of emotion she returned to the beach.

*****

As dawn broke over the calm, mirror-like lake Ealdgith rowed to Yan Island. The only movement in the still air was of thin wisps of blue smoke rising from the pile of ash surrounding the flat boulder. The cloying smell of burnt bones hung over the water and Ealdgith grimaced as she forced herself to continue rowing. As she got closer she could see embers still glowing within the ash.

Using a spade from the boat, Ealdgith cleared a way through the smoking ash towards the boulder. The rock was warm to touch, but not so hot as to burn. She gritted her teeth and blinked away tears as she looked at the grey line of grist-like ash and scorched bone. Trying not to gag as the bitter air caught in her throat, and fighting the nausea rising within, Ealdgith began gently collecting pieces of bone and grit, and placed them methodically into a metal urn.

At last, with her fingers blackened by burnt bone and her tears mingling with sweat from her brow, Ealdgith stood and carried the urn back to the svanmeyja. She breathed a little more deeply as the air freshened by the lake shore and placed the urn carefully by the central thwart.

The boat barely rippled the lake's still surface and, as she reached a wider stretch of water, with Blowick Bay to one side, the long strand of Glynrhedyn Bay to the other and the wide waters of the first reach of the lake ahead, Ealdgith shipped the oars and wept. It was the first time that she had been truly alone and her only chance to cry without drawing the compassion of others. Gradually, as the gentle rocking of the boat, and the soft lapping of the water against the hull, eased her mind, her tears ceased to flow.

"Come, my love." She spoke out loud, but to herself. "Let this be your final resting place." Ealdgith took hold of the urn and, resting it on the side of the boat, tipped Hravn's ashes gently onto the water.

As ash fanned slowly across the surface, Ealdgith watched other of the fragments sink deep into the clear water, fascinated as shadowy fish rose to nibble them. She was thankful that Hravn was now part of the lake's circle of life. She glanced up, her attention caught by a movement reflected on the surface, and gasped as a raven, high above and silhouetted against the clear blue sky, uttered a deep-throated kraa. Surely, this was an omen, a sign that Hravn, his spirit still alive, was watching over her and their family. She tracked the raven as it soared east, until it was lost against the sun, and then looked once more into the depths of the lake. The boat had drifted on and there was now no sign of ash. Her reflection smiled back at her.

Chapter 15

"Your fader wasn't an ostentatious man, he valued practicality more." Ealdgith stood facing Bear and Gytha in her private chamber which was screened from the rest of the hall by heavy red curtains. Her voice was serious, almost reverential. "But I know that he would want you to have these." As she spoke Ealdgith gestured towards a polished oak cabinet and the items upon it. "Nadr is the best of swords, Bear. It was a gift from Gunnar, along with your fader's first mail hauberk, and has served him well in many a fight since." Bear picked up the sword, slid it from its leather scabbard bound with silver and bronze, and weighed it in his hand to feel its perfect balance; it was always a joy to hold and swing. Then, holding it in front of him he squinted along the long, light blade. The natural patterning of the beaten metal caught the lamp light, and enhanced the twists of an engraved lattice of serpent bodies and heads surrounding a line of Norse runes. They spelt its name: Nadr.

Ealdgith continued speaking as Bear held the sword. He was in awe of the honour and significance of its possession. "I don't know how much your fader told you about it. Gunnar said that it was crafted in the Norse-Irish lands before his people came to Westmoringaland. It is one of a pair, Tyr now has the other. It is said to have a power of its own and the speed of its namesake, the adder. Hravn always felt that it had when he fought with it."

"Thank you, Moder." Bear was about to embrace Ealdgith when she picked up a ring. "This too, Bear." She passed him a heavy gold ring with an embossed crest. "Hravn didn't wear it generally for fear of losing it. It was given to him by my uncle, Earl Gospatrick, as a seal and symbol of his authority.

Keep it safe. Your fader was the Earl's man. You are too now, as his successor."

One item remained. "And for you, Gytha." Ealdgith passed her an ivory horn. "This was given to Hravn by his fader when he was your age. Æsc said that it was made from the bone of a sea monster caught in the cold northern ocean. It too has served him well many a time. We first used it when we trained our hounds to hunt." Ealdgith looked wistful as she recalled days of innocent pleasure before the Norman harrying destroyed her childhood.

Gytha took the horn carefully in her hand and ran her fingers around the delicately engraved silver rim, then traced the etched line of coiled serpents until they came to the silver mouth piece. Anticipating her daughter's intention, Ealdgith said softly. "Blow it outside, Gytha. Not in here. Use it on the lake to control your fleet of svanmeyjas. That most certainly is what your fader would have wanted."

"Oh, Moder!" Gytha stepped forward and hugged her mother tightly, then wiped the back of her hand across her cheeks as she blinked away tears. "Thank you. I will, of course."

"But what of Freya? Is there nothing of Fader's that can pass to her?" Bear asked, quietly.

Ealdgith shook her head, sheepishly. "Nothing that I can think of. She ..."

"There is, Moder." Gytha interrupted quickly. "Fader's slim seax. The little one he uses for eating when he's on patrol with Bear. Freya would value that. I know she would. Osberht has just been given a short seax and she will want to keep up with him. It's what I would have wanted when I was ten."

Ealdgith looked surprised, then smiled. "Of course. She is yet another little Valkyrie. There's no point in trying to keep her out of harm's way, is there? Thank you, Gytha."

Bear cleared his throat and spoke hesitantly. "Moder, whilst the three of us are together, there is something else." He paused, seeing Ealdgith's questioning frown. "I have spoken with Ulf and we sense that the people need something to lift their spirits. The Normans could come at any time now. Agnaar can't keep drawing their attention away from the lake for much longer. We need to raise everyone's morale ahead of any attack."

"Yes?" Ealdgith agreed and encouraged him to continue.

"Well, as I say, I have spoken to Ulf and he agrees." He paused, "A wedding. Eir and I will have our wedding and a feast for all."

Ealdgith gasped, then pulled Bear to her. "Of course."

"And not before time!" Gytha laughed and poked her brother under his ribs.

*****

"Hah! Timing is everything, young Bear, and the one thing we don't have time for is to brew more ale and mead, not that we have either honey or barley to spare at this time of year." Ulf slapped Bear on the shoulder, then winked. Having just confirmed to Ulf that Ealdgith had approved a wedding feast, Bear was now wondering how to provide the food and drink. "It's just as well that Cynburg made the most of last year's honey, isn't it? She's been waiting for this moment for so long and was sure you would be wed in lencten."

"We would." Bear agreed, laughing. "But circumstances got in the way. I suppose we might have to water the mead down a bit?" He looked at Ulf questioningly.

"I suppose we might, Bear. But not too much." Ulf winked, then continued, "I've spoken to Mungo, the Reeve, and he agrees that we can only afford to slaughter the older and infirm sheep for the feast. We've got smoked char too though, and Ada has set the new women to work, baking. Eir says that she expects a bridal loaf."

"Thanks, Ulf. Your help means a lot, especially at the moment. If you'll excuse me I need to find Eir and then we'll go and see Father Cedd. We want to make sure everything is kept as simple as possible. The chapel is so small that we want the service held at the door so that all who want to come, can see." Bear tapped Ulf on the shoulder by way of farewell then set off up the track to Grassthwaite Howe Hall to look for Eir in the A-framed outhouse that she was preparing to use to care for any injured in the fight to come. He whistled as he went.

*****

Eir stirred as the dawn's first light and early-morning birdsong filtered through the cracks in her chamber's shutters. She wrapped her mantle around her shoulders and over her shift, pulled on shoes and slipped out of the hall. As she ran light-footed down the grassy track towards the chapel, dew darkened her leather footwear and spattered her bare legs. She paused at the bottom of the short flight of steps to the chapel to admire the swathe of woven ferns bedecked with white daisies that surrounded the entrance, and went inside. It was still dark within, save for a shaft of light through the slit window behind the altar.

Eir hesitated, gathered her breath, and then knelt in front of the simple wooden altar and carved cross.

"Our Father..." Eir spoke softly, then paused, listening. She turned at the sound of feet on the steps, then the door opened. "Father?" She gasped.

"Eir, my child?" Cedd's surprised frown melted quickly. "I pray every day at dawn and wondered why the door was open. Is anything amiss?"

Cedd knelt beside Eir and turned his head towards her.

"Nothing is amiss, Father. I couldn't be happier, but I am worried too."

Cedd looked kindly at Eir and nodded encouragement.

"I want a long marriage, with children, Father. But I'm scared of what is to come. How can we really stand against the Normans? I don't want to lose Bear, nor anyone else, and I don't want to fail should I have wounded to care for. I came to ask for Our Lord's help. Is that wrong?" Cedd glimpsed tears in Eir's eyes.

As he stretched out and took her hand Cedd said gently, "No, Eir, it is not wrong. Our Lord knows what is in your heart without your speaking to him, though he welcomes your prayers. We cannot change God's Will but if we have faith in the rightness of our actions, and faith in Him to see us through, then we will have faith in our future. Let us pray together, then you must go and ready yourself." He released Eir's hand, clasped his own together and spoke with a firm softness, "Our Lord..."

*****

The sun had passed its zenith as Eir, wearing a dark blue dress, stood to Bear's left in the chapel entrance. Cedd faced them, raised his arms and called loudly to the throng of villagers clustered outside. "Is there anyone here who knows of a cause why this man and this woman should not be wed?

The silence, broken only by the mew of a buzzard overhead, was all the answer Cedd needed. He turned his attention back to the couple, heard their vows and then blessed their marriage tokens.

Eir gave a small gasp of delight as Bear slipped a ring onto the fourth finger of her left hand. The gold band was engraved with delicately entwined leaves wrapped around a series of amethyst stones.

Bear smiled proudly as Eir gave him a broad gold ring inset with a diamond-shaped bezel of cut glass and garnets. He had seen it before; Ulf had taken it from a merchant that he had ambushed in Ghellinges-scir many years ago. It had been the pride of his treasure. As he felt the firm embrace of the ring upon his finger, Bear leant forward and, raising Eir towards him gently, kissed her deeply on her lips. The crowd's loud cheer echoed around the valley. The sun seemed suddenly brighter and the valley to be suffused with a preternatural warmth. It was good to be alive and amongst friends.

Blue wood smoke curled from several fires along the lakeshore and, as Bear and Eir walked hand in hand from the chapel, they saw that spitted sheep were already being turned slowly above glowing embers. As they walked they watched Ada supervising women around the cooking fires. The breeze gusted briefly and they smelt roast mutton and a hint of freshly baked bread as the smoke flicked past them. Godric appeared through the haze, waved and gestured towards a long table, before turning away to direct a group of young men and girls serving mead.

"Where did you get my ring? It has such exquisite beauty." Eir asked, holding her finger in front of her.

"I should say that it is a secret, but I would be found out for sure. Godric was with me when I called on a goldsmith after speaking to Dolfin in Carleol last sumor." Bear glanced apologetically towards his wife. "I wanted us to be wed last haerfest but the chance was never there."

"Well, we are now, and that's all that matters to me." Eir squeezed Bear's hand in hers.

Early-evening shadows fell across the broad bay as the couple took their places at the centre of a long trestle table set on the short grass by the lakeshore. Platters of hot mutton and smoked char were set in front of them as soon as they were seated. With their backs to the lake they faced a swelling crowd. Bear was surprised by their numbers and strove to quash a cynical thought that it was the offer of free food rather than respect that drew them there. Their cheers as first his mother, and then Ulf, stood to speak dismissed his doubts.

Ulf concluded and raised his horn of mead in yet another toast to the couple. It was time for Bear to speak. He stood, raised his hands for silence, and spoke for all to hear as he turned to Eir. "My love, we are married in the eyes of God, have already exchanged our marriage vows and our families are bound ever closer together, but now I have one more gift for you. In honour of the old ways so dear to my fader, I gift you the sword with which I have fought and slain our enemies. Keep it safe and one day, give to our son." As he spoke Leofric stepped from behind and placed the sheathed sword on the table in front of Eir.

Bear turned to him with a smile, "Thank you, brother," he said quietly.

Eir stood as Bear sat. Hearing the sudden sharp intake of her breath, Bear worried that the gift might have been a gesture too far. She looked quickly at the expectant eyes of those around her: Bear, her mother-in-law, her parents, Gytha. Her head swam slightly but, seeing understanding in Ealdgith's eyes, she calmed. She knew what to say.

Eir turned to the crowd, unsheathed the sword and raised it above her head. "Today has been about more than the joining of two people, or two families. It has been about joining all the people from broken communities into one new family. We are all of one family now and we all know that we will soon face a great threat. Let this sword be a symbol of our unity and our strength in the times to come. God's Will is for him to decide. Let us all have faith that He is the strength of our future."

Bear jumped to his feet and clasped his hand over Eir's upon the hilt of the sword. Together, they held the blade aloft and faced the wildly cheering crowd.

Ulf used the distraction of the resounding cheers to draw Bear to one side. "What plans do you have for the bedding? I've heard voices in the crowd demanding a fulsome scene."

Bear almost gagged on his mead. "I feared as much. The more we raise their spirits, the more we raise their enthusiasm." He leant close to Ulf's ear. "Worry not. I've made a bower on yon side of the lake. Neven is going to see to it that a svanmeyja is left on the beach. We'll be gone and into the shadows before anyone can follow."

Ulf's face creased with laughter. "You're your fader's son, Bear, I'll give you that."

Bear nodded wistfully, "Aye, Ulf. Thank you." He paused, "Come let's get the dancing started."

Bear put his arm around Eir and they sat and watched as Godric ushered the first entertainers forward. "Ragnaar and Alv, my Lord and Lady." Godric stepped back quickly as the boat builder and his son leapt into the small space in front of the long table.

"Hah, the spear dance!" Bear guided Eir backwards a few paces, knowing what was to come. "I always thought there was something wildly Viking about our Norse boat building family." The crowd stepped back too.

The two men stood to attention in front of Bear. Each held a spear with a polished tip, as sharp and lethal as broken glass in the setting sun. They stepped smartly apart and spun wildly around, holding the spears at arm's length. Eir flinched as the whirling glinting tips wove up and down, missing the dancers' heads by a hand's span. The crowd fell silent and Bear slowed his breathing almost to a halt as the gyrating men stopped abruptly, faced each other, and began to dance with, and around, the spears: stepping over and around them and, at times, clubbing them together, and at all times within inches of their deadly tips. At last, panting to control their breath, they stopped, bowed to the table and sprinted smartly away.

As they did so, a quick rhythmic drumming came from the lake to echo around the strath, and was joined by the swift strumming of a lyre. "Ah, Gytha!" Bear muttered under his breath. "I should have guessed."

With two swift backflips, Gytha appeared in front of him. She held her arms wide and bowed before starting a dance of her own. Moving in time to Leofric's lyre and Neven's consistent drum beat, she swayed, twisted, turned and rolled as she merged all her fighting moves into one flowing dance. At last, breathless and more than a little dizzy, she stood, bowed again and ran to join Leofric.

Bear stood and, gesturing after Gytha, shouted. "Gytha! Come back. That deserves a special thank you." As Gytha returned he swept her into his arms in a tight hug, then swung her around before placing her down with a kiss on her head. "You're full of surprises. Thank you."

The drumming stopped as suddenly as it had started. On cue, Leofric began to play. Eir nodded her head in time. She had heard Leofric practising and smiled as her mother's clear gentle voice began to sing in the accent of the Old North, the words floating softly through the evening air as the crowd strained to catch them.

Let us go, lassie, go
To the fells o' Glynrhedyn
Where the bleaberries grow
Among the bonnie Cumbric heather
Where the deer and the raven
Live under God's heaven
Spend the long sumor day
On the fells o' Glynrhedyn

I will build thee a bow'r
By the clear silver fountain

And I'll cover it o'er
Wi' the flooers o' the mountain
I will range through the wilds
And the deep glyns sae dreary
And return wi' their spoils
Tae the bow'r o' my dearie

Let us go, lassie, go
To the fells o' Glynrhedyn
Where the bleaberries grow
Among the bonnie Cumbric heather
When the rude wintry win'
Idly raves roun' oor dwellin'
And the roar o' the linn
On the nicht breeze is swellin'
So merrily we'll sing
As the storm rattles o'er us
Till the dear shielin' ring
Wi' the licht liltin' Let us go,...

It was a song for them all: of their loves and their lives in the fells around Glynrhedyn. Eir felt a tear trickle slowly down her cheek and, as she looked cautiously down the table, she saw moisture in Ealdgith's and Gytha's eyes too; even Ada's.

Cynburg's voice silenced the crowd and few spoke in the moments after she finished singing. In the silence Eir heard Adelind ask, "Wealmaer, why didn't Agnaar return with you? This could have been our wedding too. It breaks my heart that..." her voice, and Agnaar's reply, were drowned by a sudden shout.

"The beacon! Look! One's lit, no two!"

"Three!" A second voice shouted as the beacon directly above them burst into a column of flame and smoke.

"Quiet!" Ulf yelled loudly. His deep voice, seasoned by shouting over the sound of battle, brought immediate silence. "We all know what this means, and we all know what we must now do. Return to your homes and await my call in the morning. This is our fight, and I know it is one that we will win." He turned to those at the table.

"Bear, Eir, this is still your night, go and enjoy it now. Edie, will you let me deal with what must be done?" As Ealdgith nodded, Ulf continued, "Gytha, find Neven. I want your two svanmeyjas off Pulhoue soon after first light to find out exactly what is happening. Don't risk sailing in the dark, but you'll be safe to sail in this breeze once the false dawn starts to break."

Chapter 16

Gytha gave a short blast on her horn and pointed to the lakeshore a couple of furlongs to her left. Neven, following in her svanmeyja, waved in recognition and altered course to follow. "There're people on the track ahead and they're not Norman." Gytha called forward to Leofric who was squatting at the bottom of the mast. "I want to cut them off and find out what's happening."

Glancing over her shoulder as she guided the boat towards the shingle beach, Gytha saw that Neven had seen the group and understood her intention. Both boats grounded together and, as she leapt out close on Loki's heels, Gytha called across, "Leave someone to guard the boats, then follow quickly."

Gytha strove to control her breathing after her quick dash through the scrubby lakeshore woodland. She waited, listening to the sound of approaching footsteps.

"Stop there!" She stepped onto the track from behind the cover of a large boulder. An arrow was already notched to her half-drawn bow string. A group of three men and a woman halted, startled. One of the men raised his staff in defence as shadowy figures clad in rough green and brown clothes, with streaks of ash breaking up the outline of their faces and exposed skin, appeared around them. Loki stood close to his mistress with his head lowered and gave a low growl that prompted the two unarmed men to step back.

Ignoring the man with the staff held across his body, Gytha addressed the woman. "Relax. I'm Gytha. My moder, Lady Ealdgith, holds these lands. Are you fleeing the Normans?" Gytha studied the woman as she spoke. In her twenties and with dark hair and eyes, it was obvious that she was exhausted and scared. Judging by her clothes Gytha surmised that she was a farmer's wife and that one of the men was her husband. As the woman's eyes flitted from Gytha, to Neven and then to Duwe, she seemed to relax, perhaps feeling less vulnerable in the presence of women.

"We are. I'm Agatha, this is my husband and these are my brothers." The man lowered his staff as his wife scowled at him. "Forgive us, but we heard that we would be safe if we could get to Patrichesdale."

Gytha smiled, having caught her breath at last. "You will, I assure you. We…" she glanced around, "…are here to find out what the Normans are doing. We saw the warning beacon last night and I assume they are now at the lake foot? I asked Thorkel of Pulhoue to fire it once they arrived at Bartun or Dacor."

"They are, or at least they are at Dacor. They came yesterday in early afternoon. Herded us all into the big barn and warned us that any who tried to leave the vill would be hanged. They meant it too. When they let us out we saw Swarti and his sons hanging from the big oak. I..I, didn't see his wife, but we had heard her scream. She might have…" Agatha gasped for breath and stifled a sob as her husband took over.

"Aye, well, be that as it may." He spoke gruffly, but not harshly. "After they let us out of the barn they took it over for themselves. There were mayhap a score of them. They set some of our men to work building a stockade for their horses, and our women to cooking. We hid in our house trying to decide what to do when, as night fell, the top of Dunmallard burst into flame. There was an uproar and the Normans mounted and raced off. We escaped into the dark. Others may have too, but we haven't seen them."

Gytha nodded understanding, then involved Leofric and Neven in the conversation for the first time. "I think we should get them back to Bear and Ulf as soon as we can. There might be more that they want to ask. I want to get a look at Pulhoue before I go back."

"I agree. Why don't we get them to make their own way to our camp on the headland? Owst can keep an eye on them and when we finish at Pulhoue we'll sail back with them. "Leofric suggested.

"Of course, thanks." Gytha smiled appreciatively whilst she inwardly cursed herself for not having seen the obvious solution. She turned back to Agatha. "Follow this track until you get to Wethermeloc and see a headland off to the left. We've built shelters there and my men will be setting up camp as we speak. Find Owst and tell him I've told you to wait until we return from Pulhoue." She looked for understanding in their eyes before continuing. "You'll find the track is blocked in places. We intend to slow the Normans when they make a move against us. Just skirt past the blockages and keep out of the woodland and stick to the track until you are level with the headland." Gytha chuckled, "I don't want to make your journey any more difficult than needs be." Then, noticing their puzzled expressions, she explained, "The Normans could ride to Patrichesdale in a day. We intend to make it take a week and buy time for my brother to ready our defences." Lightening the mood, she added, "And when you get there he'll give you something better than that staff to fight them with, now you'd best get on your way."

*****

Gytha slumped, exhausted, onto the sheep-grazed grass of the Wethermeloc headland and gazed skyward, too tired to bat away the midges hovering above her.

"Here, take this." She half rolled then sat up, smiling thankfully as she took the proffered bowl of broth.

"Thanks, Leo. I'm glad you stayed back here to get the camp sorted. Ye gods, but this is just what

I need." Gytha sucked thirstily. "I've done nearly three lengths of the lake today, and thanks to the wind dropping, I've rowed over half of it."

"It's all good exercise. I always thought you needed more strength to pull that bow of yours," Leofric teased her, knowing that with a cupful of broth in her hands Gytha couldn't take revenge. "What did Fader and Bear say?"

Gytha shrugged. "Same as we thought. The Normans have always shown a fear of ambushes. They won't risk following the track in the dark and will probably take a day or two to gather their forces. We'll keep a boat down at Pulhoue during daylight, anchored just out of bow shot. Ulf's given me another horn for them to use to signal any advance. We'll use different blasts to send different warnings. You know: one for movement on the north shore, two for the south shore, and so on."

"Good, that's pretty much what I've told Owst, Kali and Gufa, and the horn will really help too. One of Kali's sections is down there now."

Gytha nodded, listening whilst she finished off the broth, then with the sweetest of smiles asked, "Any more, Leo? I feel brighter already."

Whilst Leofric went to refill the bowl Gytha glanced around the clearing to catch sight of the girl on whom she was relying increasingly as a personal assistant as well as one of her section leaders. "Neven! Can you find Owst, Kali and Gufa please, and join us? We need to plan for tomorrow before the light fades."

Gytha had taken to heart her mother's advice that, if she was going to live amongst a band of men, she would find it much easier to have a woman alongside her in whom she could confide. She sensed that Neven appreciated the status that this responsibility gave, and she realised too that it was Neven's blunt, earthy honesty that had prompted her initial outburst. The pair were rapidly becoming close friends.

Leofric returned with more broth and an oatcake. As Gytha dipped the oatcake to soften it she noticed a svanmeyja rowing briskly up the lake. "That'll be Kali's men on their way back. Let's greet them and see what's happening at Pulhoue before we speak to the others." Succumbing to Loki's plaintive stare, she tossed him the last of the oatcake and walked down to the shore.

Leif, Kali's deputy, jumped from the svanmeyja and walked briskly across the shingle, leaving his men to haul the boat partway out of the water. He gave Gytha a slight nod, then said, "There were only a handful of men-at-arms in Pulhoue all day. As you thought, Thorkel and his family must have left when he fired the beacon. But as the sun started to set a scorc or more rode in along the south bank of the Eamont. They must have come from Bartun."

"Thanks, Leif. You've done well. Get your men across to the fire There should still be some broth and oatcakes for you. Now, Leo, let's decide what we do next." Gytha's eyes sparkled. Rejuvenated by the food she was impatient to put their battle plan into action. Their long wait and constant training were over.

*****

Loki's low growl and Neven's hand on her shoulder roused Gytha from a deep sleep. "Uh! The night's too short," she grumbled, rubbing her eyes.

"It was your idea," Neven teased. "The night guard shook me as the first glow of dawn lit the fells. He's warmed more broth for us."

Gytha stretched, licked a finger and held it up to catch the light breeze. "Good, with this sou'wester behind us we'll have a quick sail down to Pulhoue. I'll catch you by the fire when I've pulled my boots on." Then, bending to give a snoring Leofric a kiss, she whistled to Loki and followed Neven.

Minutes later the two young women lowered the sail and let Brynhildr drift quietly across the shadowed waters of Pulhoue bay. As the svanmeyja slowed, Neven lowered the rope-bound boulder that served as the anchor. The little vill was dark and appeared deserted, though Gytha could smell wood smoke. "They'll have a guard with a fire in one of the houses. It's best we keep our heads low. I doubt they'll realise that there is another boat in the bay." She spoke quietly, aware that any sound would carry across the still water.

Their suspicions were confirmed a little while later when, as the surrounding fell tops caught the first light of day, a house door creaked open and a man walked around to the side. "What's he doing?...Ugh!" Gytha's question was answered by Neven's giggle. They watched as Pulhoue's encampment came to life with a brisk efficiency.

"It looks like they are readying their horses, so much for them waiting a day or two before moving against us. We need to haul the anchor in and get ready to leave." Gytha was suddenly worried that they might have stayed too long.

"I'll ready the oars and turn her around once the anchor's clear of the lakebed." Neven settled herself on the centre thwart. If we stick to the centre we can watch both shores."

"You're right. I want to get level with our first ambush point, then take her to which ever shore they're moving along before I use the horn." Gytha spoke between deep breaths as she hauled the anchor up and lifted it into the bow.

Brynhildr swung around and glided steadily away into deeper water as Gytha and Neven rowed with long slow strokes, taking care to avoid any sudden movements or splashes that could draw attention.

"Rest a moment and watch." Gytha held her oars clear of the water with one arm and used her free hand to shield her eyes against the rising sun. "They're riding. Yes, look, they're fording the Eamont at the far side of the fish pool. Pull for the north shore." Gytha rowed until they

183

were out of sight of Pulhoue then blew a long blast followed by three short ones. Roosting pigeons exploded from the woods on the shore line, whilst startled crows cawed overhead.

"Well, that woke things up." Neven spoke quietly as they strained to hear a reply. When it came, the three horn calls, carried on the morning breeze, were louder than expected: long, short, long. "That means 'message understood'. Well done, Gytha, it works. Leo and the sections should be here within fifteen minutes" Neven beamed at her friend.

"Good. Let's row back out a bit. I want to see what those men-at-arms are up to on the track and how quickly they're moving. Leo will get the men into position for the ambush." Gytha's mind was a turmoil of thoughts. The little time that she had been able to spend with her father helped, as did the days since, spent working with Bear. She understood the relationship of time, distance and speed. Now she really needed to see how well the Normans were coping with riding horses along the heavily overgrown track.

Neven rowed diagonally across the lake whilst Gytha crouched in the bow, scanning the wooded shore line for signs of movement.

"I can see them, Neven. Move closer to the shore." Gytha was silent for a few moments. "Yes! They're on foot. The branches over the track are too low for them to ride those chargers of theirs. They've taken them to the back of the column and are leading them, and they're moving slowly." She paused, listening. "What's that?"

Neven cocked her head to one side. "Axes, I think. They must be clearing the overhanging branches as they go."

"Just the sort of distraction we need." Gytha said cheerfully. "We've time to get the sections into position."

"And here they come. They'll be at the meeting place before us at this rate." Neven called over her shoulder as she swung the boat around.

They joined the cluster of svanmeyjas drawn up on the edge of boggy ground by the mouth of Ramps Beck.

Gytha winced as she stepped over the side and cold water flooded into her boots. Loki hesitated before launching himself with a splash, then leapt for the shore where he circled menacingly before choosing a person against which to shake himself. "Sorry!" Gytha called whilst trying not to laugh, then she tapped the top of her head with her hand as a signal for her section leaders to join her.

With the six section leaders squatting in front of her, and Leofric standing at her side, Gytha confirmed her orders from the night before. "They've moved sooner than I thought, but otherwise there is no change. We'll spring the ambush as planned. It looks as if they have a handful of dismounted men-at-arms in front, followed by a party with axes who are clearing the overhanging branches. Their horses are being led by hand at the rear. I want the sections to work in pairs, with two pairs on this side of the ford from where they can hit the men-at-arms and the axemen. The third pair is to hit the horse party before they cross the ford. Aim for the horses and cause as much confusion as possible. Remember, I doubt we'll kill anyone, it'll be a bonus if we do. We just need to stun and wound. Hit hard, hit quickly, and then fall back when I sound the horn. Work in twos and cover each other. I've chosen the ground so that we get maximum protection from the trees. We can't risk any of them getting a clear line for a spear throw." She glanced at the faces around her, "As I said, this is pretty much what we agreed last night. Are there are any questions before we get in place?"

Owst looked up. "After the attack, do we still move on to the next ambush site as planned?"

Gytha nodded, "Yes, but stay clear of the shore. Leo and I will watch from here and see what they do next. Wait for my call. Any other questions?"

Everyone shook their heads, then Owst jumped up. "Let's go, then. I for one can't wait to give a Norman a sore head."

Gytha stood on the track and stared at the undergrowth in front of her. She found it hard to believe that there were over a score of green-clad men and women within a short stone's throw of her. A sudden thought worried her: if the ambush didn't go to plan, or she failed as a leader, then all her credibility would be lost; as a woman, she wouldn't be given a second chance. Satisfied by what she saw, she gave a nervous grin, flicked a quick thumb up, then set off along the track at a cautious jog with Loki at her heels. She wanted to see how quickly the Norman party was approaching. As she ran she realised that, other than the low branches over hanging the ford, this part of the track was relatively clear, which meant that the Normans would cover it quite quickly. She stopped behind a thicket of coppiced birch on the edge of the wood and waited until men-at-arms entered the far side of the clearing. "Come, Loki." Gytha spoke softly, back-tracked cautiously and then ran down the track to the ford. "They are on their way, get ready," she called before turning off the track beyond the ambush site and making her way carefully to rejoin Leofric. Taking an arrow from her quiver, she notched it to her bow string and chose a point of aim in the centre of the ford.

A sense of detachment came over Gytha. It was as if she was watching herself as well as the approaching men-at-arms. She realised that whatever happened in the next few minutes her life would change: the violence that she was about to unleash would mature her from adolescent to adult in an instant.

The speed and nonchalance of the Norman advance surprised her. It was obvious that they did not expect to be attacked. Six men-at-arms, their swords sheathed and unencumbered by shields, led the way, followed by more carrying axes. Others led the party's horses on long reins in groups of three. On reaching the little ford they clustered around the crossing whilst two of the axemen worked to clear the dead ash trunk that Gufa had forced across the track only days before. Gytha bided her time, recalling Ulf's advice about timing and positioning an ambush. She waited until the party moved again and, raising and drawing her bow, tracked one of the axemen with her arrow tip. Judging when the lead Norman was level with the centre of her left-hand section, she released the arrow and watched as it slashed through the air to strike the mail covering the side of the man's neck. As he spun around, Gytha could see that the arrowhead must have penetrated the metal rings, but only sufficiently far as to inflict a shallow wound. "Damn!" She cursed as she notched a second arrow, a fraction further forward and she would have pierced his cheek.

The twang of Gytha's bowstring had been the signal for the ambush. As the target of her attack fumbled to draw his sword, a score of arrows and sling-shot battered the men on the track. The speed of some of the slingers was such that a second stone was in the air before the first hit its target. Three men slumped down, dazed by blows on their helmets. Others ripped arrows out of their mail and padded under-jackets, but none were killed. As the men-at-arms drew their swords and turned to face the ambush they realised the folly of leaving their shields strapped to their saddles. Two fell instantly: one immediately dead, pierced through his eye, and another cried out as he grasped at the side of his throat. The scream of panicked horses and the shouted curses of men trying to control them told Gytha that chaos had descended on the other side of the ford.

"Charge!" The order, shouted in Bretton, was immediately understood by the green men.

"Hold! Wait! ... Now!" Gytha's loud high-pitched order carried clearly through the trees. The charging Normans slowed momentarily then pitched forward into the undergrowth, hit by more missiles and tripped by the long ropes of entwined briars that protected the ambushers' front. Gytha seized the opportunity to signal their withdrawal by giving a long blast on her horn. As the green men fell back in pairs she shouted to Leofric, "Wait, we need to see if they continue along the track. We've injured several and mayhap killed one, but I doubt we've stopped them."

Leofric stumbled on a root as he ran across to Gytha, then grabbed her arm. "No! You can't delay. Listen!" He pointed over to their right. "They're already cutting around our flank. "Run!"

They bolted through the thick woodland of birch, ash and rowan, using the many low trees to shield their backs from a spear throw. Leofric splashed across the boggy lakeshore, vaulted over the gunwhale into Brynhildr and started to lower the oars into the water. Loki followed whilst Gytha pushed the bow clear of the mud. Her eye caught movement fifty paces away at the edge of the trees. Her heart pounded. "Spear! Get down, Leo." Her scream coincided with a loud crack inches above her head as a spear point stabbed into the tall S-shaped bow. It stuck there, vibrating. Gytha heaved the boat into the water and threw herself over the side to lie gasping in the bow. "Row, Leo, Row."

Leofric strained as he rowed stern first out into deeper water. Moments later he swung the boat around as Gytha shouted "We're clear, Leo."

*****

The sun was dipping towards Helvellyn's ridge when Gytha called all her sections to her. She had been right to assume that the Normans would continue to clear the track. Having recovered their horses, they had sent three wounded back with the dead man-at-arms and then resumed their advance along the track. Gytha had anticipated correctly that the first ambush would force a change in her opponents' tactics and the Normans now moved slowly and methodically, checking the area around each cluster of felled trees that blocked the track and then screening the axemen with shields whilst they worked. The horses were kept well to their rear.

The sections had worked well, setting repeated hit and run ambushes as they used their boats to leapfrog along the lakeshore. It had been late in the afternoon before the Normans halted, mounted and rode back along the track, proving that it was now clear to be ridden at speed.

As Gytha looked at the faces in front of her, she could tell that they were as tired and elated as she was. Each had had their own close escape, had enjoyed the thrill of the fight and relished the surge of adrenalin. She leaned on the spear that she had wrestled from Brynhildr's bow, and looked around at the weary, but attentive and hardened faces gazing at her. "We've done well. Each and every one of us. The Normans have cleared less than a league of the track and have many more to go. We know we can't stop them, but we can slow them, tire them, wound them and make it easier for Bear and Ulf to defeat them. We must keep a guard out tonight, though I am sure they won't risk moving in the dark. Get a good sleep and then we'll move camp at first light. I am sure they will reach here tomorrow and, although the track passes us by, we can't risk being cut off. Owst, I want your section to set up the new camp on the headland below the Knotts, whilst the rest of us continue to give them another day to remember us by." She ended with a grin, "Any questions?"

Neven jumped up to face the gathering, "Only one, Gytha. Why did any of us ever doubt you?"

Chapter 17

Bear pulled Gytha clear of the ground in a hug worthy of his name. "Well, I can no longer call you 'little sister'. You've achieved more than I ever hoped for in this past week." She blushed as he lowered her, but welcomed his praise. "Go and find Leo, then join me here when I brief all the sections."

Gytha groaned inwardly. She was so exhausted that she could no longer remember how long they had been harrying the Normans' approach by setting a sequence of ambushes every few hundred paces along the track. The dense wild woodland of birch, oak, rowan and alder interlaced with thick undergrowth had provided ideal cover for very close confrontations, and had caused the men-at-arms to move very slowly as they tried to clear the sides of the track. Unfortunately for them, their long kite-shaped shields hindered progress, snagging on the undergrowth and constantly tripping them. Forced to move without shields the men-at-arms had provided more open targets and several had fallen to arrows shot at very close range. None of the green men had fallen, though many were grazed and bruised from slips and trips. Gytha thanked the gods that the maze of tree trunks had always screened them from the few arrows and crossbow bolts that had come after them.

On the last day Gytha had deliberately laid ambushes to the right of the track, hitting the Normans' unprotected flank and drawing their attention away from the lake and up onto the wooded fellside slopes. She hoped that this would help entice the men-at-arms to follow the road up the valley and into the jaws of Bear's intended ambush. Now, all she wanted to do was sleep.

The huscarles and section leaders squatted on top of a fifty paces long man-high earth rampart watching Bear finish making a model on the turf below. He stepped back and looked up.

"Those at the back, move a bit closer so that you can see better. My fader taught me the benefit of making a model of a battle plan, so here's ours for tomorrow. I don't know which of our forebears built the rampart that you are seated upon, but they chose the site well, as you will see." Bear tapped the ground with his spear point. "The model relates to the ground in front of you, on yon side of the trees. We'll fight in four groups and I want us all ready for first light tomorrow. We know the Normans are now using the headland below Knotts as an outpost and that they have cleared the track as far as Aira Beck, so it won't take them long to cover the two leagues to reach us. Gytha, your slingers and archers will be involved first. As you've seen, we've dug up the stone road from its junction with the track. You've got three tasks. The first is to keep one section in a boat just this side of the Norman camp. They need to be there from last light tonight and are to use a horn to signal when the Normans move. That should give us up to an hour's warning. Second, place most of your men in an ambush astride the old track, just in case the Normans aren't deceived and keep following the lake shore. Harry them and fall back whilst attracting my attention. We'll ride down and take them in the flank if needs be. Finally, I want a section to be on the road just far enough up from the old junction for them to be seen clearly enough to entice the Normans up the dale. Tell them to flee into the woods and rejoin you once the Normans react." Gytha nodded understanding, then Bear continued.

"Ulf, I want you, with Wealmaer and Ari, to take command of Tyr and the other refugees you've mustered and trained in the last couple of weeks. Hold the rampart here as a final block if the Normans do persist along the shore-side track. The boulder field we've made in front of it should hinder any that do try to come through."

Bear shifted position and tapped the model again. "This represents the line of the stone road running up Matterdale alongside Aira Beck. The fellside is open for a couple of furlongs before it runs into woodland as it starts to cut around the steep flank of Round Howe. Tófi, your section is with me. Once we see that the Normans have taken Gytha's bait we will ride onto the track and trot up towards the woods. We'll allow them to close up to within a score of paces by the time we get to the woods. That's when Lady Ealdgith and Godric will close the trap with the remaining five sections, and hit them from the higher ground with a hail of crossbow bolts. Once most have been taken down then Tófi and I will ride back in and finish them off. Is everyone clear so far?"

Bear leant forward on his spear as he looked for confirmation. "Good. Tófi, I want you to try to take two prisoners in order that I can find out exactly which Norman lord is behind all this. It's becoming obvious that whoever it is, is determined to take the lake, or us. Finally, all of our wounded, should we have any, including any of theirs with a chance of survival, are to be sent back to Eir at Grassthwaite Howe. My moder will treat and return any Norman wounded as she wants to prove that we live and fight by a code of decency."

*****

The sun's first rays burst over Cross Fell's distant summit to turn the lake's still surface from deep woad to red and then burnished gold. Bear swung himself onto his fell pony and turned to watch as Ealdgith and Ada mounted, whilst Hati ran in circles around them. He marvelled at the sight of his mother adjusting herself in her saddle. The fine steel, copper and brass rings that formed her suit of mail shimmered in the golden light. Her mail, thought to have been made centuries before for her distant forebear, Queen Aethelflaed, had been given to her by her uncle, Earl Gospatrick, along with the Carolingian sword that graced her hip. The sight of Ealdgith armed to fight inspired confidence in her ability to lead in battle and, although it was a score of years since she had last done so, he knew her people would follow her today just as they had then.

The sound of a pony galloping along the metalled road drew Bear's attention and he waited for Ari to ride up to him. Ari's nod, as he wheeled his pony around, told Bear that it was time and he signalled to Ealdgith to take the lead and trot down to where Ulf had marshalled all who would fight.

Ealdgith slowed and turned to halt her pony in front of a sea of expectant faces. Some, newly recruited, appeared nervous. The slingers seemed exhausted, but determined, whilst the men within Bear's sections had the confident smile of those trained to fight.

Ealdgith's expression was grave as she looked from face to face, but then smiled. "I can see that some of you are confident of victory, and so you should be. Others are understandably nervous, and you are right to be so, for you'll not have fought before. Be reassured," she gestured towards the mounted sections, "many of these men rode alongside Hravn and me when we fought the Normans before ever we took charge of these lands. They will tell you that when we fight the Normans on our own terms, we always win. Today we will fight the battle on our ground and on our terms. It is a battle that we will win. It is a battle that we must win. It may not be our last battle, but it will set the pattern for those yet to come." Ealdgith drew her sword and waved it above her so that its shimmering blade could be seen by all around her. "Let today be ours. Make it one that your children, and your children's children, will always remember. One that bards, down our generations, will recount with pride."

A loud cheer erupted that resounded across the lake and echoed in the dales. As it died away the sound of a horn replaced it. Battle had been called.

*****

Gytha settled the slingers into a line across the dug up and disguised track, choosing a spot a hundred paces from the track junction where it forded a shallow beck. Any men-at-arms leaving the track would have to move on foot through woodland to where the slingers could strike in the open from behind the added protection of the beck, and then fall back to the rampart, across a wide stretch of heathland strewn with rocks and boulders that would trip horses and men alike.

Content that Leofric could fight any battle on her behalf, Gytha took Neven and her section back onto the track a couple of hundred paces from the junction, where it turned a sharp bend. "This is ideal, Neven, we can see down through the trees to the lake track and should have a few moments warning. When they come, we'll make sure they spot us, lead them on by running around the bend then cut through the trees back down to the beck. Bear will be on the track a furlong further up. It'll be his fight then."

They didn't have long to wait. Catching sight of movement, before the sound of galloping horses reached them, Neven gasped at how many horses seemed to be on the track. "D'you see that! There's well over a score. Your moder is going to have quite a fight."

Gytha didn't get a chance to reply. "We're on!" She shouted loudly as the first horsemen burst into the junction. They didn't waver, seeming to accept that the metalled surface heralded a sign that they must be nearing their objective. "Quickly! They're fast!" Gytha and Neven sprinted after the rest of the section. Adrenalin drove their legs as their lungs gasped painfully for breath. Gytha caught a brief glimpse of Bear's men circling their ponies higher up the road before she flung herself into the undergrowth and slid frantically down towards the beck.

Bear heard his sister's warning shout, swung his pony around and urged it to start walking up the hill. "Ready, lads. Move to a trot and then a gallop once they start to close on us. At the pace they are going, their horses will already be feeling winded." He marked the point at which he would come level with the start of the ambush then glanced backwards. The Normans were closing, but still some distance behind. He wanted them to be within twenty paces when the attack came. "Steady, Tófi, ease up slightly. We've got them in play," he shouted across to his section leader.

The sudden heavy thrum of a score of cross bow bolts through the air, and the scream of wounded men and horses that followed, told Bear that his mother had sprung the ambush. The section slowed and wheeled around immediately to face the carnage behind them. The leading Normans were all down, along with several of their horses. A roan charger with a foam flecked muzzle staggered past, then galloped on up the hill, neighing in panic.

"Wait, Tofi," Bear cautioned unnecessarily. "We can't move until the bolts stop flying." They continued to watch as Ealdgith's sections methodically destroyed the Norman cavalry. Pinned by steep ground on either side, and the road ahead blocked by dead and dying men and horses, it was impossible for the Normans to carry the battle to their attackers and there was nowhere for them to flee.

"Look!" Tofi pointed down the hill. "Two have got away."

"Aye," Bear nodded, "my money is that they were at the tail and just outside the killing ground. A witness to this slaughter will be no bad thing if it deters them from coming back."

"Hold!" Ealdgith's clear call cut through the noise of battle.

"Come." Bear jerked his head towards the fallen, then dismounted, leaving his pony's reins hanging. Taking his spear, he walked forward and started prodding the bodies.

"This one. Here, and him." Bear methodically pointed out casualties for his men to attend to, as others slid down from the fellside to help.

"This is the part I hate." Bear turned to find Ealdgith beside him. "When it is kill, or be killed, we have no choice. But it makes it no easier. When I learned to fight, I vowed to only take life to save others. These men would have brought suffering to us all, but it is their lord that is to blame. They simply followed the orders they were given."

"I know, Moder, but..."

"There are no buts. That is simply the way of it. Now, we must tend to those whom we can help and finish the suffering of those we cannot save."

Tófi, standing behind Ealdgith and over hearing the conversation, interrupted. "Let me, My Lady. It's a foul task. Tell me who you cannot save and I will see that they have a quick end. It's what all of us would want in their place." The giant Dane at times spoke with a gentleness that still surprised Ealdgith.

Ealdgith smiled her thanks. "It's been a long time since we fought together, Tófi, but nothing has changed."

*****

"We've two more here, Eir." Wulf ducked back out of the door way and gestured to his men to lift the wounded men-at-arms down from a pair of ponies. Ducking back in again, he added, "Bear says he will be down shortly. He's just sorting out the bodies and all the weapons we've taken."

Eir smiled her thanks, then took a deep breath. She already had three Normans demanding her attention, as well as one of their own who had been bitten viciously by a panicked war horse. Checking first that Adelind and Cynburg were coping, she showed Wulf's men where to lay the casualties on the fern-strewn floor of the outhouse she had prepared for the care of the wounded.

Both had leg wounds. Although one was grinding his teeth in pain from a twisted knee, it was the man whose leg was oozing blood that Eir knew she must attend to first. "Aebbe, bring me mead, salted boiled water and clean lint please. Oh, then see if Godric or one of the other men is to hand. I'm going to need their help." She called to her mother's friend, thankful for her assistance.

Eir had already realised that all the wounded must be Bretons because they understood her Cumbric. She probed gently around the thick blood-soaked clothing clinging to the man's thigh. She could see that the flesh at the back of his thigh had been sliced by a cross bow bolt. "I'm going to cut away all the clothing around your leg then bathe and stitch the cut. It will hurt." Eir tried to reassure and warn the man as she started to cut the sodden material with a small sharp blade. He stared at her, understanding her meaning, but cautious as to why he was being attended to.

"What's your name?" Eir asked by way of reassurance rather than interest.

"Mihael." The man grunted, then spoke through clenched teeth. Eir could tell that he was trying to control his breath in reaction to the pain.

Eir heard Godric come in and was relieved that she could proceed. She continued speaking conversationally. "I would say you've been lucky, Mihael. Your horse must have taken this bolt in its belly. Any further forward and your thigh bone would have shattered. Now, roll onto your right side, please." As Mihael shifted painfully, Eir placed the remains of his breeches to one side for Aebbe to throw onto the fire outside, then she soaked a piece of soft linen in salt water and gently washed around the slice in his flesh. "Mmm, good." Eir talked out loud to herself, then added for Mihael's benefit. "It's a clean cut. The bolt head sliced you without driving much material or dirt into the wound. I've cleared away everything I can and washed it with salty water to promote healing. Now, I'm going to bathe it with mead. The alcohol helps stop infection. It will sting, mind you. But it's a good pain, not a bad one." She looked into Mihael's eyes. He nodded, understanding, and asked, "Why are you doing this? We brought you violence, yet you tend me like one of your own. Why?

Eir paused. "It's Lady Ealdgith's way. She leads us in battle, as she did against you just now, and will fight like a wildcat; but she treats everyone with care and respect. By caring for her foes, she hopes to better our understanding of each other and to foster peace. It was she who taught me the skills of healing."

They both fell into a reflective silence, then Eir continued.

"Once I'm happy with the wound, I will sew the edges together." She hesitated, a slight smile on her lips. "I'm not bad at needlework, you know."

Mihael forced a weak smile. "Anything that holds it together will do for me."

"When I've finished stitching I will add a salve of honey and egg white to help soothe and heal, then I'll bind it. First, though, you're going to drink this." Eir took a cup from Aebbe. "It's strong mead. It won't stop the pain, but it will dull the sharpness. Then, in case you can't help but lash out, Godric will hold your legs and Aebbe your shoulders."

Nodding, Mihael took a long draught, lay flat, and stared at the wall. Eir unrolled the medicinal roll that Ealdgith had given her and chose a thin steel needle and a length of cat gut.

*****

Ealdgith and Bear rode down to the rampart to join Ulf where he was waiting with Gytha. Bear dismounted whilst Ealdgith spoke from her saddle. "Well, at last we know for certain that Count Alan is behind this. These men are Breton and they wear his colours. Count Ivo's men are Norman."

"There were a score and half of them." Bear interrupted, still fired with the thrill of the ambush. "Two escaped and five are being treated for wounds."

"Hah! Add in those that Gytha and Leo took down and the Count has paid a high price. I doubt he has the strength to come back at us in a hurry." Ulf was enthusiastic. "What do you propose next, Edie?"

Ealdgith didn't hesitate, already sure what she would do. "As soon as one of the wounded is fit to be moved by boat, I will send him back with a letter and a verbal message from me to the Count to say that these lands are mine, by word of the Scots' King, and written into a charter. I will tell him that I have treated and returned his wounded by my grace. Others might not be so fortunate in future. I will also tell him that any Frenchman found on my land will be killed."

"Mayhap keep some of the wounded here, as hostages. We need to stop any further incursions along the lake shore too." Ulf spoke advisedly.

"We will, Ulf. Bear, take all your men now, before the Count's men can gather and react, and fell trees this side of their camp at Knotts. Block the track properly. Then, when they evacuate the camp, as I'm sure they will, do the same down towards Pulhoue. And Gytha, from now on I want two boats on the lake every day, one watching Pulhoue bay and another in between. They can communicate by horn and get warning of any movement back to me."

Haerfest 1092

Chapter 18

"Ye gods! I'm glad that's done." Bear eased himself onto the grassy bank outside the big barn at the foot of Grisedale valley, then propped himself up on one elbow as he heard Godric chuckle behind him.

"You're like your fader, for certain. There're not many lords that would do the work meant for their villeins. He always threw himself into it too."

Bear, dog-tired, nevertheless smiled at the compliment. "Aye, well, it's fair enough. I ask them to fight for me. Anyway, we'd never have got the harvest in and the sheep shorn if we hadn't all rallied round. I'm just grateful that Count Alan hasn't pestered us again. I'm surprised, though. I can't see him giving up, and now that he knows moder has out-witted him he will doubtless want revenge. Mayhap Agnaar's kept him distracted."

"Mmm, talking of Agnaar, your moder wants him back here. When your fader was killed, he told Wealmaer that he would return in Æfteraliða and it is now Hāligmonath; that was two months ago. She was talking of sending you to fetch him."

Bear sat up suddenly. "What! That's hardly wise. The threat hasn't gone away. We'll need all hands to fight one day soon, I'm sure of it. It was enough of a risk when you took a section to escort the jaggers to Rengles in Weodmonath, though we had little choice. It was the only way we could pay for Aedan to buy and store extra grain for us until later in the year."

Godric sat down next to Bear. "Worry not, that's much as I've just told her. I said Ulf should go, with Ari. If anyone can talk sense into Agnaar it's his adopted fader, and Ari was working with Agnaar until he came back here. We've agreed that Ulf will take Ketel the charter that Hravn died saving. That will secure William and Aebbe's land rights. Then he can seek Ketel's help in finding where Agnaar has based himself."

"Good." Bear sighed. "Thanks, Godric, that was well advised and Moder heeds your counsel. It's time to get the sections back into shape, but I wouldn't mind taking a look at what's going on around Bartun and Dacor. Can you work with Wealmaer whilst I take Dai? We'll go by way of Brethstrett and make our way down towards Askum. Ulf will head off over Kirkstein."

Godric nodded sombrely, "Aye, that'll work. I think we should leave Gytha and her boats working from Haugr-tun. They've got the foot of the lake pretty well sewn up, and have given several Normans a sore head whenever they ventured along either shore. I have to say that she's really impressed me; she reminds me more and more of your moder at that age."

Bear rolled his shoulders, stood up and stretched. "Come on, let's give Ulf the good news. I think we need to summon Gytha back too, just so that we can discuss everything properly before Ulf goes. We'll need to share out his responsibilities in case the Normans come calling again whilst he's away."

*****

"That's the best idea I've heard in days...what?" Ulf's enthusiasm for the trip was dampened immediately by Cyneburg's concerned frown. "I'll be fine, my love, what would our Adelind say if I didn't go and bring her Agnaar back? I'm sure he's safe and doing a good job of tying those bastards down, but we do need him here. Though I could do with a couple more of the lads with me. Poor Ari can't look after a one-armed old warrior on his own. What do you say, Bear?"

Bear laughed, "Whatever you say, Ulf, though you said 'old', not me. Choose whom you like. I've sent for Gytha, so Moder will hold a counsel tomorrow. Can you be ready for the morning after?" However much he sensed that the balance of the scales of responsibility was shifting, Bear was still reluctant to directly tell Ulf what to do.

Ulf clasped Bear on his shoulder. "Hah! I wish I felt your age, young Bear. I'll take Cerdik and Nudd with me. Cerdik could do with the experience and I'm sure you can redeploy his other two lads. I'll go and warn them."

*****

Ulf grimaced at the sight of the cloud-shrouded fells whilst, with his good hand, pulling his cloak tight around his shoulders. Water dripped from the edge of the porch and puddled on the slate flags. He grunted. "Ugh. The days are shortening and the weather's turned, thank the gods that we are going over Kirkstein and not Brethstrett. At least on the old road we can find our way in the mist. I don't envy Bear crossing those tops without a clear track to follow."

"You've got me for company, that should brighten things up." Ari joked good- naturedly. "I'll bring the ponies around. Wealmaer's with Cerdik and Nudd getting rations."

Their ride up the long incline of Kirkstein was slow and tedious. They made a sombre sight, their dull green cloaks dripping with water as the ponies pushed their way through the dying bracken. The going improved after they passed the chapel-shaped Kirkstein and dropped down to Ameleseta, from where they made their way in a south-eastward loop towards Ketel's hall at Kircabi Kendala.

The wind increased as the sun dropped, howling in from the south west and whipping rain across their faces whilst they battled through it. Ulf released the reins and used his knees to guide his pony, struggling to keep his cloak together and the wind-driven water out. Ari, riding ahead, turned and pointed. His shouted 'There's the Hall' was lost unheard, ripped from his lips by the wind.

Cerdik and Nudd led the ponies off to the stables whilst Ulf hammered on the door. He burst inside as soon as it opened, laughed at Ketel's astonishment, and apologised. "That accursed wind! I'm sorry, Lord, but it blew me in, though mayhap it underwrites the urgency of my mission."

Ketel's loss of composure was fleeting. "Come, Ulf, join me at the hearth. You too, Ari isn't it?" Turning to a house servant, he called. "Bring mulled ale. I can see these men need it." Ketel listened attentively, nodding gravely, whilst Ulf informed him of Hravn's death and the Norman incursion along the lake.

"To think that these words on parchment are worth my friend's life. We should never have need for such a charter, though I fear that in these times we will. Thank you, Ulf, and thank Edie too." Ketel took the leather-bound scroll containing the land rights and stuffed it inside his jerkin as he spoke. "I'll secure it properly later, and see that William gets it. He's away checking some of our land in Amounderness."

"Have you heard owt of Agnaar?" Ulf asked, keen to progress the search for his adopted son.

"Not directly. Whatever he has been up to, it hasn't affected us. My fader-in-law is yet to get properly involved. He seized the pass at Tibeia, just as Hravn supposed he would, and was then called away to deal with matters on his estates south in Lincolia-scir. I've heard that he is now to be granted lands across much of the upper vale of Eden, north of those that were Hravn and Edie's. At the moment, Count Alan seems to be making free with them whilst he takes charge of those he has his eye on north of Penrith. Discretion being the better part of valour, I've kept out of the matter, though I've heard that the Count has paid a high price to move his supplies over the tops at Stanmoir. I had surmised that was Hravn's doing, but it must surely be young Agnaar."

"Aye, good, that it must. He's fired with vengeance for his family, but we now need him and his men to bolster our defence of Ulueswater." Ulf took a long draught from his cup of ale whilst Ketel continued.

"He's taken care to avoid drawing attention to my estates, that's for certain, and to any of Hravn and Edie's old lands. From what I hear, the Count has had men searching along the east fellside. Wherever he's based it would seem to be yon side of the stone road. Though, that said, I haven't heard of any attacks these past few weeks"

"Mmm, now that's a surprise." Ulf sat up sharply. "The last we heard, he had agreed with Hravn to work out of Mallerstang."

Ketel took a deep breath. "He could still be. If you know the lie of the land it's easy enough to cut across to the east and then give the impression you are based there. That would be a sound plan."

Ulf put his cup down and looked at Ketel. "Lord, I need to get Agnaar and his men back to Patrichesdale as soon as possible. We were lucky in the sumor. If the Count is still active across the vale of the Eden, I'm sure he'll have another go at taking the last of our lands, particularly if he thinks Hravn is there. He too, seems to be driven by revenge and I'm sure he knows Hravn was behind that first day's slaughter at the top of the pass. It will simply have fired his want of retribution. If Agnaar has been quiet these past few weeks mayhap something has befallen him, in which case I must find out what. Or the Count could be deliberately switching his men away from the fellside towards Ulueswater."

Ketel's decision was immediate. "Ulf, I've sat on my hands too long. Now I know that the Count has taken Bartun, he has gone too far. The vill was one Edie gifted to Aebbe, and it is William's to defend. Pulhoue and Dacor are still Edie's by right. Thanks to these charters I can show that William and I have the right to march on Bartun, and I intend to do so. But first, you must find out what has happened to Agnaar. Take five of my men and ride in the morning. They will ensure that you have free passage across all of my lands. I will start to muster our men. It will take a while to raise the two score that I can call on now that they can be spared as the haerfest is over."

"Thank you, Lord. I'll start at Mallerstang. Mayhap I'll find out all I need to know there."

Ulf's words were prophetic. After a long, wet ride during which they had followed the old road towards Hep, then cut over the fells to the upper Lauen valley in order to avoid Norman lands south of the Haugr-gill fells, Ulf finally approached the gated entranced to the hall at Mallerstang.

Bran, who was standing guard at the gate, brightened as he recognised Ulf riding towards him at the head of a group of armed men.

"Your face is as red as your beard, Bran, there must be too much ale for you hereabouts." Ulf teased as he rode up. "How's that arm of yours? I heard you fell foul of a Norman spear tip."

"Hah! It's good, Ulf, though the spear left a mean scar. I'll show you later." Bran laughed, then spoke seriously. "Thank the gods you came, but how did you hear?"

Ulf swung down from his saddle. "I've heard bugger all, Bran. That's why I am here. You'd best show me to Agnaar and get one of the lads to tell Ari where to stable the ponies."

Bran lowered his voice and spoke urgently to Ulf, then pointed to the hall. Ulf strode up the steps to the high oak door, took a deep breath, pushed the door open and stepped inside. Agnaar, ashen faced, lay propped on a bench at the far side of the hearth in front of the remains of a feeble fire. He attempted to push himself upright, then fell back weakly.

Ulf closed the door whilst sniffing the air in the hall. Relieved that he could not smell the sickening scent of infection, he picked up a stool and strode across. He stooped to throw a log and some kindling onto the fire, before sitting opposite Agnaar. "It's alright, son, Bran's explained. I've cracked a rib before now, and it's a right bugger to get over. How's your foot?" Ulf's manner was deliberately matter of fact.

Agnaar shook his head. Ulf could tell from his expression that Agnaar was in pain, though his eyes showed that the hurt was more than just physical.

"Not good, Fader. I can't stand on it. A pony stamped on it before kicking me in the chest. Mildred has bound it to a splint of wood and leather, and she wraps fresh leaves around it every couple of days, but I can't say what good it does. Edie might know better."

"Mildred?" Ulf questioned.

"The healing woman. She did a good job with Bran's arm, and my chest has eased a bit, but this is something else."

"Ah." Ulf nodded as he rubbed his chin. "We'll get you back to Eir and Adelind all in good time. But first, I want to hear in your words, not Bran's, just what happened."

Agnaar lowered his gaze. "I failed, Fader. That's what happened."

"No, son. Don't judge yourself harshly. Just tell me the facts."

Agnaar's shoulders slumped as he looked up at Ulf. He appreciated being called 'son'. Ulf didn't do so very often. When he did, it generally reflected sympathy rather than censure.

"I wanted to keep hitting the Normans from the east fellside in order to keep them away from what were Edie's lands. It was what Hravn wanted. We found a high, almost hidden valley behind the pikes east of Aplebi. It was long and broad with steep curved sides and high crags at the end, like a great horse shoe. I thought that if we were caught in there the ponies could out-climb any Norman horses. By working from there we could hit the Normans at both their forts and anywhere in between. I lost count of how many times we caught their waggons. Anyway, it must have worked because they started combing the whole of the fellside. I set a watch and, whenever they got within a couple of leagues, we pulled out onto the high tops and circled our way back here, to Mallerstang, to rest and clean ourselves up."

Ulf smiled reassuringly. "Well, there's nothing amiss there. Hravn himself could have done no better."

Agnaar brightened a little. "It went well until we had that storm a few weeks back. You must have felt it too. The build-up of humidity, and then clouds that towered higher and higher. They seemed to grow directly over our heads and then plunged us into darkness."

"Aye, I do. It stayed clear over the lake fells, but I recall seeing the great pillars of cloud along the Pennines. By the gods, it was muggy though."

"It broke in one sudden clap of thunder late in the morning, right above the head of the valley. It was all we could do to keep hold of the ponies. We were drowned just standing there, then the water started to run down the fellsides and came down the valley in a torrent. It was as if someone had spilt a cup of ale over a table. Within moments we were up to our ankles, then our calves. I led the men out, cutting across the slopes to higher ground overlooking the pikes. There was no risk of being seen, we could barely see ourselves. I hoped that it would be drier underfoot the higher up we were, so we made our way onto the tops and headed for Stanmoir. So much water came down that the clouds must have emptied. They cleared suddenly and it wasn't that long before the sun burst through and steam started rising all over the valley. It was the strangest of sights, yet it favoured us as we couldn't be seen from the fort below us at Burc. In the end, we overnighted at our old camp below the pass, and in the morning, I sent two sections back here and took Brandr and Ewen's section up to the main fort thinking that we could monitor the pass whilst continuing to dry out."

Agnaar paused with a sigh. "That was my mistake. I sent one of the lads, Cardok I think it was, to check the fort. He didn't go in, but assumed it was clear, and waved us forward. Our minds were elsewhere and we were fooling light-heartedly when we rode up. That's when they hit us."

"Ah." Ulf said quietly. "Go on."

"Half a dozen men-at-arms must have ridden up from Bogas and were resting their horses. They had obviously heard us and jumped us from both sides of the gateway as we came through. I was thrown, then kicked and stamped on by one of our ponies. Brandr and Cardok were pulled from theirs and hacked to pieces. I can still hear their screams. Bada leapt down, pulled me up, and pushed me back onto mine whilst Ewen and Wemba slashed left and right to keep them back. But Bada fell to a spear before he could remount. Then we were away, with Wemba leading my pony whilst I gasped for breath and clung on. We went straight across the moors, which is probably why the Normans didn't trust their horses to give chase."

"Who's in charge now?" Ulf questioned without judging.

"Toudwal's the most experienced, Godfrid and Ewen listen to him. But it should be me, Fader. That's how I'm failing them. They're keeping the men busy by patrolling the approaches, but I'm stuck here. I...I can't even get to the privy without help. They've put a bucket behind that screen at the end of the hall. I slept for days at first, I think Mildred made me, but I can't think clearly. It's the pain in my foot, it just overwhelms me at times."

Ulf dew his stool closer and rested his hand on Agnaar's shoulder. "Aye, lad, I understand. Sometimes it's more than just the pain that numbs the mind." He peered into Agnaar's eyes as he spoke, hoping to see some understanding. Pausing, he came to a decision.

"I think you would be better at Ketel's hall. Safer for sure, and his physic can take a look at you. If you were lifted onto a pony and then led, could you manage a day in the saddle?"

Agnaar shut his eyes to think, then grimaced as he opened them. He nodded slightly. "I've nothing to lose. I can't fight any longer and I know the men are needed." Forcing a weak grin, he added, "And it's closer to Adelind."

Ulf squeezed Agnaar's arm in appreciation. He knew the ride would be a physical and mental challenge. "Good. You'll have time to rest once there. It'll take Ketel a while to muster his men and I won't force you to move

208

until you're ready. If needs be we can ride on ahead. Let's just see how you go."

Chapter 19

The distant blast of a horn hung over the lake, its sound muffled by the rain and distorted by the wind.

"That must be Neven." Leofric turned his head to hear better, whilst he sorted through sheaves of newly made arrows. He ducked inside the barn where they slept and called up to Gytha who was working with Duwe on the platform that she shared with the two women. "Gytha, quickly! Neven's calling for assistance. I'll rouse Owst's crew. They can row you down there, and I'll get others on standby if you call for us."

"What! Thanks, Leo, I'm coming." Gytha slid down the steps, her feet barely touching the rungs, then ran out of the door with Loki at her heels. She stopped on top of the bank and stared across the rain-swept lake. Owst pushed his svanmeyja into the water as his men took to the oars. She could barely see across the lake, let alone the two leagues to Pulhoue. As soon as Owst had taken his place by the steering board, Gytha ran down and splashed through the shallows to swing into the bow.

"Keep to this shore and head for the bay at Sharrow. I doubt we'd have heard the horn if she had blown it from beyond there." Gytha was already building a picture of the lake in her mind. "I sent her out at first light to check on what's happening in Pulhoue. She'll have found the Normans up to something." Gytha spoke with more confidence than she felt, fearing that events might just be turning for the worse on the very morning that Bear and Ulf departed.

The crew rowed the svanmeyja out into the bay and turned towards the foot of the lake, keeping close to the shore, conscious that they could lose visibility and their sense of direction in the next rain squall. They worked hard and started to sweat from the exertion of rowing through a grey world of silvern water, sluicing white rain and leaden clouds.

"There! A furlong away and further out. That's them!"

Owst acknowledged Gytha's shout with a nod as he pushed the arm of the steering board to his right, swinging the svanmeyja sharply to the left. Moments later, Neven's svanmeyja swung towards them, closing rapidly. The crewmen shipped oars as the boats drew together.

"The bastards are on the lake, Gytha. Those old Káras that were drawn up on the beach, well, they are in the water now along with a couple of smaller ones." Neven called across, breathlessly.

"Are they planning on fighting from them?" Gytha questioned, aghast at the sight of two crossbow bolts embedded in the side of Neven's boat.

Neven gave an embarrassed grin. "Sorry, Gytha. They nearly caught us out. We were watching from behind the shelter of a headland this side of Eusemere when two of them spotted us and cut across the lake to get behind us. Those Káras make a good platform for archers," she laughed, "but they're not as fast as a svanmeyja."

"Do you think they're going to come up the lake?" Gytha already knew the answer to her question.

Neven shrugged. "They looked pretty capable to us. I'd bet good coin that they have pressed some of the Pulhoue men into crewing for them. It was hard to tell in the mist, but the archers could have been wearing mail."

"I feared as much. You've done well. If they intend to get us at Patrichesdale they'll leave Pulhoue at first light, so they won't attack today."

"Yes, but they could surprise us at Haugr-tun at any time."

Gytha kept talking to Neven, but sensed both crews' eyes upon her. She knew her decision could affect the start of the coming fight. "I agree. We need to pack up and leave Haugr-tun now. I'm going to go straight back to Patrichesdale to warn Moder and Godric, and start getting the log-booms in place. Tell Leo to make sure that Bjarni gets all the boats here out of the water and hidden; we don't want Normans having an excuse to come ashore.

He's to get word to those at Sandrwic to do likewise. Then get back to join me as quickly as you can."

*****

"Thanks, Leo, you're God-sent." Gytha took the cup of reheated broth and hunk of bread from Leofric, warming her hands on it whilst watching the grey dawn break over the lake. She had felt relief flood through her the previous afternoon when Godric had praised her quick action and then taken charge of preparations: tasking Ragnaar and Alv to start positioning the booms and readying the mangonel. He had also endorsed Gytha's plan to place two sections on Tethera Island and herself and four more on the craggy headland on the shore beyond. Owst's men had then spent the hours before Leofric's arrival building crude shelters for them all amongst the rocks.

"I hope they come. We're as ready as we can be and I just want this over now." Leofric's calm confidence reassured Gytha, as it did all around him. She realised as she drank the broth just how much he too had changed over the summer. Though lacking his father's build, he certainly had his self-confidence.

"They're coming alright, look!" Gytha pointed to the beacon above the bluff upon which the mangonel stood, guarding the line of the boom between the west shore and Tethera Island, less than one league north of Glynrhedyn. Flames flickered at the base of the beacon, then spread quickly upwards. "They can see as far as Haugr-tun from there. My guess is that the sneaky bastards moored at their old camp by Wethermeloc overnight. They could be on us in an hour."

Gytha drank the broth in a long gulp, grimaced at the sudden heat in her throat, then shouted, "You've time to finish up, but the sections on the island need to get over there as soon as possible to raise the wicker shields, get a fire going and prepare arrows for lighting." She referred to the strips of cloth soaked in pine tar and wrapped around the arrow heads.

"Godric's on the move, listen. Ponies are galloping up the track from Glynrhedyn. There. See them?" Leofric stilled Gytha with a wave of his hand, then pointed across the lake.

*****

Ealdgith shouted to Godric as they led the gallop along the lake shore track. "Stay with me, I want Wealmaer to take charge of the mangonel. He can take Wulf and Ranald's sections in case they break through the boom and try to come ashore. Keep Tófi's, Ivar's and Osric's with us." Ada closed up alongside Ealdgith whilst Godric fell back to give Wealmaer his orders. Hati, her hunting instincts alive, ran ahead. Ealdgith passed the track to the mangonel, slowed, then halted at the edge of a wood on a low hill overlooking the mouth of the Glencoyne Beck.   Ealdgith turned in her saddle and shouted to the sections behind. "If they try to come ashore to storm the mangonel we will hold them here. Tófi, go forward and guard this side of the ford. Osric and Ivar will cover you from here, you'll still be within crossbow range." She dismounted and tethered her pony. "Godric, Ada, come forward to the edge of the trees. I want to watch without being seen."

Godric rested his back against a tall pine, staying in the shadows and keeping his green cloak wrapped around him to avoid any reflection off his mail hauberk. "They're barely moving in this low breeze, they'd have done better to row."

"Aye, possibly," Ealdgith agreed, pursing her lips in thought, "but they'll save strength this way. What they don't know is that they'll lose all headway and have to row when they reach this promontory and turn into the southern stretch of the lake."

Godric interrupted, chuckling, "And run straight into the boom whilst they do so."

"I hope they drown." Ada said coldly, under her breath.

Ealdgith was about to speak, then held her reply, as she saw the look of pure hatred on her housecarl's face. She knew that any drowning Normans who made it ashore would find little sympathy from Ada. When she did speak, it was to assess their chances. "Four káras and two smaller tubs, they could have thirty men-at-arms there. If they caught us unawares and came ashore it would be a close-run thing, shield wall against shield wall. As it is, I fully intend to catch them unawares. If we sink or disable two of those káras they'll have to withdraw, given that I'm sure they still don't have a real grasp of our strength."

Time seemed to stand still as the six boats approached slowly; the káras leading and the two tubs lagging behind. "It looks like they're going to keep close to this side of the island to give them room to swing around. I'm impressed at how those wicker screens are hidden by scrub. I can see just the faintest wisp of smoke from the fire for the arrows. I doubt it'll be seen from the boats. Gytha and Leo have done well." Ealdgith spoke softly, her voice calm and controlled in anticipation of battle.

'They're distracted by dropping the sails and shipping oars by the look of it," observed Godric as the two boats nearest the island began to turn and lose headway.

"Ah, any moment...now!" Ealdgith half jumped at Ada's sudden shout, as a silvern shower of smoke-trailing arrows tore across the short stretch of water and struck the nearest kára amidships.

A second flight of fire arrows was in the air before the screams and shouts of pain and panic following the first flight broke the silence on the lake.

Two fire arrows struck a man-at-arms on the foredeck. He fell clutching his thigh, then thrashed desperately as his thick cotton breeches began to burn. He couldn't extinguish the quickly-burning pine tar, nor could he pull the barbed arrow out of his leg. Ada smiled thinly as an anguished scream rent the air.

Another wave of arrows ripped into the central space between the fore and aft decks, embedding themselves in the vertical planking. Flames spread upwards as the pine tar caulking between the boards caught fire, igniting the dry wood beneath the deck.

The three on the promontory watched spell-bound whilst two of the crew ripped at the old boards with their bare hands. Ealdgith winced inwardly, sensing the burnt and shredded flesh the men would suffer. It was a poor reward for serving their new Norman masters. Another crewman had collapsed over one of the thwarts whilst the fourth thrashed at his shoulder trying to break a protruding arrow shaft in half. Men-at-arms, split between the fore and aft decks, tried to steady themselves to shoot back, but staggered as the kára drifted sideways, rocking and uncontrolled. It stopped suddenly and listed to the right, caught on the half-submerged boom. More arrows thumped into its sides or into mail. As one man fell, and then another, they were forced to shelter behind their shields as fire took hold in the centre of the boat.

Ealdgith heard a distant cheer from the island. It was masked, moments later, by the sharp crack of the mangonel and a sudden swooshing sound.

"By the gods!" Godric exclaimed, almost in disbelief, as a shower of fist-sized rocks pounded the kára nearest the shore, catching the fore-deck and momentarily hiding the boat in a shower of spray. One man-at-arms pitched forward and slid over the side in a swift fluid movement, his body dragged directly to the lakebed by the weight of his mail. Another collapsed backwards, his neck bent grotesquely by the force of a blow that had cracked his helmet open. Panic-stricken cries cut across the lake as the crew strove to drop the sail and man the oars.

Realising that there was every likelihood that the boat would hit the rocks below them, Godric yelled to Osric. "Get your section across to the side of the promontory. Hit them hard if they come ashore."

"No, Osric!" Ealdgith yelled, countermanding Godric's order. "I want prisoners. They'll be key to ending all of this."

Osric's shouted orders were drowned out by the mangonel. Having found the range, Wealmaer chose to sink the kára and had ordered a head-sized rock to be loaded. Ealdgith watched, stunned by the weapon's potency, as the rock rose slowly into the air, hung momentarily high above the lake, then dropped with increasing speed to smash into the hold. The crack of snapping timbers and the sudden jolt of the boat were followed by a loud cheer from the promontory.

Chaos erupted as the surviving men on the fore and aft decks threw their helmets off and struggled to pull mail hauberks over their heads as water spurted up through the shattered hull. The stricken kára sank ever lower in the water then foundered, resting on rocks below the surface. Osric watched with a sense of detachment as two men flung themselves into the water and thrashed on the surface trying to reach the shore. They sank, choking, unable to swim. Three remaining survivors clung in desperation to the edge of the aft deck. Osric watched for a few more moments then shouted over his shoulder. "Fetch a rope. We've caught our prisoners."

Gytha and Leofric stood on top of the crag at the south side of the lake watching as disarray seized the Norman fleet.

"They'll try this side of the island next, Gytha, I'm sure of it." Leofric advised as he saw the two remaining káras begin to back paddle and slowly extract themselves from the range of the mangonel. He could guess at the fear driving the oarsmen as a deluge of rocks fell between the two boats, followed moments later by another just short of the retreating foredeck of the one nearest the far shore. "See, they're out of range and turning this way."

"Look, Leo!" Gytha shook Leofric's shoulder and pointed to the kára pinned against the boom. As she did so, a column of water shot up just short of its bow. "They're going to pound that to pieces."

"Good, then we can concentrate on those heading for us." Gytha formed a trumpet around her mouth with her hands and shouted as loud as she could. "Kali! Forget that boat. Concentrate on the káras crossing your front."

Gytha's order focused Kali's attention just in time. The first of a series of crossbow bolts thrummed across the water and smacked into the fleece padding behind the wicker screens. An anguished cry followed, though Gytha couldn't tell whether it was in surprise or pain.

"Owst, try and get the range of those káras." Leofric called to the sections on the crags. "Kali's in danger of being pinned down. Draw those káras' attention until they hit the boom by the island."

"Leo, the tubs are moving away from the káras. I think they're going to try and get men ashore in the bay beyond the headland and move up to engage our archers from behind." Gytha shouted urgently.

Leofric switched has attention away from the island, seeing the new threat immediately. "Oh no they're not. Leave it to me, Gytha, I'll take Gufa's sections and block the shore." He ran off, shouting to Gufa to move position.

The men-at-arms on the two káras, raked by arrows along their left flank, were forced to shelter behind their shields. Gytha ran across to Owst. "Keep aiming for the men-at-arms. Pin them down and they can't shoot back." Shooting at extreme range, many of the arrows fell short or behind the káras as the oarsmen rowed frantically, gradually increasing speed. The shock, as the boats crashed into the boom, was dramatic. The bows of both vessels rode up onto the half-submerged logs, then listed sharply before slipping back down. The boats turned slowly in a welter of thrashing oars and churned water whilst the close range of Kali's archers began to take their toll on the exposed men-at-arms. The hail of flame-trailing arrows continued whilst the káras moved doggedly back past the island towards the middle of the lake. Gytha watched with an increasing sense of relief as the two tubs joined the káras and continued moving away towards the foot of the lake.

"We've done it! We've seen them off. Look across the lake." Gytha turned to see Neven pointing towards a mass of wood, sails and a couple of lifeless, floating bodies.

Gytha waited until Leofric and Gufa re-joined them and then ordered her elated band of warriors to cross the lake.

*****

"Keep those two separate. They're from Bartun and were forced into this." Godric pointed to two roughly dressed and bedraggled men. "Get the other four up to our Lady. Bind them first."

"Aye, right enough." Osric and his men used the rescue rope to bind the captured men-at-arms' wrists and link them together.

The prisoners grunted, slipping on loose earth and bare rock, and staggered as they tried to scramble up the steep side of the promontory.

Ealdgith watched impassively whilst the men were arrayed in front of her. They regarded her with sullen disrespect until she spoke, first in Norman and then in Cumbric. "In what tongue should I speak to you?"

Looks of disrespect turned to surprise, then one spoke. "We're Bretton, not Norman."

"Good. Who speaks for you?"

The prisoners cast questioning looks at each other, then the same man spoke. "I do. There is no one of any rank here." He jerked his head sideways, indicating the lake. "They're down there, somewhere."

"Well, who is, or was, in charge of this...this waste of your lives and unjustified attack on my lands?" Ealdgith paused in mid question to highlight the futility of the men's mission.

"Felix de Kiberen...Lady." The prisoner spoke hesitantly, gradually realising that a woman wearing expensive mail, speaking French tongues, and commanding the respect of her own men-at-arms, was probably someone he too should respect.

Ealdgith smiled thinly, the sun's sparkle in her green eyes adding a sense of mystique to her expression. "Ah, is he now? Our paths have crossed before." She paused, partly for effect and partly to gain time to think. "I'm sure de Kiberen values his men-at-arms, even if he seems wasteful with their lives. You, and one other, will return to him with a message from me. The other two will remain captive as my hostages until he complies with my conditions. Is that understood?"

"Yes, Lady."

"My men will escort you to Pulhoue. Tell your master that he is to meet me on the headland at Wethermeloc this mid-afternoon. He is to come with one man for his protection, as shall I. I will allow him free passage along the shore road, or he may come in one boat but without archers; that's if he has anyone left to crew a boat." Ealdgith gave a wry smile.

"What if he does not comply, My Lady? What of the hostages?"

The cold in Ealdgith's eyes chilled the prisoner. "They will be sold into slavery in Dyflin, have no doubts." Ealdgith held the prisoner's stare a few moments longer, confident that he had no inclination of her bluff. "Godric. Have two sections escort these men close to Pulhoue, then ensure they watch the track and give warning if de Kiberen tries any tricks. We need to prepare for this afternoon."

*****

Four svanmeyjas grounded on the long shingle beach that fronted the Wethermeloc headland, whilst two more stood off in the middle of the lake. No other boats were visible. Ealdgith stepped over the gunwale of her boat, accompanied by Hati, as Godric, Gytha and Ada followed from their respective vessels.

"It looks like he's coming on horseback, if he's coming at all." Ealdgith gestured towards the empty lake to their north.

"I'll check." Godric waved towards the trees at the edge of the open headland, then tapped his helmet with his right hand. Moments later, Osric's pony broke clear of the wood and trotted over. Osric halted with a brief salute to Ealdgith.

"My Lady, Master, he's coming. Wulf sent word back that he has been seen on the track, and there's just the one man-at-arms with him. I'll stay out of sight with the hostages and will bring them as arranged."

They turned at the sound of a low whistle from the woods.

"That means they've just left the track for the headland." Osric reassured Ealdgith as he wheeled his pony and cantered back to the woods.

"We should stay in the middle of the headland to reassure them that we are alone." Godric advised, then added, nodding towards the trees, "That's them now."

Ealdgith waited, standing with Gytha to her right, Ada to her left and Godric behind. The two hounds lay at heel.

Felix de Kiberen rode cautiously across the headland, halted twenty paces away, dismounted, then strode towards Ealdgith. His escort followed suit. They stopped a pace away from the group.

De Kiberen spoke with a frosty haughtiness. "I understood that we were to have one man apiece, not a war band."

Ealdgith laughed spontaneously in reply. "What? I'm impressed that you think my daughter, my maid and my dogs are that frightening. I thought that you Normans so disparaged the value of women that we count for nothing."

De Kiberen snorted, then said, "I've a score to settle after my sojourn in what passes for a castle at Carleol. I won't be tricked by you, or your husband, again. Where is he? Why isn't he here to speak for his lands?"

Ealdgith sensed the women by her side tense, but ignored the jibe. "You've only yourself to blame, de Kiberen. You volunteered all that information about Count Alan's invasion plans yourself, helpful though it was. As to Hravn, he is here in spirit, all around us." Ealdgith hesitated and bit the inside of her cheek in an attempt to quell her rising emotion. "I thought a man of your intelligence would have known that Hravn was killed in late lencten, whilst harrying the Count's invasion of our lands."

"What?" The Bretton's surprise was genuine as Ealdgith had known it would be. "Then who has been attacking the Count's convoys all sumor?"

Ealdgith shrugged. "I wouldn't know, for you have been attacking me. I would say that you Frenchmen, be it Norman or Bretton, have a penchant for making enemies. I do know that you have not been attacked from what were my husband's lands, for these were gifted to our daughter and her husband, Lord William of Kircabi Kendala. His family is joined by marriage with that of Count Ivo de Taillebois, so you dabble in my affairs at your peril. The lands here are mine by right. On whose authority have you been trying to seize them?"

"Count Alan has given me leave to seize the lands of those who have betrayed him."

Ealdgith felt her emotions freeze. "Has he? Then I would be within my rights to kill those who are his agents. Mayhap I should seize you and sell you to Dyflin slavers alongside the hostages. They would demand a high ransom for you from the Count, would they not?"

De Kiberen bristled with anger. "Bitch!" He raised his right arm and was about to slap Ealdgith across the face when he staggered backwards, gasping as a slim dagger sliced through the edge of his bicep. Godric, forewarned by Ada's twitching fingers, drew his sword just as she flung the dagger under-arm. His twitching sword tip was sufficient to stop the Bretton man-at-arms from moving to protect his master.

Ealdgith frowned at the knight as he slowly stood upright, blood oozing through the fingers grasping his wound. "Think on, de Kiberen. My maid is also my huscarle and has many a good reason to kill any Norman, as do we all. Let me remind you that your Count's men slew my family and seized our lands to build his castle at Richemund. Don't talk to me of betrayal. Go now and tell Count Alan that unless he leaves all the lands south of the Eamont and west of the Eden alone, he will he answerable through Count Ivo to Lord William. That includes leaving my vills of Dacor, Bartun and Pulhoue. The life of any Norman seen on the lakeshore tracks will be immediately forfeit. Oh, and I will continue to hold your men hostage until you prove your good will. My threat of their sale to the Dyflin slavers was not idle. Remember, if anyone raises their hands against my people we will strike them off. Man, or woman, we will all fight."

Chapter 20

"I still can't believe I missed it! After all the planning and the training, then Ulf and I miss it." Bear kicked a rotting tree stump dejectedly whilst watching the lake from the promontory.

Godric laughed and patted him on the back consolingly. 'Well, it just proves how good all that planning and training was, we barely missed you. I bet de Kiberen's arse is still smarting."

"His shoulder too, thanks to Ada, so I hear. Though he doesn't appear to have heeded Moder's words. From what Gytha has just reported, nothing has changed at Pulhoue."

"Aye, their archers are still taking a shot at any of her boats that come too close," Godric agreed, "and from what you saw at Bartun, de Kiberen has established himself there. I'm surprised that he can command so many men-at-arms."

"Mmm, he certainly has more clout with the Count than we thought when we took him prisoner and sent him to Carleol. I can see why he seems bitter. We've humiliated him whenever he's showed his face." Bear kicked the stump again, sending a flake of sodden bark over the edge, onto the rocks below. "I can see another fight coming before we settle this. I wonder if we should reinforce Gytha at Haugr-tun? It's the only route he hasn't tried."

"Aye, mayhap." Godric didn't sound convinced. "If we did have sections there, we would struggle to move them in time if he came along the north shore again. I'd keep them here if I were you."

Bear's thumb nail rasped the stubble at the base of his beard. He wasn't convinced either way. "At least we should ride over there and take another look at our defences on the hause. I'm worried about Ulf too. It's over three weeks since he left. It'll be Winterfylleth soon and the nights will start to close in."

Gytha turned to Leofric whilst watching Bear and his men on ponies ascending towards Boredale Hause. "I'm glad they trained the villagers. I agree with Bear; if de Kiberen is going to try again it has to be soon and I think it may well be through here. It's the only route he hasn't tried to force."

Leofric was quick to agree. "I was thinking the same. We could keep a svanmeyja in Pulhoue bay during daylight, swapping them during the day, and another two sections in ambush on the track for a full day and night at a time. That way we'll know if they start to gather for an attack. They can get warning back to us so that we can then send to Bear, and hinder any initial move on the south track."

Gytha threw him a quick smile, "Yes, we saw how our first ambush on the north track slowed them. My guess is that they will try to catch us out by moving as quickly as they can at first light, but they'll be more cautious if they know there is a likelihood of ambush. I told Bear that we would light a single beacon on Hallin if they are sighted on the north track and two beacons if they are on the south track. That way, Bear will know how to react. He said that he could have men here inside of two hours."

Squeezing Gytha's hand quickly, Leofric said, "No time to waste then. I'll tell Owst to get his sections ready to start the boat watch, and Gufa to move his two sections down to the hill north of Sharrow. The track enters the wood and is forced close to the water's edge there. It's ideal for a quick ambush and escape by boat, and they can post a couple of men on the hill to watch the open ground between there and Pulhoue."

Gytha's green men settled into a steady routine. Nothing happened for three days, but on the fourth, Neven returned from the midday change-over with news that mounted men had been seen by the lakeside at

Pulhoue. "A dozen, at least. I warned Kali on my way back up the lake" She reported to Gytha.

"You did right." Gytha thanked her. "Get some food, then I'll see you back here with Gufa."

Gytha waited for the men lounging on the dry earth in front of her to settle down. Leofric and Neven stood beside her. Gytha leaned on her spear in the manner of her father, but she had not gone to the bother of making a model. Their battle plan was simple and known to all there. This was the first time that she had really studied the men of Haugr-tun and was struck by their mix of ages, with more than a few grey and balding heads amongst them. She saw, too, how they all had the hardened wiry physique of those bred to a hard life on the fells, and that they had the strength and determination to stand their ground. The men watched her closely. Most had initially, and instinctively, questioned her authority and competence to lead anyone in a fight: what could a woman barely out of girlhood know? But the last three months had taught them otherwise. Most of the men of Haugr-tun respected Gytha as much as her own slingers and archers.

Background chatter stopped as she spoke. "Neven reports that men-at-arms are mustering in Pulhoue again." Gytha pointed to her friend, wanting to emphasise the value of women within her war band. "It is obvious that they took little heed of their humiliation on the lake and that they will make yet another attempt to seize our lands and force us into servitude." She paused, letting the meaning of her words strike home. They knew that their liberty was at stake. "I am sure, as is my brother, Lord Æsc, that this time they will try and force their way through here. If they can take Haugr-tun they will, in time, be able to take Patrichesdale from behind. But they won't, will they?" Gytha paused; a hint of a smile played on her lips as her cold green eyes looked from face to face inviting a response.

Neven took her cue. "No, my Lady," The men followed with a unanimous response. Then one spoke. He was older than the others.

"Lady, I respect your authority, but if Lord Æsc believes the attack will come through here, why isn't he with us? He built the defences and knows where the secret paths run."

Gytha was unperturbed. "Mayhap you forget that I too helped build the defences. We think the Normans will attack here next, but we can't be certain. If we hold all our men here we leave the north side of the lake open to them. By holding our men at Patrichesdale, Lord Æsc can respond quickly to wherever I detect the attack is coming from." The man nodded.

Gytha banged the butt of her spear against the dry floor of the barn and caused a small cloud of dust to spiral and hang in the still air. "Good! They won't pass because we all know what we have to do. I want everyone, I mean everyone," she tapped the butt again, "to be up on the hause behind the crags and the stone walls as soon as we get warning. No one is to be left in the vill to be taken hostage. Is that understood?"

The men of the vill nodded, surprised and impressed by Gytha's authority.

"All of you must put everything into our defence: throwing rocks, heaving boulders, bringing ammunition forward, preparing food and...tending to any who are wounded." She paused again.

"My brother will be here within two hours of the attack, three at the most. Our job is to hold until then. My men will keep guard day and night. As soon as they hear the warning horn they will light the beacon on the summit of Hallin. That is your cue to rouse everyone and get them into position." Gytha smiled. "Any further questions?"

*****

Although the smoke that hung above Hallin merged into low grey clouds, it was visible from all around the lakeshore.

"Here they come!" Leofric's voice carried clearly in the still, early-morning air. Warned just before dawn, the villagers had reacted as Gytha had ordered. Leofric stood overlooking the top of the track that wound its way up the hause. He commanded Gufa's section and half the village men. Gytha commanded the left flank from the opposite side of the track, with Kali's section and the rest of the village men. Owst and most of the vill's women blocked the head of the track. Kali lounged with his back against a crag face, his chest heaving for breath. His men had rowed frantically, having ambushed the leading Normans, and had only just got into position.

"The bastards must be keen to come up the track quickly in the half light. I thought our ambush might have slowed them up."

"It's no matter." Gytha reassured him. "You gave us warning and returned in time, that's all that counts."

The first riders halted in the centre of the cluster of houses and, remaining mounted, banged on doors with spear butts. Realising that the vill was deserted, and casting around for evidence of where the villagers had fled, they caught sight of the motley clothing of people half hidden in the crags above Haugr-tun.

Gytha heard a shouted order that caused six men-at-arms to ride forward, dismount, and form into an extended line to make their way up the lower slope of the hause. The remaining dozen or so riders observed from their mounts. One man stumbled, then another. "Hah! The boulders under the bracken. Let's see." She whispered to herself. Seconds later two men popped forward from the cover of low rocks and hurled rocks at the stranded men-at-arms. Their shouts of annoyance floated up the valley, followed by howls of derision from the villagers on the fellside. The men retreated clumsily, stumbling as they tried to protect their bodies with their shields.

Two mounted men-at-arms rode forward, following the track as it wound up the hillside. As they rounded the first bend they stopped, their way blocked by a swath of boulders. They dismounted to lead their mounts across or around the piles of rocks, but their horses could not move without stumbling. Frustrated, and annoyed by rocks beginning to land around them, they remounted and retreated down the slope. Having been thwarted on horseback, all of the riders hobbled their mounts and advanced up the track on foot. Gytha waited, watching them labour up the increasingly steep track, weighed down by their mail and padded under-jerkins.

Every few moments men burst from cover, ran forward, and hurled rocks at the men-at-arms below, before retreating up the fellside. Most of the rocks missed or were deflected by shields, but each attack needled and hampered the Normans. Curses echoed from the valley sides as tempers frayed. Gytha continued to wait, with one eye on Leofric across the little valley, whilst the men caught in the midst of the lower boulder field picked their way across to the track. Then, whoever was in charge of the main body came to a decision and the men-at-arms spread out and began clambering up the slope towards her, and the score of men alongside her.

"Stand by!" Gytha cautioned them and raised her arm to alert Leofric.

On her signal, men on both sides of the valley flung rocks upon the Normans below. Kali moved through the defenders, urging them to work as a group, and to distract the men below with showers of rocks before rolling larger boulders down towards them. These moved slowly at first, then gathered speed and momentum, clattering and bouncing before smashing onto and over the track. Two men-at-arms were bowled over. Another fell, his body battered. The remainder took flight and retreated down the track in disarray. Curses gave way to jeers and ribald laughter.

Kali patted a couple of his men on the back, then grinned over his shoulder towards Gytha. "Well, that's slowed them."

"But not for long. Look, they're stripping off their mail. Get your archers forward along the slope, then wait for my word." Gytha waved to attract Leofric's attention then yelled loudly, pointing at the Normans. "Archers, now!"

Leofric acknowledged, sending four of Gufa's men forward, into effective range. As soon as they were in position Gytha gave two short blasts of her horn.

The half-dressed Normans looked up, then realised their folly as steel tipped arrows first soared and then plummeted towards them. A few grabbed shields and managed to cower under them. Others, caught ill prepared, staggered and stumbled further down the hill, to take cover behind the lower crags. One lay still.

"That, slowed them." Gytha laughed across to Kali.

As the would-be attackers regrouped below the steep hause, Gytha could tell from their posturing that there was debate about what to do next. Realising that she was holding her breath, willing them to delay further and hoping that Bear would arrive soon, she spoke to Kali to reassure herself. "We've given them a quandary. They've lost the advantage of their horses and their armour. Swords, spears and shields are all they have left."

"Aye," Kali answered wryly, "precious few of which we have."

"Yes, but they have to get past slingshots and arrows to make them count. We still have our pieces on the tafl board" Gytha tried to sound confident.

"They've decided upon something, look!" Kali nodded towards the Normans, "They're splitting up."

"Damn!" Gytha cursed under her breath. A small group had detached itself and was running towards the lake. She gave a quick blast on her horn to attract Leofric's attention and then shouted loudly, her voice just about carrying across the valley. "They are cutting around behind us. I'm taking Owst's section. Take charge here." Turning briefly to Kali, she added. "You know what to do. Just don't let them get further up the track than before. Stop them getting near the women blocking the top." Then she ran with Loki at her heels, calling for Owst to follow.

They ran over the shoulder of Hallin, knowing that if the Normans found the gap in the crags on the north slope of the fell, they could clamber up through Hag Wood and attack them from behind.

Gytha spoke breathlessly to Owst as they ran. "They could come up almost anywhere. We'll spread out as we drop down the fellside, you on the left, me on the right and the others in between. We'll regroup once someone shouts that they have found them." Owst nodded, panting, and fell back to organise his section.

The slope steepened and Gytha moved off to her right, slowing her pace on the rough slippery ground above the edge of the trees. She could see the lake below but nothing of the men-at-arms. Slipping as she dropped down past a rocky outcrop, she grabbed the trunk of a young alder to steady herself, and spun around as she stopped. Her heart jumped with shock.

A man-at-arms, without his mail but with a shield slung over his back and his sword drawn, stood at the base of the rocks. Gytha cursed as she realised that he had heard her. She moved her right hand to the hilt of the dagger at her waist, and then froze. The man's expression chilled her. The look in his eyes was more than just physical aggression; she knew instinctively what he wanted from her.

Gytha felt suddenly sick and unable to breathe or call out. He edged towards her and started to grin. Loki's low growl broke the silence and provided the prod she needed to react. No longer transfixed, she drew the dagger.

"My hound's not eaten today. Mayhap he'll break his fast on your balls." Gytha spoke with a cold confidence that belied her dread.

The man paused, surprised. "How come you speak Breton?"

Gytha spat. "Breton be damned! I'm Cumbric." The action bolstered her confidence a little more. This was a situation her mother had prepared her for, and for which she had trained. Her gaze swept over the man, registering how he stood and the ground around him, and then focused on his eyes. In doing so, she drew his attention to her face and away from her body. She knew that she must use his weight and aggression against him. Tall, powerful and with heavy shoulders, the man stood with his legs apart, one braced against the base of the crag and the other lower down. She could tell that he was keeping his balance by leaning back slightly.

"Heel, Loki!" Gytha cautioned under her breath. If Loki moved towards the man, he wouldn't hesitate to slash out and, in all likelihood, disembowel the hound.

The man moved quickly. As he switched his sword to his left hand, Gytha realised that he intended to grab her with his right and pull her against the crag. She cursed her long hair that she had left braided and hanging down her back; why hadn't she tucked it under her jerkin?

The man spoke with a smile that sickened Gytha. "If I take you, and you please me, mayhap you'll live. Come closer." But she saw how his arrogance opened the way for her.

"Mayhap I will." Gytha took a half pace up the hill with her left foot. This brought her closer, but also gave her a firm stance from which to move quickly. She goaded the man; waving the fingers of her left hand invitingly whilst forcing a faint smile. "You have to come to me too."

She held his gaze whilst he edged his left foot forward. "Now!" a voice in her head screamed at her.

Gytha sprang, cat-like, through the gap between the man's legs, turned onto her back and stabbed upwards as she moved.

The man's sudden scream of rage, then pain, was cut off by a metallic thud. His knees buckled and he toppled forwards slowly, before dropping heavily down the slope. Loki pounced on top of the body, worrying with his fangs, until Gytha called him off lest he develop a taste for human blood. She stood up, braced her shoulders and shook her head to try and clear the shock and raw emotions within her; surprising herself by wondering if the man had felt pain in his groin before he fell. She turned, startled by a friendly laugh behind her.

"I had to let that play out, I couldn't get a clear sling-shot at the bastard until you moved. But you were remarkable."

"Neven! That's why he collapsed so suddenly!" Gytha exclaimed, then rushed to hug her friend.

"Come, the battle's over." Neven said, slowly releasing Gytha from her hug. "The rest of those we were after ran into Bear and his men. He's on top of the fell."

Gytha clambered frantically up the fellside, grabbing handfuls of grass and bracken to pull herself up more quickly, desperate to join her brother and Leofric. As she got to the top Leofric was striding up towards her. Lower down, Bear was leading his men on their ponies through the hidden pathways they had left in the boulder fields. Then, with a surge of pure joy, she saw a one-armed giant on a black pony. Ulf! His shouted orders drifted up to her. "Put the skittas in with the swine. Strip them of mail and weapons first though. We don't want them harming the pigs."

It wasn't so much the warmth of Leofric's embrace, nor his kiss, but the words he spoke next that brought a smile to Gytha's face and tears to her eyes. "We've beaten them, Gytha. Ulf's brought word that Lord Ketel is riding to Bartun with his own men, intent on reclaiming the vill. It is his now, or rather it belongs to William and Aebbe. Agnaar is on his way to tell your moder. She is to join us here."

Chapter 21

Agnaar clenched his jaw and focused on the back of the man in front. Every one of his pony's jolting steps sent pain shooting up the back of his leg. He willed time to pass, but didn't dare to look at the sun again. The last time he had, it had barely moved and was still well below its zenith.

"Whoa!" He heard Ulf shout from the head of the column and slowed to a halt. At least the rest brought temporary relief. Moments later Ulf rode up alongside him and pointed into the valley below.

"It looks like there's strife in Haugr-tun, son. I knew when I saw the smoke from the beacon that something was amiss somewhere. It looks as if people on the hause are keeping men-at-arms at bay. There's no sign of ponies, so I doubt Bear has managed to get there yet, but Gytha and Leo may have made it."

Agnaar knew Ulf had a duty to respond to whatever was happening, particularly if there was a good chance Leofric was involved. "You go, Fader. I'll get to Patrichesdale, and get the news to Edie." He forced a smile, "Just leave a couple of good lads to help."

Ulf leant across and patted him on the shoulder. "Keep Ewen and Wemba. Follow the ridge round the valley head, drop down into Martindale and then head over the back of Beda to Boredale. You'll be home before midday."

Agnaar watched with a pang of regret whilst Ulf led ten green-clad men steadily down and across the fellside, their spear tips glinting. He had a nagging sense that his injured foot might never recover sufficiently for him to ride to battle again.

Fixing a false grin on his face, he forced himself to take the lead and urged his pony on. The battle below added a new urgency to their journey.

*****

Adelind stood in the porch looking dejectedly towards Place Fell. Tattered cloud hanging in grey shrouds over the upper slopes matched the gloom of her mood. Agnaar had been gone for months, her father for weeks, and now Bear had rushed off to battle once again. She felt alone, dejected and with no purpose. Eir was finding fulfilment as their healing women and as a wife, young Gytha was sharing her mother's place as a warrior leader; but what could she offer? She doubted Agnaar would ever return, and feared that whatever fate had befallen him had now overtaken her father.

Sudden movement on the track below caught her attention. Two, no three green-clad men on ponies were riding towards the hall. She felt nauseous with worry. If these were Bear's men, where were the rest of them? As the riders left the wood and came into clear view, Adelind felt faint and gripped a post momentarily. It was Agnaar! But why were the men helping him from the saddle?

Adelind lifted her skirts and ran, heedless of the soft mud under her feet. She stopped, frozen, seeing the pain-fighting set of Agnaar's jaw whilst he rested his weight on his spear butt.

"I'm sorry, my love. I should have come back to you sooner, then I couldn't come at all." Adelind saw moisture in Agnaar's eyes as he spoke.

Longing to hug, but fearful of hurting him, Adelind placed her arm around Agnaar's waist. "Come, lean on me and we'll go in together." She could feel the tension in Agnaar's body.

As he walked Agnaar talked through clenched teeth. "Ulf is well, I know you want to ask. As is Bear, whom I met on my way. But I must speak to Edie urgently. Where is she?"

"She's at the hall at Glynrhedyn, but we can call her after you're settled."

"No! This can't wait." Agnaar looked around, his face haunted by the need to convey Ulf's message. "Ewen, ride there now. I must speak to Lady Ealdgith before I do anything more. Bring her here, please." As Ewen mounted and urged his horse into a gallop, Adelind led Agnaar into the hall and felt some of the tension ebb from within both of them.

Ealdgith's annoyance about Agnaar's late return passed as soon as she saw the state of his foot and his obvious pain. She said little as he blurted out the need for her to ride to Haugr-tun, and of Ketel's intention to confront the Normans at Bartun the next day.

She bent down and touched him gently on the shoulder. "You've done well, Agnaar. I can't say that I wasn't displeased when you failed to return as promised, but I can now see why, and your actions on the east fellside doubtless helped us this past sumor."

Standing, and turning to Ada, Ealdgith said, "Find Godric, Eir and Wealmaer. The four of us will ride to Haugr-tun now. Eir may need to attend to wounded, and I want Wealmaer to secure the north shore track and wait for me to contact him at Wethermeloc."

Ada looked surprised, "Surely you want all our men at Haugr-tun. That's where the Normans are."

Ealdgith shook her head. "No. That's where we know some of them are. We've fought too many battles to risk stumbling at the last hurdle. I have to be confident that they can't attack here whilst we are away. Wealmaer can ensure that."

*****

Men from the vill were retrieving stones and boulders from the track down the hause as Ealdgith rode by. Seeing Bear and Ulf standing at the edge of the vill, she spurred her horse forward to join them.

"I've got Agnaar's message," she said, as she dismounted, "and before you ask, Ulf, he's being clucked over by Adelind. I doubt she'll let him out of her sight again. She hasn't looked so happy for months."

"It's what he needs. The lad did well but he's been in a lot of pain for weeks now and is still racked by guilt over the loss of his men, though that was more the Norns' doing than his." Ulf sounded relieved.

Ealdgith caught sight of Gytha behind Bear and noticed with concern that she looked wan and withdrawn. "Ulf, gather all our commanders, I want to talk through what we must do next. Pieces are falling into place on the board, and I want to finish the game. Gytha, I can see we have something to talk about. Come, we'll walk down to the lake. Do you want Leo to come too?" Gytha gave a smile of gratitude whilst shaking her head.

Ealdgith took her daughter's hand as they walked towards the lake. Gytha talked whilst they walked, she felt it was easier that way. "I killed a Norman this morning, but that isn't what's upsetting me. It was the other thing that you warned me could happen one day. He didn't want to kill me, not straight away. He wanted..."

Ealdgith stopped and pulled Gytha to her, hugging her closely. "I know, I know. There's a side to men, some men, that you've been sheltered from until now. But you know you can protect yourself whereas other women can't."

Gytha gave a low sob. "It was the way he looked at me. I had to play up to him at first. I felt ashamed at what I was doing, but I needed him to move towards me before I could fight him."

Ealdgith released Gytha, then wiped a tear from her cheek. "It doesn't shame you, my love. It shows your strength. You didn't freeze in fright, you fought and you used what skill and cunning you had. I'm proud of you and your fader would be too...just as Leo will be. Talk to him. He'll understand."

*****

"Can you see any sign of life, Leo?" Gytha called to Leofric whilst she and Neven rowed Brynhildr towards the shore at the end of Pulhoue Bay.

Leofric, squatting in the bows, turned and spoke softly, "No, but keep your voices low in case there is. Take us right into the shore and I'll go and check the house they seem to use." He jumped over the gunwale as the bow touched the beach, and ran to the side of the house.

The girls back watered a couple of strokes clear of the shore and turned Brynhildr, in case they needed to make a quick escape, whilst watching Leofric. "He's gone inside," Gytha spoke quietly.

"Now he's out the back and running to the next." Neven replied.

Leofric returned moments later, splashed up to the boat and vaulted in. "They've been gone a while," he panted, "the hearths are cold and there's no sign of horses either."

"Good." Gytha looked at them both conspiratorially. "Although Moder's orders were for Wealmaer to take Pulhoue first thing in the morning, he could get established here this evening and be ready for when Moder and Bear ride in tomorrow."

"I agree, Gytha. With this breeze, we can sail back to Wealmaer at Wethermeloc in a matter of minutes, get him moving, then cut across to Haugr-tun and tell Edie of the change." Leofric was enthusiastic, as was Neven.

"You're right, but we will have to row back down here afterwards. I think we need to be on hand just in case Wealmaer has a problem and we have to get word back." Both Neven and Leofric were keen to keep close to Gytha and to keep her busy, sensing that the morning's incident still nagged at her.

Gytha grinned at the pair. Her eyes were alight with excitement. "Yes, the more I think about it, Pulhoue is key to Moder's march on Bartun. If we hold Pulhoue we know that both lakeshore tracks are clear of Normans. She can ride without worry in the morning whilst our section leaders bring the svanmeyjas down the lake. Come on, let's get the sail up."

*****

Dusk's red glow had long faded by the time they returned to Pulhoue, and the three rowers were thankful for the glow of Wealmaer's hearth fires to guide them down the lake. Ealdgith, appreciating the logic of Gytha's change to her plan, had made a point of praising her in front of her commanders, but had then insisted that Gytha wait until Bear returned from meeting Ketel and William at Askum.

Grateful for food and a place by Wealmaer's hearth, Gytha waited until Wealmaer's section commanders had settled close to her before briefing them.

"Bear has met Ketel and we have a plan for tomorrow. Moder interrogated the prisoners and they were quite open with her. De Kiberen has all his men at Bartun, and there is probably only a score or so fit to fight by now. They take supplies from Dacor, but don't have men there. She got the impression that after all the men de Kiberen has lost, or who have been wounded, he is no longer in the Count's favour. The plan is that Moder will ride at first light and move through here straight to Bartun. Lord Ketel will also ride at first light. He has more than a score of men with him. They have half the distance to ride and will be at Bartun before Moder. If there are any problems there, then Moder's arrival will doubtless sway the balance."

Wealmaer nodded, a relaxed smile on his face as he pictured how the morning's action should play out. "So far, so good. Where do we come into it?"

Gytha continued, enjoying their respect and attention. "All my slingers will be here first thing. We are to work with you and block the way from the ford over the Eamont, along the track to Dacor, and the land either side of the Dacor Beck at Dalman."

"And?" Wealmaer asked as Gytha hesitated, smiling at him.

"It'll be your battle, Wealmaer, if there is one that is. But I was thinking that the slingers could form a series of ambush points, and that your men should be mounted behind them to react quickly. What do you think?"

Wealmaer guffawed loudly. "What I think, Gytha lass, is that you have spent far too much time talking to that cunning master-at-arms, Ulf. Of course it will work and, by the way, you're now every bit our captain, second only to Bear and your moder. It's your battle, not mine."

*****

Ealdgith knew that Bartun lay in a hollow, separated from the confluence of the River Eamont with Dacor Beck by a long low hill. She kept the Eamont to her left as she led her war band around the side of the hill, and ordered them into line abreast before cresting the broad summit.

She smiled thinly at what she saw. Two lines of mounted men faced each other a couple of furlongs away at the far side of the vill. Bear sidled his pony towards Ealdgith who spoke as he approached. "It looks like a stand-off. Ketel's men are those furthest away, and it looks as if William is in the centre of their line; and that must be Ketel close to the Norman line."

"Aye, and he is vulnerable there. De Kiberen could take him prisoner if he was of a mind." Bear saw immediately that Ketel had allowed himself to be drawn far too close to the Normans. "I doubt they have men on watch, all will be in that line, but if any turn and see us it could provoke them to snatch Ketel."

Ealdgith sighed, cursing Ketel's lack of battle experience. "You're right. Have the men fall back and lead them around the south side of the hill, keeping in dead ground. Go through the vill on foot and get into crossbow range of the Norman line."

Bear nodded, understanding. "What about you?"

"I'll take Godric and Ada, go around by the north and ride up past the edge of Ketel's line." She gave a low laugh. "De Kiberen thinks he has a score to settle with Ada. He'll recognise us and let us come close."

They backed-up quietly and then moved quickly. Ealdgith used the cover of Ketel's men to move up behind them. She observed the vill closely, watching Bear's men move cautiously into concealed positions close behind the Normans. Satisfied that they were in place, she led Godric and Ada at a canter past Ketel's men and halted a dozen paces short of de Kiberen. Her mail caught the low sun and glistened in a medley of gold and copper hues, drawing the immediate attention of all. Her sword was already drawn.

"I'm sorry to interrupt, de Kiberen, but I sense that Lord Ketel's instructions to you are being ignored." Ealdgith spoke loudly, ensuring that de Kiberen's men could hear and understand.

"Ah! Lady Ealdgith and her maid." De Kiberen spoke with a deliberate arrogance designed to irk Ealdgith and prompt her fiery housecarl into a rash move. "How pleasant to meet yet again. I was just telling Lord Ketel that he is welcome to this paltry vill of his, but that my interest in your lake is far from finished. I was just informing him that by coming so close to my line, he has little choice but to accept my terms, lest I take him prisoner."

Ealdgith gave a loud derisory laugh. "Really? You are a fool, de Kiberen. Do you not think that Lord Ketel and I had planned our move beforehand? You are the last piece standing in this game of Hnefatafl, and we are about to remove you from the board."

De Kiberen bristled angrily and took a deep breath, about to speak.

Ealdgith stayed him, holding up her hand with a seductive smile. "I suggest you look behind you before you speak. Everyone of your men is marked by a crossbow. I assure you that at this range they will not miss." She watched her warning register on the faces of the Norman men-at-arms.

As her words sank in, she gestured that Ketel should move back towards her.

"How many men have you lost? A score, two score, more? Is that a price that Count Alan is prepared to pay?" Ealdgith saw pure anger flash across de Kiberen's face. She goaded him further.

"Or mayhap you haven't told him yet? I suggest you do, though you would be right to be fearful. I met him once, you know. Quite charming as I recall, but dismissive of fools."

Ealdgith saw a ripple of smiles on the faces behind de Kiberen. "I would hate to see more of your men die needlessly, and I have no intention that they should. Unless of course you provoke me. Do you undertake to leave my lands and those of Lord Ketel and our joint families'?" Ealdgith raised an eyebrow in a very theatrical expression.

De Kiberen hesitated, then nodded curtly.

"Good." Ealdgith smiled pleasantly. "Now, be so kind as to unsheathe your sword and hand it, hilt first, to the lady you so deliberately called my maid."

De Kiberen complied slowly as Ada rode up to him, her eyes fixed coldly on his.

"I won't humiliate you further. Lord Ketel and I have drawn up a short charter for you to sign. There are four copies: one for you, one for me, one for Lord Ketel and one for Count Ivo de Taillebois. Just in case you conveniently lose your copy, there will be plenty for other interested parties to present to your overlord. Oh, and if you are wondering who the scribe was, it was me. Do please always remember that English women can be every bit as accomplished as Normans, if not more so."

Ealdgith turned her head and spoke to Godric. "Please find us a table to write upon. Once our good Norman knight has given us his written promise to leave all these lands and never return, he will be free to depart along with his men." Ealdgith switched her attention back to de Kiberen. "I have brought those of your men who are my prisoners. They are free to leave too. Though your sword, de Kiberen, will remain with my lady huscarle as proof of your word."

Aere Yule

Chapter 22

"Ugh! I wish this weather would lift. We've had cloud down to The Dodd for the past week and constant drizzle. Why can't we have some decent cold and snow? At least it might be sunny." Gytha grumbled whilst shaking drips from her cloak. "Ulf's just coming too. I saw him stomping up the track."

"Hah! Don't let him catch you saying that he stomps." Ealdgith laughed, chiding her daughter. Then added, as the door re-opened. "Ah, Ulf. I have a seat for you here by the hearth fire, and some mulled ale. Don't bother chuntering about the weather. Gytha's already done that, again."

Ealdgith began the meeting. "Before we discuss Yuletide plans, not that I feel like celebrating without Hravn, I want to run over what Bear and I have done since banishing de Kiberen. As you know, I've just been to see Aebbe and William at Kendala. All are well and, as you would expect, little Gunilda is now walking and beginning to chatter as much as her mother. I met Lord Ketel too, and he assured me that Count Alan is no longer a threat. However, the news is mixed. Ketel's fader-in-law, Ivo de Taillebois, has, as I suspected he might, been granted the lands of the upper Eden by the King."

"Huh! So much for returning the land to the Scots' king." Bear blurted sarcastically.

"Indeed." Ealdgith continued, ignoring her son's interruption. "What should concern us is that Count Ivo intends increasing the size of the settlements on those lands by moving in people from his other lands in Lincolia-scir. Ketel assumes that they will be brought as soon as possible after Winter, possibly in Sōlmōnath if the weather permits, so that they can start working the land in Hrēðmonath."

"Phoor!" Ulf blew through his cheeks. "The poor bastards. What's more, it means that Count Ivo intends working the land and the people hard for his own profit."

"My uncle always said he could be brutal. This just proves it. Ketel is determined not to follow suit, as is William, but in time I'm sure the King will demand equivalent returns in tax from them. It's as well that we can look to our own defences and have lead of our own to sell. Now, Bear, do you have better news from your trip to Rengles?"

"It went well, Moder. Aedan gave us a good price for the little lead that we smelted over the sumor, and I brought back all the grain he was holding for us. Mungo says we should be good until well into lencten. What came as a surprise, and a very pleasant one, was news from Aedan's wife's fader, the Jarl of Garth. Having discovered that Moder and he are cousins of a sort, and hearing from Aedan about our problems with the Normans, he has offered us sanctuary on Mann should we need it. He gave me his ring and seal for Moder as a token of friendship between our families. I promised to return with a token from us. Quite what that should be, is for you to decide Moder." Bear paused, his face bursting into a large grin. "There's one more thing. Eir has just this morning told me...she is with child. Mayhap we do have something to celebrate at Yuletide."

The hall, as it exploded into a cacophony of congratulations, was stilled by a loud rap on the door. It was pushed open by two bedraggled men.

"Grimr! What a surprise! What's happened?" Bear jumped up, his hand outstretched to greet the Ameleseta publican.

"Lord, Lady," Grimr turned quickly to Ealdgith, "This is Hákon. He has a message from Jarl Buthar for Lady Ealdgith."

Those around the hearth stood instinctively and welcomed the strangers to a place by the fire whilst Ealdgith ordered more mulled ale.

Hákon spoke quickly. "My message has an urgency, My Lady, because the days are short and the high fell passes could close if the weather turns to snow."

Ealdgith was intrigued and motioned for Hákon to continue," Please..."

"My master, Jarl Buthar, has heard of your fight with the Normans and offers you his support. He understands that it would be as difficult for you to leave your lands as it would be for him to leave his, but he would like to meet with your Captain before the snows come. He says there is an urgency and that it is to our mutual benefit. He says too that Gytha of the Lake should come too, whoever that person may be?"

Gytha gasped, and Ulf chortled. "You're a Valkyrie indeed, lass. If a Norse Jarl summons you to his hall it can only be because you have a reputation for valour. Though only the gods know why." He laughed again.

Gytha blushed. Ealdgith's expression changed from consternation to amusement.

"My son, Æsc, though we know him as Bear, is my captain. He will return with you. Gytha though, is my daughter. I can see why she is 'of the Lake', for it was her boats that fought the Normans on the lake, but how did Jarl Buthar hear of her?"

Hákon's face remained grave despite the levity that permeated the hall. "That is for the Jarl to say, my Lady. He has many who spy for him. That is one reason our lands have been so secure and have never yet been troubled by the Normans. If I may speak frankly, it is because we have never been troubled by the Normans that we have little experience of fighting. The Jarl has heard what you have achieved here and in the vale of the Eden. It is your experience of fighting that is of value to him, and of using boats to fight from."

Bear seized the moment. This was his chance to secure the Jarl as an ally. "I understand, Hákon. I will be ready to return with you tomorrow, as will Gytha. I will ready two sections of my men to escort us."

Hákon cleared his throat nervously. "Ahem, no Lord. One of our strengths is that very few know where our lands lie. The Jarl will show only the most trusted of men the routes to his valley. You may bring a huscarle, but that is all."

Ealdgith spoke quickly, looking at Ada. "In which case Gytha must take hers too."

Gytha pre-empted Ealdgith's command. "Neven will come with me. After all, my battles are her battles and we have fought together all sumor."

"Very well." Ealdgith agreed after a pause. "See Cenhelm. If Neven is to serve you, she must be dressed and equipped appropriately."

*****

Bear rode alongside Hákon, Gytha and Neven followed, whilst Wealmaer brought up the rear. Neven had been surprised, and initially a little over-awed, by her new-found status: it meant leaving her own family who had struggled during the sumor to cope without her and Duwe. Her doubts had been as momentary as had her doubts about Gytha when they first met, and she was delighted with the clothes that Gytha and Cenhelm had provided: Gytha's spare leather breeches, calf length boots, a padded leather jerkin, a thick lanolin-soaked Glynrhedyn Green cloak and a hard leather helmet. Cenhelm had been unable to find a light sword, like that used by Gytha, but had given her a long slender dagger and scabbard supported on a leather belt braided with copper thread. Both women were armed with their bows and slingshot. The small war band blended well with the fading greens and browns of the damp vegetation and mossy grey rocks as they rode up the long Glynrhedyn valley.

Hákon had insisted that they leave at first light, saying that if they rode hard they would reach Jarl Buthar's valley by dusk, and adding that they would not want to be benighted on the fells. The ponies panted as they zig-zagged up the steep earthy track from the valley towards the shoulder of Stibarro Dodd and the pass that would lead them down towards Wythburndale.

As they leant forward in their saddles to encourage their ponies, a large night-black raven soared behind them and hovered in the strengthening wind, lifted higher and higher. Carried at last to the base of the looming clouds, it rolled and dived low over their heads, calling with a deep kraa as it passed. The symbolism was not lost on Gytha. She glanced back at her friend who had seen it too.

The westerly wind hit them as the ground levelled out. "Thank the gods it's blowy, it'll keep the mist clear of the tops. I suggest we quickly make a few cairns as we go. You'll be needing markers to keep you on the right track for your return." Hákon shouted across to Bear. He waved in reply, appreciating that they would all have to improve their fell craft if they were going to be making regular trips over the tops.

Whilst Bear and Wealmaer piled a few larger rocks to form a cairn, Gytha took the opportunity to study the maze of ridges and valleys before them. "Fader brought me here once. It was when he was trying to teach me to see the ground like a bird does. He always said we should think of the ground like the back of our hand, with the fingers as ridges and the gaps as valleys, and remember how they shape and connect. Look, that must be Wythburndale below and Kesewic will be somewhere in a valley to the north."

Neven stared, open-mouthed and over awed. "I've never been this high before. What a fastness! Normans could never find us in there."

They turned as Hákon spoke gruffly behind them. "Your fader was a wise man, Lady Gytha. You won't survive long in the fells without understanding how they lie, and how the weather plays around them. I'll show you more as we ride, but you're right, that is Wythburndale and the route through the valley to Kesewic. It is an ancient way from north of Kesewic to Ameleseta and the big bay to the south, and one the Normans may start to use. That is why the Jarl wants your help. It is only by taking ownership of the land and ambushing and killing those who venture in, that we can keep it as our fastness, as you so rightly call it, Neven."

"Hákon, can you show me our way from here? That really will help me see it as a bird might." Gytha asked.

Hákon's laugh surprised her. "Hah! Aye. Just like yon raven back there. He's prince of the lands hereabouts, under the watchful eye of our eagles. Mayhap you'll see some of them too. Now, we'll follow this spur down to Legburthwaite, cut between the two lakes that you can see in the valley bottom, then we'll go straight over that low fell that's pretty much in line with us and the gap between the lakes. Do you see it?"

Gytha followed the line of Hákon's arm and finger. "Aye, it's to the left of a saddle."

"Good. Beyond that is the little tarn of Watendlath. We can't see it from here; but mind, it is in a wet and boggy bit of land and is not a place to stray about in. We'll go past the tarn, taking our line from that of a steep valley rising up in front of us. We'll drop down into the vill of Rosthwaite, which is in the dale called Borgarárdalr. The dale is named for an old fort on a crag guarding the way in. You'll see it as we pass, but it's a wee bit north of our route. Then we'll follow the beck up the steep valley. It's a back door into our hidden dale."

"Thank you, Hákon, and for your trust." Gytha stared ahead a few moments longer, working out how the rugged grey ridges linked together, and burning the image into her memory. It was something she was to do many times before the day was over.

*****

The sun had already dropped below the mountains on their left by the time they halted at the top of the long steep valley. Awed by the towering cliffs of black crags rising on both sides, they could see that a steep descent followed, beyond which two lakes glimmered through the shadows. "A fastness indeed." Gytha muttered to Neven.

Hákon looked around radiantly. "Welcome to Buthar's mere. My Jarl's hall is on the neck of land between the two lakes. We'll see it soon."

The hall was really a cluster of halls, all built in a similar style and focused on a tall wooden building, erected on a high rocky foundation, and with a steep turf-clad roof that almost touched the ground. The thick roof beam, protruding beyond the ends of the hall, was carved into great dragons' heads just like those at Morlund. Blue wood smoke curled from the roof vents.

"By the gods!" Bear spoke an aside to Wealmaer, "It's even bigger than the hall at Mallerstang."

His mission achieved, Hákon appeared to relax. "Come inside, my Lord will be waiting."

Buthar's hall reeked of wood smoke and the stale sweat of too many bodies. They blinked, trying not to cough whilst their eyes adjusted to the gloom and the atmosphere. Loki growled at the hearth dogs whilst Gytha stroked his raised hackles, calming him.

A sturdy, well-built man strode forward. Though tall, he was still half a head shorter than Bear. "Sir Æsc, welcome." Bear appreciated the honour of a title he hadn't been granted, but suspected it was probably little different to Buthar's own appendage of Jarl.

"Jarl Buthar, the honour is mine. May I introduce my sister, 'Gytha of the Lake'." He chuckled, "for that is, I believe, how you refer to her. Then, our respective huscarles, Wealmaer and Neven." Buthar grasped Bear warmly by the forearm. Bear held the grasp momentarily, trying to read the expression behind the grey eyes and thick blond beard. Buthar was hard to age: late twenties or early forties? Bear guessed the former, assuming that an older man might have been less willing to ask for assistance in training his men.

"Come, eat and drink, then we will talk. I have much to ask of you, and you should be away again on the morrow. My shepherds tell me that this weather will change soon."

Bear formed an immediate bond with the secretive Jarl, who divulged little of his past other than that his people had come from Mann and settled in the then deserted dale some generations ago.

Buthar listened attentively, scrutinising Bear as he did so, whilst Bear talked of his family's past. His parents' raids against the Normans in Ghellinges-scir, their taking of their Eden lands, the debacle of 1080 and then the resistance to the latest Norman invasion.

When Buthar finally spoke, his praise was fulsome. "A warrior family indeed, and one in which the women are as militant as the men."

"Indeed so, Lord Jarl." Gytha interrupted impetuously. "My moder is descended from the English warrior, Queen Aethelreda of the Mercians. Her blood still runs in our veins."

Buthar reacted explosively, striking the broad table with his fist and laughing at all around him. "And there you have it. I knew there had to be a reason I was drawn to stories of 'Gytha of the Lake'. Now regale my warriors with tales of your valour, as any good shield maiden should."

Gytha was speechless, and silent momentarily, whilst she wondered if the Jarl was teasing or taunting her. Bear was silent too. Both decided, in their own way, that Buthar's good-humour was intended to draw Gytha to the attention of his men.

She took her cue and spoke in earnest to the Jarl, describing how her father's foresight had led to the creation of small fast craft with sails from which parties of archers and slingers could quickly set ambushes along the forested lakeside tracks, and then escape without fear of pursuit. He had called them svanmeyjas, named after the Valkyries.

Gradually Gytha became aware of men falling silent and listening. Some looked suspicious, and others appeared doubtful of a young woman's ability, but more seemed enraptured, as if imagining the tales recounted in Valhalla. The women in the hall, standing behind the men, pushed forward agog at what they heard. When she involved Neven in the story about the four-day battle which had slowed the Norman advance and given her mother time to prepare a devastating ambush, in which women stood behind and supported the men, they gasped with open admiration. But it was her description of the boom and how it had blocked the head of the lake to Norman boats, pinning them for destruction by the mangonel and her archers, that prompted Buthar to strike the table again. "Aye, lass, that is what we want. I can see how all this will work. It is just what I need here."

The Jarl turned back to Bear. "Sir Æsc. If you are of a mind, I can see grounds for a close alliance between our people. There is much that you can teach us, for I see a day coming when we must fight to block the Normans from the routes through these valleys. We both know we cannot stand and fight, but we can keep them at bay by bringing them enough sudden death and injury through the use of ambushes alone. A score of well-trained green men, as you call them, will be worth a hundred in a shield wall. And with swift boats, a boom and a mangonel, I can hold the head of this lake for eternity. Only you can teach my people how to do this. In return I can offer you the sanctuary of these valleys, and the empty spaces within them, should a time come when the Normans decide that your lake should be theirs. I fear that the more their presence in the vale of the Eden grows, the more they will put pressure on you, not least to claim access to the lead upon which you rely so heavily. Let us work together to hold this, our homeland, together."

Bear appreciated the prescience of Buthar's warning. He caught Gytha's eyes upon him as she mouthed, 'Count Ivo'.

"I agree, Jarl Buthar. I suggest that Gytha and I return as soon as the passes are clear after the winter snow, and that I bring some of my more experienced commanders with me. I will also bring my master boat builder. I am sure that there are those amongst your men who have the skill to build and sail a svanmeyja after a little instruction. In the meantime, gather ponies and men who can ride well, and identify those who are good at hunting. Gytha and Neven will refine their skills with the bow and sling. Mayhap we will be patrolling these valleys together by next sumor."

Buthar struck the table a third time. "Bring ale and mead. My men will drink to that."

*****

Bear deferred their return by a day and insisted that Buthar show them the lake and the surrounding fells before they departed. It proved to be a close-run thing; the skies had cleared and the wind had shifted to the north east by the time they crested the ridge above Glynrhedyn.

Pausing to let the ponies regain their wind, Gytha asked her brother, "How did Buthar know so much about me? Who do you think informs him?"

Bear responded with a broad smile. "Grimr for one, and Aedan too. After all, Buthar and Aedan have Manx blood. Buthar's a canny one. He'll have several men in his pay. Mayhap that's a lesson for us too. As to how he heard about you, I can only think that I might have been rather too fulsome in your praises when I last spoke to Aedan." He laughed at Gytha's surprise and added, "Well-deserved, that it was."

Gytha glanced up and held out her hand. A white flake settled on her palm. "It's snowing! Let's get back. There's lots I need to tell Leo." She turned as Bear spoke, moved by the warmth in his eyes and his voice.

"Come on, my Lady of the Lake. We've more to celebrate than just Yuletide.

~~~~~

The lakeside communities enjoyed several more peaceful years and avoided the dramatic changes that affected the Eden Valley. Norman incursions into the heart of the

Lake District, as it became known, were largely deterred. It was a place that they learned to fear.

Everything changed in 1100 when Henry I took the English throne and developed a renewed interest in the North. Ealdgith's people would once again have to fight for their existence and call upon the support of their allies.

Glossary

Aefter Yule. After Yule. January, the month after the Yuletide festival that became Christmas.

Aere Yule. December, the month before Yule.

Atheling. Old English. A royal prince eligible to be king.

Blōtmonath. November. The month of blood sacrifices.

Breeks. Breeches. From Old English, brec. Northern dialect.

Burh. A Saxon fortified settlement. Typically, a timber-faced bank and ditch with a palisade on top, enclosing a manor house and settlement.

Castle. A European innovation, castles originated in the 9th and 10th centuries. Many castles were built initially from earth and timber, but had their defences replaced later by stone. Motte and bailey is a relatively modern term. These castles were introduced to England by the Normans. Each consisted of a circular moat surrounding an earth mound (Motte) upon which a wooden tower (Keep) was built. The Baily was a wooden palisade inside the moat that encompassed the motte and flat land upon which the castle's domestic buildings were built.

Churl. The lowest rank of English freemen.

Conroi. Old French. A group of five to ten knights who trained and fought together.

Dale. Old English and Norse for a valley.

Ealdmoder. Grandmother.

Earl. An Earl is a member of the nobility. The title is Anglo-Saxon, akin to the Scandinavian form: Jarl.

Ēostre. Easter

Eostremonath. April. After, Eostre, goddess of spring and fertility.

Fader. Father.

Fell. Norse for a high hill, mountain or high moorland.

Fettle. Northern English. Various meanings, including: to sort out, fix or repair.

Freyja. Norse. Goddess of love, fertility, and battle.

Furlong. Old English. An eighth of a mile or approximately 200 metres.

Fyrd. The local militia of an Anglo-Saxon shire, in which all freemen had to serve.

Haerfest. Harvest. Autumn.

Hāligmonath. September. Holy month.

Hall. Old English: Heall, a large house.

Hefted. The instinctive ability of some breeds of sheep, including Cumbrian herdwicks, to know intimately and return to the land where they live.

Hel. Queen of Helheim, the Norse underworld.

Hide. An area of land capable of supporting an extended family of up to 50 people.

Hnefatafl. This Viking board game, pronounced 'neffa-tafel', was ubiquitous in Nordic settlements in the early Middle Ages.

Holmganga. Norse: "going to an island", a special place for a duel governed by rules of combat.

Hrēðmonath. March. Hreða, or Rheda's month. A Germanic fertility goddess.

Hundred. Most of the English shires were divided into 'Hundreds;' groups of 100 'Hides'.

Jagger. Northern English. Someone who controls a team of packhorses. A Jagger way is a packhorse trail.

League. A league is a classical unit of length. The word originally meant the distance a person could walk in an hour. This distance has been defined variously as between one and a half and three miles. I have used the Roman league which is 7,500 feet or one and half Roman miles.

Lencten. Spring.

Liða. June and **July** were together known as *Liða*, an Old English word meaning "mild" or "gentle," which referred to the period of warm, seasonable weather either side of Midsummer. To differentiate between the two, June was sometimes known as *Ærraliða*, or "before-mild," and July was *Æfteraliða*, or "after-mild."

Logi. Norse god of fire.

Longhouse. A Viking equivalent of the English manor house, typically 5 to 7 metres wide and anywhere from 15 to 75 metres long, depending on the wealth and social position of the owner.

Manor. An estate of land. The manor is often described as the basic feudal unit of tenure. A manor was akin to the modern firm or business. It was a productive unit, which required physical capital, in the form of land, buildings, equipment and draught animals such as ploughing oxen, plus day-to-day management and a workforce. Its ownership could be transferred, by the overlord. In many cases this was ultimately the King.

Moder. Mother.

Nadr. Norse. Viper or adder.

Norns. Norse. The Norns were female beings who ruled upon the destiny of gods and men. They roughly correspond to other controllers of humans' destiny, the Fates, elsewhere in European mythology. (See Wyrd.)

Ratch. Yorkshire slang. To rummage.

Reave. To plunder or rob. Reaver: a raider. From Old English: reafian.

Reeve. An administrative officer who generally ranked lower than the ealdorman or earl. Different types of reeves were attested, including high-reeve, town-reeve, port-reeve, shire-reeve (predecessor to the sheriff), reeve of the hundred, and the reeve of a manor.

Seax. The seax is a type of sword or dagger typical of the Germanic peoples of the Early Middle Ages, especially the Saxons. The smallest were knives, the longest would have a blade over 50 cm long.

Shire. Groups of hundreds were combined to form shires, with each shire under the control of an earl.

Silvatici. Norman term for the 'men of the woods' or the green men.

Sōlmōnath. February. The month of cakes, possibly referring to the cakes' sandy, gritty texture.

Skíta. Old Norse: shit.

Snekke. Or snekkja, meaning 'thin and projecting' was typically the smallest long ship used in warfare, with at least 20 rowing benches. Typically, 17 m (56 feet) long and

2.5 m (8.2 feet) wide with a draught of only 0.5 m (1.6 feet). It would carry a crew of around 41 men (40 oarsmen and one helmsman).

Sokeman. Ranked between free tenants and bond tenants (or villeins). A free man within the lord's soke or jurisdiction.

Staddle stones. Supporting bases for granaries, hayricks, game larders, etc. Mushroom-shaped staddle stones lifted granaries above the ground thereby protecting stored grain from vermin and damp.

Stane. Scots' word for stone.

Strath. Commonly used in rural Scotland to describe a wide valley, even by non-Gaelic speakers. In Scottish place-names, Strath- is of Gaelic and Brittonic origin.

Sumor. Summer.

Tafl. These games, known also as hnefatafl, are a family of ancient Nordic and Celtic strategy board games played on a chequered or latticed game-board with two armies, usually of unequal numbers.

Thegn. A member of several Norse and Saxon aristocratic classes of men, ranking between earls and ordinary freemen, and granted lands by the king, or by lords, for military service. The minimum qualifying holding of land was five Hides.

Thrimilce. May. "The month of three milkings," when livestock were often so well fed on fresh spring grass that they could be milked three times a day.

Vill. Medieval English term to define a land unit that might otherwise be described as a parish, manor or tithing.

Wapentake. An administrative area. The Dane-law equivalent of an Anglo-Saxon Hundred.

Warg. In Norse mythology, a warg is a wolf and in particular refers to the wolf Fenrir and his sons Sköll and Hati.

Weodmonath. August. Plant month.

Historical Note

The background to the main historical characters and events is told within the narrative of the story. Whilst Hravn and Ealdgith, and their wider household, friends and associates, are fictional the principal protagonists, other than Felix de Kiberen, are real. Within Ealdgith's family, Dolfin and Ketel are both from my Curwen family line.

As the Harrying of the North series evolved I developed Ealdgith's character to reflect that of a young English noblewoman of the pre-invasion period. She would have been educated alongside her brothers and schooled to support her husband in the management of his estates. This would often have been in the role of 'peace-weaver', enabling disputes to be resolved diplomatically rather than by force. Now that the story has jumped forward twenty years it was time to introduce the next generation. They would have been raised in the way of life that Hravn and Ealdgith had experienced and established.

By the end of the 11th century the Eden Valley was a medley of Cumbrian, English and Gallo-Norse communities that were largely independent, though technically under Scottish rule. This was ended by the Norman invasion of 1092.

Little is known for certain about the power-play that underwrites the events of this time. I have striven to weave Ealdgith's and Hravn's story around what is credible, to create a coherent and logical narrative.

The reason for King Malcolm's invasion of Northumbria in May 1091 is not known. The timing of his attack, in May, was unusual and might imply that he had been goaded into doing so; and his decision to attack Durham implied a deliberate attempt to seize control of the North.

It is possible that Malcolm considered that he was in a strong position to oppose William Rufus, or conversely, he felt threatened by rising Norman power. Quite possibly both. The Normans reacted forcefully by despatching an army and a fleet north in the autumn to force a military decision. When it became clear that the Scots had fallen back, William Rufus followed them into Lothian. Losing his fleet, and sucked into a Scottish winter, William Rufus was forced to negotiate, reaffirming the Abernethy agreement of 1072. Malcolm swore fealty to William who promised to return the twelve vills that Malcolm had held under William the Conqueror. These twelve vills have been assumed to mean Cumberland.

William Rufus then mixed aggression with deceit. In 1092 he led an army north and ejected Dolfin, the ruler of Cumberland, from Carlisle. The king then had a castle built at Carlisle, moved or 'planted' peasants in from lands in the south and established a self-sufficient colony from which he could control the Eden valley and the west Cumbrian seaboard.

King Malcolm appears to have given no sign that he viewed this as an act of aggression. In 1093 he went south peacefully, laid a foundation stone at Durham Cathedral and then went to meet King William at Gloucester. It is reported that William refused to meet Malcolm, insisting that he abide by a judgement of his Court. Malcolm withdrew in a rage, summoned his army and attacked into Northumbria in November. William's retention of Carlisle may have been a ruse to force Malcolm to attack. Earl Robert de Mowbray, who held the North for William, already had his army in the field waiting for the Scots; surprising and roundly defeating them south of Alnwick where Malcolm and his heir were killed.

The Normans quickly subdued the Eden Valley. William Rufus ordered the building of Brough Castle on the site of the Roman fort in 1092. Also in 1092, Count Ivo de Taillebois built an earthen motte and bailey castle at

Appleby, much as Hravn surmised might happen. Later in the decade, Ranulph de Meschines, Count Ivo's successor, ordered Pendragon Castle to be built in Mallerstang. During the course of the building, Count Ivo also settled his lands in the Eden Valley with peasants transported from his lands to the south.

Elftred was a prominent Anglo-Cumbrian noble. He is sometimes referred to as The Baron of Kendal. This is a misnomer because the barony wasn't established for another one hundred years when it was bestowed on one of his heirs. His son, Ketel, married Christiana de Taillebois, and their son William married Gunilda who was a daughter of Earl Gospatrick. I have applied a sleight of hand, aging Willian by a decade or so and marrying him to Aebbe, thereby linking into the fictitious family of Hravn and Ealdgith. Between 1092 and 1125 Ketel granted lands by charter to various religious houses. These included charters gifting the Hospital of St. Nicholas in York land and a mill at Barton, and a fishery at the outlet of Ullswater, and to St. Mary's priory in York the church at Morland. The latter charter was witnessed by Ketel's wife, Christiana and his son William.

Jarl Buthar is an enigma. He is apparently mentioned in 12th century Norman documents, but much of his story appears to be based on local legend and archaeology, enhanced later by Nicholas Size's popular novel, 'The Secret Valley' and Rosemary Sutcliff's 'The Shield Ring.'

A final thought about Ullswater. Is it just coincidence that the century-old lake steamers plying between Glenridding and Pooley Bridge are called Raven and The Lady of The Lake?